W9-BZZ-467

GREGOR
and the Curse of the
WARMBLOODS

GREGOR
and the Curse of the
WARMBLOODS

Suzanne Collins

Thorndike Press • Waterville, Maine

Recommended for Middle Readers.

Published in 2006 by arrangement with Scholastic Inc.

Thorndike Press® Large Print The Literacy Bridge.

The tree indicium is a trademark of Thorndike Press.

The text of this Large Print edition is unabridged.
Other aspects of the book may vary from the original edition.

Set in 16 pt. Plantin by Al Chase.

Printed in the United States on permanent paper.

Library of Congress Cataloging-in-Publication Data

Collins, Suzanne.
  Gregor and the curse of the warmbloods / by Suzanne
Collins.
    p. cm. — (Underland chronicles ; bk. 3)
    Summary: Eleven-year-old Gregor and his younger sister,
Boots, return to the Underland beneath New York City to
find the cure for a terrible plague that threatens the life of
their mother, as well as the lives of the people, bats, and rats
who populate the underworld.
  ISBN 0-7862-8083-2 (lg. print : hc : alk. paper)   1. Large
type books.   [1. Brothers and sisters — Fiction.   2. Animals
— Fiction.   3. Plague — Fiction.   4. Fantasy.   5. Large
type books.]   I. Title: Curse of the warmbloods.   II. Title.
  PZ7.C69716Gre 2006
  [Fic]—dc22   2005022129

For Charlie and Isabel

PART 1
THE PLAGUE

CHAPTER 1

Gregor stared in the bathroom mirror for a minute, steeling himself. Then he slowly unrolled the scroll and held the handwritten side up to the glass. In the reflection, he read the first stanza of a poem entitled "The Prophecy of Blood."

As usual, the lines made him feel sick to his stomach.

There was a knock on the door. "Boots has to go!" he heard his eight-year-old sister, Lizzie, say.

Gregor released the top of the scroll and it snapped into a roll. He quickly stuck it in the back pocket of his jeans and pulled his sweatshirt down to conceal it. He hadn't told anyone about this new prophecy yet and didn't intend to until it was absolutely necessary.

A few months ago, right around Christmas, he had returned home from the Underland, a dark war-torn world miles beneath New York City. It was home to giant talking rats, bats, spiders, cockroaches, and a variety of other oversized creatures. There were humans there, too —

a pale-skinned, violet-eyed people who had traveled underground in the 1600s and built the stone city of Regalia. The Regalians were probably still debating whether Gregor was a traitor or a hero. On his last trip, he had refused to kill a white baby rat called the Bane. For many Underlanders, that was unforgivable, because they believed the Bane would one day be the cause of their total destruction.

The current queen of Regalia, Nerissa, was a frail teenager with disturbing visions of the future. She was the one who had slipped the scroll into Gregor's coat pocket when he was leaving. He had thought it was "The Prophecy of Bane," which he had just helped to fulfill. Instead it was this new and terrifying poem.

"So you can reflect on it sometimes," Nerissa had said. Turned out she'd meant it literally — "The Prophecy of Blood" was written backward. You couldn't even make sense of it unless you had a mirror.

"Gregor, come on!" called Lizzie, rapping on the bathroom door again.

He opened the door to find Lizzie with their two-year-old sister, Boots. They were both bundled up in coats and hats, even though they hadn't been outside today.

"Need to pee!" squealed Boots, pulling

her pants down around her ankles and then shuffling to the toilet.

"First get to the toilet, then pull down your pants," instructed Lizzie for the hundredth time.

Boots wiggled up onto the toilet seat. "I big girl now. I can go pee."

"Good job," said Gregor, giving her a thumbs-up. Boots beamed back at him.

"Dad's making drop biscuits in the kitchen. The oven's on in there," said Lizzie, rubbing her hands together to warm them.

The apartment was freezing. The city had been clutched in record-breaking lows for the past few weeks, and the boiler that fed steam to the old heating pipes could not compete. People in the building had called the city, and called again. Nothing much happened.

"Wrap it up, Boots. Time for biscuits," said Gregor.

She pulled about a yard of toilet paper off the roll and sort of wiped herself. You could offer to help, but she'd just say, "No, I do it myself."

Gregor made sure she washed and dried her hands, then reached for the lotion so he could rub some into her chapped skin. Lizzie caught his sleeve as he was about to

11

squeeze the bottle.

"That's shampoo!" she said in alarm. Almost everything alarmed Lizzie these days.

"Right," said Gregor, switching bottles.

"We have jelly, Gre-go?" asked Boots hopefully as he massaged the lotion into the backs of her hands.

Gregor smiled at this new pronunciation of his name. He'd been "Ge-go" for about a year, but Boots had recently added an *r*.

"Grape jelly," said Gregor. "I got it just for you. You hungry?"

"Ye-es!" said Boots, and he swung her up onto his hip.

A cloud of warmth enveloped him as he brought Boots into the kitchen. His dad was just pulling a tray of drop biscuits out of the oven. It was good to see him up, doing something even as simple as making his kids' breakfast. More than two and a half years as a prisoner of the huge, bloodthirsty rats in the Underland had left his dad a very sick man. When Gregor returned from his second visit at Christmas, he brought back some special medicine from the Underland. It seemed to be helping. His dad's fevers were less frequent, his hands had stopped shaking, and he had regained some weight. He was a long way from well, but Gregor's secret hope was that if the medicine kept working, his dad might get to go back to his job as a high school science teacher in the fall.

Gregor slid Boots into the cracked, red plastic booster seat they'd had since he was a baby. She drummed her heels happily on the chair in anticipation of breakfast. It looked good, too, especially for an end-of-the-month meal. Gregor's mom got paid on the first of every month, and they were always out of money by then. But his dad served each of them two biscuits and a hard-boiled egg. Boots had a cup of watery apple juice — they were trying to make that last — and everybody else drank hot tea.

His dad told them to start eating while he took a tray of food to their grandma. She spent a lot of time in bed even when the weather was milder, but this winter she'd rarely left it. They'd put an electric space heater in her room and she had lots of quilts on her bed. Still, whenever Gregor went in to see her, her hands were cold.

"Jel-ly, jel-ly, jel-ly," said Boots in a sing-song voice.

Gregor broke open her biscuits and put a big spoonful on each. She took a huge bite of one immediately, smearing purple all over her face.

"Hey, eat it, don't wear it, okay?" said Gregor, and Boots got a fit of the giggles. You had to laugh when Boots laughed; she had such a goofy, hiccuppy little-kid laugh, it was contagious.

Gregor and Lizzie had to hurry through breakfast so they wouldn't be late for school.

"Brush your teeth," reminded their dad as they rose from the table.

"I will, if I can get in the bathroom," said Lizzie, grinning at Gregor.

It was a family joke now. How much time he spent in the bathroom. There was only the one bathroom in the apartment, and since Gregor had taken to locking himself in to read the prophecy, everybody had noticed. His mom kept teasing him about trying to look good for some girl at school, and he pretended she was right by doing his best to act embarrassed. The truth was, he was thinking about a girl, but she didn't go to his school. And he wasn't worried about what she thought of his hair. He was wondering if she was even alive.

Luxa. She was the same age as him, eleven, and already she was the queen of Regalia. Or at least, she had been queen until a few months ago. Against the Regalian council's wishes, she had secretly flown after

14

Gregor to help him on the mission to kill the Bane. She had saved Boots's life by taking on a pack of rats in a maze and allowing his baby sister to escape on a devoted cockroach. But where was Luxa now? Wandering lost in the Dead Land? A prisoner of the rats? Dead? Or had she by some miracle made it home? And there was Luxa's bat, Aurora. And Temp, the cockroach who had run with Boots. And Twitchtip, a rat whose nose was so keen she could detect color. All his friends. All missing in action. All weaving through his dreams at night and preoccupying his thoughts when he was awake.

Gregor had told the Underlanders to let him know what happened. They were supposed to leave him a message in the grate in his laundry room, which was a gateway to the Underland. Why hadn't they? What was going on?

Not knowing about Luxa and the others . . . trying to decipher the mysterious prophecy on his own . . . the combination of these things was driving Gregor crazy. It was a huge effort to pay attention in class, to act normal around his friends, to hide his worries from his family, because any hint that he was planning to return to the Underland would throw them into a panic.

He was constantly distracted, not hearing people when they spoke, forgetting things. Like now.

"Gregor, your backpack!" said his dad as he and Lizzie headed out the door. "Think you might need that today."

"Thanks, Dad," said Gregor, avoiding his father's eyes, not wanting to see the concern there.

He and Lizzie took the stairs down to the lobby and braced themselves before stepping out into the street. A bitter blast of wind went right through his clothes as if they weren't even there. He could see tears spilling out of Lizzie's eyes; they always watered in the wind.

"Let's hustle, Liz. Least it will be warm at school," said Gregor.

They hurried through the streets, as fast as the icy sidewalks would let them. Fortunately, Lizzie's elementary school was only a couple of blocks away. She was small for her age, "delicate" his mom called her. "One good strong wind would blow you away," his grandma would say when she hugged Lizzie. And today Gregor wondered if she might be right.

"You'll pick me up after school, right? You'll be here?" asked Lizzie at the door.

"Of course," said Gregor. She gave him a

reproachful look. He'd forgotten twice in the last month, and she'd had to sit in the office and wait for someone to come get her. "I'll be here!"

Gregor plowed back into the wind with almost a sense of relief. Even if his teeth were chattering, at least he could have a few minutes without anybody interrupting him. Immediately, his thoughts turned to the Underland and what might be happening there now, somewhere far beneath his feet. It was just a matter of time before Gregor would be called back down — he knew that. That's why he spent so much time in the bathroom, studying the new prophecy, trying to understand its frightening words, desperate to prepare for his next challenge in any way he could. The Underlanders were depending on him.

But the Underlanders! At first, he'd made excuses for their silence, but now he was just mad. Not only was there no word about Luxa or his other missing friends, Gregor also had no clue what had happened to Ares, the big black bat whom he trusted above anyone in the Underland. Ares and Gregor were bonds, sworn to protect each other to the death. The journey to track down and kill the Bane had been dreadful, but if one good thing had come of it, it was that the relationship between Gregor and Ares had become unshakable. Unfortunately, Ares was an outcast among the humans and bats. He had let his first bond, Henry, fall to his death to save Gregor's life. Even though Henry was a traitor and Ares had done the right thing, the Underlanders hated him. They also blamed the bat for not killing the Bane although, technically, that had been Gregor's job. Gregor had a bad feeling that wherever Ares was, he was suffering.

As he pulled open the door to his school, Gregor tried to replace thoughts of the Underland with his math assignment. Every Friday, they had a quiz first thing. Then there was half-court basketball in gym, some kind of sugar crystal experiment in science, and finally lunch. Gregor's stomach was always growling at least a full hour before he reached the cafeteria. Between the cold, trying to make the groceries stretch at home, and just growing, he was hungry all the time. He got free school lunch and he ate everything on his tray, even if he didn't like it. Fortunately, Friday was pizza day, and he loved pizza.

"Here, take mine," said his friend Angelina, plunking down her slice of pizza on his plate. "I'm too nervous to eat, anyway." The school play opened that night and she had the lead.

"Want to run your lines again?" asked Gregor.

Her script was in his hand in a flash.

"Are you sure you don't mind? I come in right here."

Like he didn't know. Gregor and their friend Larry had been running lines with Angelina every day for six weeks. Usually Gregor did it, though. The cold, dry winter air aggravated Larry's asthma, so reading out loud made him cough. He'd been in the hospital last week with a bad attack and was still looking kind of wiped out.

"It doesn't matter, you won't remember a thing," said Larry, who was drawing something that looked like a fly's eyeball on his napkin. He didn't look up.

"Don't say that!" gasped Angelina.

"You'll be rotten, just like you were in that last play," said Larry.

"Yeah, we could barely sit through that," Gregor agreed.

Angelina had been wonderful in that last play. They all knew it. She tried not to look pleased.

"What were you again? Some kind of bug, right?" said Gregor.

"Something with wings," said Larry.

She had been the fairy godmother in a version of Cinderella set in the city.

"Can we start now?" said Angelina. "So I don't totally humiliate myself tonight?"

Gregor ran lines with her. He didn't mind really. It distracted him from darker thoughts.

"Keep your head in the Overland," he told himself. "Or you'll just make yourself nuts."

And he did a pretty good job of it for the rest of the day. He got through his classes and took Lizzie home and then went over to Larry's apartment. Larry's mom ordered out Chinese food for a special treat, and they went and saw the play. It was fun and Angelina was the best thing in it. When he got home, Gregor gave his sisters a pocketful of fortune cookies he'd saved from dinner. Boots had never seen fortune cookies and kept trying to eat them, paper and all.

They went to bed earlier than usual because it was just too cold to do anything else. Gregor piled not only his blankets but his coat and a couple of towels on top of him. His mom and dad came in to say good night. That made him feel secure. For so many years his dad had been absent or too ill to come in. To have both parents tuck him in seemed like a real luxury.

So he was doing all right, keeping his head in the Overland, until his dad leaned down to hug him good night and whispered in a voice his mom couldn't hear, "No mail."

He and his dad had worked out a system. Gregor's mom had put the laundry room off-limits last summer. You couldn't blame her. In the last few years, first her husband, then Gregor and Boots had fallen through a grate in the laundry room wall that led to the Underland. Their disappearance was agonizing. How his mom had kept the family going both emotionally and financially through all this . . . well, Gregor couldn't say. She had been amazing. So it seemed a small enough thing to let her have her way about the laundry room.

The tricky thing was . . . that made checking the grate that led to the Underland impossible for Gregor, but his dad knew how anxious he was for news of Luxa and the others, so once a day he would make a brief visit to the laundry room and see if a message had been left for his son. They didn't tell his mom; she would have just been upset. It was different for her. She had never been to the Underland. In her mind, everyone who lived there was somehow connected to the abduction of her husband and children. But Gregor and his dad both had friends down there.

So there was no mail. No word again. No answers. Gregor stared into the dark for hours, and when he finally fell asleep, his dreams were troubled.

He woke late the following morning and had to rush to get to Mrs. Cormaci's apartment by ten. He went over every Saturday to help her out. There had been times in the fall when Gregor had felt like she was making up work for him to do because she knew his family was hurting for money. But with the weather so bad, Mrs. Cormaci actually did need his help. The cold made her joints ache and she had trouble navigating the icy sidewalks. She talked a lot about falling and breaking a hip. Gregor was glad he was really earning his money now.

Today she had a big list of errands for him to run — the dry cleaners, the greengrocer's, the bakery, the post office, and the hardware store. As always, she fed him first. "Did you eat?" she asked. He hadn't but he didn't even have time to answer. "Never mind, in this cold you can stand eating twice." She placed a big steaming bowl of oatmeal on the table, loaded with raisins and brown sugar. She poured him orange juice and buttered several slices of toast.

When he had finished, Gregor felt ready to face any weather, which was good, since it was ten below not even counting the windchill factor. Following the list, he ran from place to place, grateful to have to wait in lines so he had a chance to thaw out. After he had dropped his purchases on Mrs. Cormaci's kitchen table, he was rewarded with a large cup of hot chocolate. Then they both bundled back up to go to the two places where Gregor could not run her errands, the bank and the liquor store. Once they got outside, Mrs. Cormaci was on edge. She clung to Gregor's arm tightly as they confronted patches of ice, pedestrians half-blinded by scarves, and swerving taxicabs. They had a chance to warm up at the bank, since Mrs. Cormaci didn't trust automatic bank machines, and they had to stand in line for a teller. Then they went to the liquor store, so she could pick out a bottle of red wine for her friend Eileen's birthday. But by the time they had made their way back home, Mrs. Cormaci's fingers were so numb that she dropped the wine in the hall outside her apartment just as Gregor got the door open. The bottle broke on the tile, and the wine splattered all over the throw rug inside the entrance.

"That's it, Eileen's getting candy," said

Mrs. Cormaci. "I've got a nice box of chocolate creams, never been opened. Someone gave it to me for Christmas. I hope it wasn't Eileen." She made Gregor stand back while she cleaned up the glass, then gathered up the throw rug and handed it to him. "Come on. We better get this down to the laundry room before the stain sets."

The laundry room! While she collected detergent and stain remover from the closet, Gregor tried to think of an excuse for why he couldn't accompany her. He could hardly say, "Oh, I can't go down there because my mom is afraid a giant rat will jump out and drag me miles underground and eat me." If you thought about it, there was almost no good reason a person couldn't go to the laundry room. So he went.

Mrs. Cormaci sprayed the throw rug with stain remover and stuffed it into a washer. Her fingers, still stiff from the cold, fumbled as she picked the quarters from her change purse. She dropped one to the cement floor, and it rolled across the room, clanking to a stop against the last dryer. Gregor went to retrieve it for her. As he bent down to get the coin, something caught his eye, and he bumped his head into the side of the dryer.

Gregor blinked, to make sure he hadn't imagined it. He hadn't. There, wedged between the frame of the grate and the wall, was a scroll.

CHAPTER 2

"Are you okay over there?" asked Mrs. Cormaci as she dumped detergent into the washer.

"Yeah, I'm fine," said Gregor, rubbing his head. He picked up the quarter and resisted the impulse to yank the scroll out of the grate. Trying to appear like nothing had happened, he returned the coin.

Mrs. Cormaci stuck the quarter in the machine and started it up. "Ready to grab some lunch?" she said.

There was nothing for Gregor to do but follow her to the elevator. He couldn't retrieve the scroll in front of her. She would want to know what it was, and since she was already suspicious about the stories he used to cover his family's time in the Underland, it wasn't likely he could come up with a believable lie. Shoot, he hadn't even been able to make up an excuse to avoid the laundry room!

Back at the apartment, Mrs. Cormaci heated up some homemade chicken soup and ladled out big servings. Gregor ate mechanically, trying to keep up his end of the conversation although he was only half-listening. As they were finishing off some pie, Mrs. Cormaci glanced at the clock and said, "I guess that rug's about ready to go in the dryer now."

"I'll do it!" Gregor sprang to his feet so quickly his chair fell over backward. He set the chair back up as casually as possible. "Sorry. I can change the rug."

Mrs. Cormaci gave him an odd look. "Okay."

"I mean, doesn't take two of us to change a rug," said Gregor with a shrug.

"You're right about that." She put some quarters in his hand, watching him closely. "So, how come your family doesn't use our laundry room anymore?"

"What?" She'd caught him off guard.

"How come you and your mother walk all the way over to use that place by the butcher's?" she said. "It's the same price. I checked."

"Because . . . the washers . . . are . . . bigger there," said Gregor. Actually, they were. It was not a complete lie if it were not the whole truth.

Mrs. Cormaci stared at him a moment, then shook her head. "Go change the rug," she said shortly.

The elevator had never moved so slowly.

People got on, people got off, a woman held the door for what seemed like an hour while her kid ran back to their apartment to get a hat. When he finally made it to the laundry room, Gregor had to wait for some guy who had obviously not done his clothes for about a month to load up six washers.

Gregor stuck the rug in the dryer next to the grate and fussed around with it until the guy left. The moment the coast was clear, he leaned down and yanked the scroll out of the grate. He stuck it up the sleeve of his sweatshirt and walked out. Ignoring the elevator, he slipped into the stairwell and closed the door securely behind him. He went up one flight and sat on the landing. No one would disturb him here, not with the elevator working.

He slid the scroll out of his shirtsleeve and unrolled it with shaking hands. It read:

Dear Gregor,

It is most urgent that we meet. I will be at the stair where Ares leaves you when the clock strikes four. We are at your mercy. "The Prophecy of Blood" is upon us.

Please do not fail your friends,
Vikus

Gregor read the note three times before it began to register. It was not what he had expected. It was not about Luxa and his other missing friends. It did not tell him about Ares. Instead, it was a flat-out cry for help.

"The Prophecy of Blood" is upon us.

"It's here," Gregor thought. His heart began to pound as a sense of dread coursed through him. "The Prophecy of Blood."

He didn't really need a mirror to read it anymore, although looking at the lines sometimes helped him figure out parts. By now he knew the thing by heart. There was something in the rhythm of the words that made it get in your head and stick there, like one of those annoying songs on TV commercials. It played in his brain now, adjusting to the beat of his boots as he slowly climbed the stairs.

WARMBLOOD NOW
A BLOODBORNE DEATH
WILL ROB YOUR BODY OF ITS BREATH,
MARK YOUR SKIN,
AND SEAL YOUR FATE.
THE UNDERLAND BECOMES A PLATE.

TURN AND TURN AND TURN AGAIN.
YOU SEE THE WHAT
BUT NOT THE WHEN.

REMEDY AND WRONG ENTWINE,
AND SO THEY FORM A SINGLE VINE.

BRING THE WARRIOR FROM ABOVE
IF YET HIS HEART
IS SWAYED BY LOVE.
BRING THE PRINCESS OR DESPAIR,
NO CRAWLERS CARE
WITHOUT HER THERE.

TURN AND TURN AND TURN AGAIN.
YOU SEE THE WHAT
BUT NOT THE WHEN.
REMEDY AND WRONG ENTWINE,
AND SO THEY FORM A SINGLE VINE.

THOSE WHOSE BLOOD
RUNS RED AND HOT
MUST JOIN TO SEEK
THE HEALING SPOT.
IN THE CRADLE FIND THE CURE
FOR THAT WHICH MAKES
THE BLOOD IMPURE.

TURN AND TURN AND TURN AGAIN.
YOU SEE THE WHAT
BUT NOT THE WHEN.
REMEDY AND WRONG ENTWINE,
AND SO THEY FORM A SINGLE VINE.

GNAWER, HUMAN, SET ASIDE
THE HATREDS THAT RESIDE INSIDE.
IF THE FLAMES OF WAR
ARE FANNED,
ALL WARMBLOODS
LOSE THE UNDERLAND.

TURN AND TURN AND TURN AGAIN.
YOU SEE THE WHAT
BUT NOT THE WHEN.
REMEDY AND WRONG ENTWINE,
AND SO THEY FORM A SINGLE VINE.

Gregor had survived two other prophecies by the man who had written this one. Bartholomew of Sandwich. It was Sandwich who had led the Underlanders far beneath what was now New York City and founded the human city of Regalia. When he died he had left behind a stone room whose walls were entirely carved with prophecies, his visions of the future. And not just the humans but all the creatures in the Underland believed Sandwich had been able to see what was to come.

Gregor went back and forth on how he felt about Sandwich's predictions. Sometimes he hated them. Sometimes he was grateful for their guidance, although the prophecies were so cryptic they seemed to mean a lot of things at once. But within the loaded lines you could usually get the general idea of what awaited you. Like in this one . . .

WARMBLOOD NOW
A BLOODBORNE DEATH
WILL ROB YOUR BODY
OF ITS BREATH,
MARK YOUR SKIN,
AND SEAL YOUR FATE.
THE UNDERLAND BECOMES A PLATE.

Gregor had figured out it was about some kind of disease, a deadly one, and a lot of people were going to get it. Not just people, but anything that was warmblooded. Any mammal. Down in the Underland, that could include the bats and rats . . . he really didn't know how many other creatures could be affected. And what was that scary line about a "plate" supposed to mean? That everybody got eaten up?

BRING THE WARRIOR FROM ABOVE
IF YET HIS HEART
IS SWAYED BY LOVE.
BRING THE PRINCESS OR DESPAIR,
NO CRAWLERS CARE
WITHOUT HER THERE.

The warrior was Gregor, no use trying to kid himself about that. He didn't want to be the warrior. He hated fighting, hated that he was so good at it. But after having successfully fulfilled two prophecies as the warrior, he had stopped believing they had gotten the wrong guy.

Then, there was the princess. . . . He was holding out hope that it wasn't Boots. The crawlers — that was the Underlander name for the cockroaches — called her the princess, but she wasn't a real one. Maybe the crawlers had a princess of their own to bring.

Other stanzas seemed to suggest that the humans and the gnawers — the rats — were going to have to band together to find the cure for the disease. Boy, they were going to love that! They'd only spent centuries trying to kill one another. And then there was Sandwich's usual prediction that if things didn't work out, there would be total destruction and everybody would end up dead.

Gregor had to wonder if Sandwich had ever written a cheerful prophecy. Something about peace and joy, with a big old happy ending. Probably not.

The thing that drove him craziest about "The Prophecy of Blood" was the one stanza that appeared four times. It was like Sandwich was trying to drum it into his brain.

TURN AND TURN AND TURN AGAIN.
YOU SEE THE WHAT
BUT NOT THE WHEN.
REMEDY AND WRONG ENTWINE,
AND SO THEY FORM A SINGLE VINE.

What did that mean? It made absolutely no sense at all! Gregor had to talk to Vikus! Along with being Luxa's grandpa and one of the most influential people in Regalia, Vikus was one of the best interpreters of Sandwich's prophecies. If anyone could explain the passage, he could.

Gregor realized he was standing on the landing of his floor, gripping the railing. He was unsure of how long he'd been there. But now he had to finish up with Mrs. Cormaci and get home.

If he had been gone too long, she didn't seem to notice. She gave him the usual forty bucks plus a big bowl of stew for his family. As he was leaving, she wrapped an extra scarf around his neck because, "I've got enough scarves to choke a horse." Mrs. Cormaci never let him leave empty-handed.

Back in his own apartment, Gregor got

his dad alone in the kitchen as soon as he could and showed him the note from Vikus. His dad's face became grave as he read it.

" 'The Prophecy of Blood.' Do you know what that is, Gregor?" he asked.

Without a word, Gregor handed his dad the scroll with the prophecy. It was crumpled and somewhat grimy from many readings.

"How long have you had this?" asked his dad.

"Since Christmas," said Gregor. "I didn't want you to worry."

"I will start worrying if I think you're hiding things from me," said his dad. "No more of that, okay?"

Gregor nodded. His dad opened the scroll to read it and looked perplexed.

"It's written backward," said Gregor. "But I know it by heart." He recited the prophecy aloud.

"A 'bloodborne death.' Well, that doesn't sound good," said his dad.

"No, it sounds like a lot of people will get sick," said Gregor.

"Vikus seems to think they need you to go down there again. You know your mom's not going to let that happen," said his dad.

He knew. It was not hard to imagine his mom's horror once she heard about the prophecy. After his dad had disappeared, she'd spent endless nights sitting alone at the kitchen table. First crying. Then silent . . . her fingers tracing the pattern on the tablecloth. Then absolutely still. And it was probably much worse when he and Boots were gone. Could he really put her through that again? "No, I can't!" he thought. Then the images of his friends from the Underland crowded into his brain. They might die — all of them — if he did not go.

"I've got to at least go hear what Vikus has to say, Dad," said Gregor, his voice choked with agitation. "I've got to at least know what's happening! I mean, I can't just tear this up and pretend it never came!"

"Okay, okay, son, we'll go and hear the man out. I'm just saying, don't be making him any promises you can't keep," said his dad.

They got Mrs. Cormaci to come over for a while, saying they were thinking of seeing a movie. She seemed to be glad for a chance to visit with his sisters and his grandma. Armed with a deck of "Go Fish" cards and a jar of popcorn, she waved Gregor and his dad toward the door. "You two go ahead. You need a little father-son time."

Maybe they did. But not this kind.

Before they left, Gregor made sure he had

a good, strong flashlight. He watched his dad slip a crowbar under his jacket. At first, Gregor thought it was for protection, but his dad whispered, "For the rock." The spot where Ares always left Gregor was at the foot of a stairway under Central Park. A stone slab covered the entrance to the stairway. In this weather, it would be frozen in place.

To reach Vikus by four o'clock, they had to take a cab to the park. Gregor thought the trek to the subway would be too much for his dad, anyway. As it was, he seemed exhausted by the time they took the short walk from the street to the Underland entrance among the trees.

In the frigid weather, Central Park was almost empty. A few visitors scurried along with their heads ducked low, their hands crammed in pockets. No one took any notice as Gregor pried the stone slab loose and slid it over to reveal the entrance.

"We're a few minutes early," said Gregor, peering down into the darkness.

"Vikus may be, too. Let's go on down. At least we'll be out of this wind," said his dad.

They lowered themselves into the hole. Gregor made sure to bring the crowbar with him — the rock would probably freeze up immediately, and he didn't want to get stuck underground. He moved the slab back in place, blocking out the daylight. It was pitch-black. He clicked on his flashlight and illuminated the long flight of stairs.

"Ares usually drops me at the bottom," Gregor said. He started down and his dad moved slowly behind him, taking each step carefully.

The stairway led into a large, man-made tunnel that appeared to be deserted. The air was heavy, cold, and dank. No sounds filtered down from the park, but along the walls there was a faint scampering of tiny mouse feet.

When he reached the last few steps, Gregor looked back over his shoulder at his dad, who was only about halfway down. "Take your time. He's not here yet."

The words had barely left his mouth when a sharp blow landed on his wrist and Gregor felt the flashlight fly out of his hand. He turned his head in time to glimpse a large, furry form leaping at him from the shadows.

The rat had been waiting for him.

CHAPTER 3

Gregor swung the crowbar, but the rat caught it in its teeth and yanked him forward. He was airborne for a moment before he slammed onto his stomach in the tunnel. The crowbar clattered into the dark as his hands barely kept his face from smacking into the cold cement floor.

"Gregor!" He could hear his father's anguished cry as the rat pinned him to the ground with its chest. Hot breath hit his cheek. He tried to swing backward but he was helpless.

"Pitiful. Just pitiful," a familiar voice hissed in his ear.

Gregor felt a wave of relief that was immediately followed by annoyance. "Get off me, man!"

The rat simply shifted into a more comfortable position. "You see, the second you lose your light, you're as good as dead."

The beam of the flashlight hit them. Gregor squinted and saw his dad approaching them with a chunk of concrete in one hand.

"Let him go!" shouted his father, lifting the concrete.

"It's okay, Dad! It's just Ripred!" Gregor squirmed to free himself but the rat weighed a ton. "He's a friend," he added to reassure his dad, although calling Ripred a "friend" was something of a stretch.

"Ripred?" said his dad. "Ripred?" His chest was heaving up and down, his eyes wild as he tried to make sense of the name.

"Yes, I try and give your boy survival tips but he just doesn't pay attention." Ripred rose and easily flipped Gregor over with his paw. The rat's scarred face was accusing. "You haven't been practicing you echolocation, have you?"

"I have, too!" shot back Gregor. "I practice with my sister."

This was true, although Gregor omitted saying that he mainly did it because Lizzie made him. She was extremely conscientious about homework. When she found out that Ripred had told Gregor to practice his echolocation, she took it very seriously. At least three times a week she'd drag him off somewhere in the building — the hallway, the stairwell, the lobby — and blindfold him. Then he'd have to stand there making a clicking sound with his tongue, trying to find her. The sound of his click was supposed to bounce off her, and somehow he was supposed to know where she was standing. But despite her best efforts, Gregor's echolocation skills weren't improving much.

Now, with Ripred getting on his case, Gregor felt defensive. "Look, I told you, that echolocation stuff doesn't work for me. Where's Vikus, anyway?"

"He's not coming," said Ripred.

"But he wrote me about 'The Prophecy of Blood.' I thought he was meeting us," said Gregor.

"And I thought you'd be alone," said Ripred. He sat back on his haunches and looked at Gregor's father. "Do you remember me?"

His dad was still clutching the piece of concrete, but it was down by his side. He stared at Ripred as if he were trying to remember someone from a dream. A long dream filled with hunger and loneliness and fear and the taunting of voices in the dark. Voices of rats. Like the one who sat before him. His brow furrowed as he tried to make sense of the jumble in his head. "You brought me food. Down in the rat pit . . . you brought me food sometimes."

"That's right," said Ripred. "And did anyone here bring *me* food? I'm famished."

Ripred did look thinner than usual. His

41

belly had shrunk down some and the bones in his face were more pronounced.

Gregor hadn't even planned to see Ripred, let alone feed him. But his hands automatically dug in his jacket pockets. His fingers found a stray fortune cookie from the night before and he pulled it out. "Here," he said.

Ripred reacted with exaggerated amazement. "Oh, heavens, is this whole thing for me?"

"Look, I didn't even know —" Gregor began.

"No, please. Don't apologize." Ripred's tongue darted out and flicked the cookie into his mouth. "Oh, yes, oh, my word," he raved as he chewed and swallowed. "I'm absolutely stuffed!"

"How come you're so hungry?" asked Gregor.

"Well, what with Solovet bent on starving the rats out —" said Ripred.

Gregor vaguely remembered Ripred bringing this up at dinner in Regalia once. The humans had taken one of the rats' rivers or something.

"And having to feed that gluttonous baby you dumped on me —" said Ripred.

"The Bane?" interrupted Gregor. "How is he?"

"He's a royal pain, frankly. He eats three times as much as the rest of us, yet he can't seem to get the knack of hunting. If we don't feed him he whines. So, of course, we do feed him and then he grows another six inches and whines louder. Believe me, he's doing a lot better than I am," growled Ripred.

The rat found an old two-by-four by the stairs and began to gnaw on it. Strips of wood curled away from the board like apple peel.

"What about Luxa? Is she home?" asked Gregor, almost afraid to hear the answer.

"No, she's not home," said Ripred, a little less brusquely. "I have it on good authority that she's not being held prisoner by the rats. It's possible she did escape the Labyrinth but . . . I wouldn't be too hopeful there, if I were you."

Gregor gave a small nod. It had been months. If Luxa had escaped the rats, why wasn't she back in Regalia?

"And the others?" he said.

"Her bat's still missing. And the lovely Twitchtip's unaccounted for as well. Oh, you know who did show up? That crawler who was carting around your sister. What's his name, Tock . . . Ting . . . ?" said Ripred.

"Temp?" said Gregor's dad.

"That's it, Temp. He got home a few weeks after you left, as good as ever. Spent some time in the Dead Land growing a new leg or two," said Ripred. "He's very excited about seeing 'the princess' again."

Gregor and his dad exchanged a look. Even if they could somehow convince his mom to let him go down, getting her to let Boots return to the Underland would be impossible.

Ripred caught the moment that passed between them. "Well, you do know she has to come back? I mean, you've read 'The Prophecy of Blood,' right?"

"I've read it," said Gregor evasively. "I'm just not sure what happens next."

"I'll tell you what happens next," said Ripred. "Vikus is sending a bat up to your laundry room at midnight. He expects you and your sister to be waiting for it. We all do."

"And if we're not?" asked Gregor.

"If you're not, there's very little chance of any warmblooded creature surviving in the Underland. There's a plague running around down there causing all kinds of trouble, or didn't you hear?" said Ripred.

"Yeah, that plague thing, that's not going to be a real plus when I ask my mom if we can go," said Gregor.

"The plague. Tell us about it," said Gregor's dad.

"Oh, it's some kind of pox," said Ripred. "High fever, pustules on the skin, eventually shuts down the lungs. They call it 'The Curse of the Warmbloods' because it only affects warmblooded creatures. The rats are dropping like flies. The bodies of a few bats who were scouts were found in the Dead Land. And nobody's heard from the nibblers yet."

"The nibblers?" said Gregor.

"Mice. That's what we call them. But listen, they've only had three plague cases in Regalia, and they're quarantined, so you'll be perfectly safe there. That's all we really need you for, the meeting in Regalia. All the warmbloods are sending representatives. Every creature's blood will be tested for the plague by the humans before they can participate. Just show up for that and you can go right home," said Ripred.

"I can?" said Gregor. Usually a prophecy required a lot more of him.

"Why not? All the prophecy says is to bring you from above. After that, what use will you be? You're eleven. No one expects you to personally whip up some cure for the plague with your chemistry set," said Ripred.

The rat was right. Curing a plague was really more of a job for doctors and scientists than for warriors.

Gregor looked at his dad hopefully. "It's just for one meeting, Dad. And no one with the plague will be there. That would be okay, don't you think?"

"I don't know, Gregor," said his dad with a shake of his head.

"Oh, the warrior will come. We know that. It's his sister we're worried about," said Ripred.

"What makes you so sure I'll be there?" asked Gregor.

"Because of that bat of yours. The big moody one," said Ripred.

"Ares?" said Gregor. "What's this got to do with Ares? Are they going to banish him if I don't show up?"

"It's worse than that, I'm afraid." The board Ripred was gnawing on snapped in two. He spit out a mouthful of wood shavings and looked at Gregor tiredly. "Those three plague cases in Regalia? He's one of them."

CHAPTER 4

"Oh, no," said Gregor softly. Of all the horrible possibilities that had been running through his mind in the last few months, this was not one of them. "How bad is he?"

"He's bad. He was the first case in Regalia. They think he contracted the plague when he was attacked by those mites in the Waterway. Then he must have passed it on to the rats in the Labyrinth," said Ripred.

"Mites? But, I thought only warmblooded animals could get it," said Gregor's dad.

"Yes, but bloodsucking or carnivorous insects can carry it and spread it from warmblood to warmblood," said Ripred.

"So, he's going to die?" Gregor said in a cracked voice.

"Well, let's not write him off yet," said Ripred. "They've got medicines in Regalia that can at least ease his symptoms, which is more than the rats have. And he's strong."

"That's true," said Gregor, feeling slightly more optimistic. "He's the strongest bat down there. And he's stubborn, too. He'll fight it."

"Yes, he'll try and hang on because he believes help is on the way. Because the warrior, his bond, will come. There will be a meeting. Then a search for the cure will begin. Of course, if you take that hope away . . ." Ripred let the sentence dangle on purpose.

"I'll be there, Ripred," said Gregor.

"Don't bother coming without your sister. It's a waste of time. According to Sandwich, the crawlers have to be involved, and they've only agreed to send a representative if Boots is there," said Ripred.

"I don't know how I'm going to get my mom to let her —" Gregor said.

"Your mom. You tell your mom this from me. If you and your sister don't show up, the rats will send an escort," said Ripred.

"What's that mean?" said his dad.

"It means, be there at midnight," said Ripred.

"But —" Gregor began.

The rat gave a groan of pain and hunched over for a few moments. "Argh, I've got to find something to fill my belly. And in another minute it will be one of you," he snarled. "Go on. Go home! You know what you have to do! So do it!"

Ripred turned and vanished into the shadows.

Gregor and his dad climbed back up to

the park, pried the stone slab loose, and pulled themselves out. They quickly repositioned the rock and headed toward the street.

"What are we going to do, Dad?" Gregor asked, as they stood on the curb, trying to hail a cab.

"Don't worry, we'll figure out something," said his dad. "Just don't you worry."

But Gregor was very worried, and he could tell his dad was, too.

His mom was home from waiting tables when they returned. She was still in her uniform, with her feet propped up on the coffee table, looking beat. She worked seven days a week, every week, unless it was one of those major holidays like Thanksgiving or Christmas when almost everybody was off. She joked that Saturday and Sunday evenings were her days off because she got finished at four o'clock. She never mentioned how she also had to show up for work at six in the morning on the weekends. No, his mom never complained. Probably because she was so grateful to have them all home again. And now he was going to have to tell her they were going back to the Underland.

"How was the movie?" she asked with a smile as they came in.

"We didn't see a movie, Mom," said Gregor.

His mom raised her eyebrows questioningly, but before Gregor could continue, the door to the kitchen swung open and Mrs. Cormaci stuck her head out. "Good, you're back. Dinner in three minutes," she said and disappeared.

"What's she still doing here?" Gregor blurted out.

"I invited her to stay for dinner. She made the stew after all. Then she and the girls wouldn't let me help," said his mom. "What's with you, anyway? I thought you liked Mrs. Cormaci."

"I do," said Gregor. "I do."

"Then go wash up and find your manners while you're at it," said his mom.

The kitchen door swung open again and Lizzie and Boots stuck their heads out. "Two minutes," said Lizzie importantly.

"Two!" Boots echoed.

"Go ahead and wash up, Gregor," said his dad. "We can tell your mom about our afternoon later."

Gregor understood. There could be no talking about the Underland until Mrs. Cormaci cleared out. But who knew when that would be? There weren't that many hours left until midnight.

He was fidgety the whole meal, wishing Mrs. Cormaci would go home. He felt kind of guilty because she was obviously having such a good time. They all were, his sisters, his mom, and even his grandma had come out and sat at the table instead of eating off a tray in her bed. There was stew and warm bread, and Mrs. Cormaci and his sisters had baked a cake for a surprise. It was practically a party. But Gregor could not join in the fun; he could not think of anything except getting to the Underland to help Ares.

The meal dragged on endlessly. Then everyone sat in the living room to talk for a while. Gregor gave big yawns, hoping Mrs. Cormaci would pick up on the hint, but she didn't even seem to notice. Finally, at around nine-thirty, she stood up and stretched and said she better get home to bed.

Everyone was so keyed up, it was another hour before his grandma, Lizzie, and Boots had settled down in their rooms. When his mom came out from kissing them all good night, Gregor grabbed her hand and without a word led her into the kitchen. His dad was right on their heels.

"What? What is going on with you two?" said his mom.

"I heard from the Underland today. We went and talked to Ripred under Central Park, and Ares is dying, Mom, and Boots and I have to go back down to save him! At midnight! Tonight!" The words that had been pressing on Gregor's chest spilled out before he could stop them. He instantly regretted his impulsive delivery. The horrified look on his mom's face told him this had not been the way to break the news.

"No, you do not! You are not! You are never going down to that place again!" she said.

"Look, Mom, you don't understand!" said Gregor.

"I understand all I need to understand! First your father locked up down there for years. You and Boots disappearing like that. Giant roaches stealing my baby! There is nothing to understand and there is nothing to discuss! You are not going down there again! Ever!" His mom was gripping the back of a chair so hard her knuckles had turned white.

His dad intervened. He sat her down at the table and tried to explain the situation in a calm, rational voice. The more he talked, the larger her eyes grew in disbelief.

"What did you tell him? Did you tell that rat they were coming? Did you tell Gregor he could go?" she asked.

"Of course I didn't! But it isn't so simple, letting a whole civilization die! There are a lot of good people down there. Good people and animals, too, who risked their lives saving me, saving the kids. We can't just turn our backs on them!" said his dad.

"I can," said his mother bitterly. "You just watch me."

"Well, I'm going," said Gregor flatly.

"Oh, no, you're not. You're not going anywhere but to bed," said his mom. "Now go brush your teeth. And I don't want to hear another word out of either of you about this." His mother's face was set like stone.

Gregor felt his dad's hand on his arm. "Better go to bed, son. I don't think we're going to change her mind."

"Nothing will change my mind," said his mom.

And that's when it started.

At first, there was just a faint scratching in the wall. Then a skittering sound. And suddenly, it was as if the kitchen were alive. Scores of small, clawed feet were running around and around inside the walls. Only a thin layer of plaster separated Gregor and his parents from them.

"What's that? What's that sound?" said

his mother, her head darting from side to side.

"It sounds like rats," said his dad.

"Rats? I thought they couldn't get up here!" said his mom.

"The Underland ones can't. But I guess the regular ones can. And they know each other," said Gregor. He looked anxiously at the walls. What was going on?

"Maybe this is what Ripred meant by the rats sending you an escort," said his dad.

The creatures began to squeak now, as if to confirm what his dad had just said.

"That must be it," Gregor thought. "The rats are going to try and scare my mom into letting us go." But how far would they take this? The Underland rats believed their whole existence was in jeopardy. That they would all die if Gregor and Boots didn't come. "They'll kill us before they let us stay here," he said aloud, without thinking.

"I'm calling the police. Or the fire department. I'm calling 911!" said his mother. She rushed into the living room, and Gregor and his dad went after her.

"It won't do any good, Mom!" said Gregor. "What's the fire department going to do?"

The rats began to pour into the living room walls. They were louder now.

"Oh, my. Oh! Get the girls! Get Grandma!" Gregor's mom grabbed the phone receiver and dialed the emergency number. "Come on, come on!" Then a look of shock crossed her face. "The line just went dead."

"Okay, we're getting out of here!" said his dad.

They all rushed into the bedroom for Gregor's grandma and sisters. His mom swept a sleeping Boots right out of her crib. "They're not getting Boots again! They're not getting her!" said his mom shrilly.

His dad pulled back the covers on the main bed and wrapped his grandma in a quilt.

"What's going on?" said the old woman in confusion.

"Nothing, Mama. We think there might be a fire in the building, so we're just getting out while they check," said his dad. He struggled as he lifted her out of the bed like a baby.

Gregor shook Lizzie's shoulder. Her eyes flew open and she was instantly wide awake. "What is it, Gregor? What's that sound?"

The rats had not followed them to the bedroom, but they were still making a racket in the living room walls.

"That's rats, isn't it?" she said. "They're in the apartment!"

"No, not in the apartment. Just in the walls. But we got to get out of here. Come on now!" He guided his sister out of bed and into the living room. As the full impact of the rat noise hit her, Lizzie began to tremble all over.

"Come on, Lizzie! It'll be okay once we're outside!" said Gregor, and propelled her across the room. He grabbed their coats as his mom flung open the front door and ran. Gregor pulled Lizzie along after her. His dad brought up the rear with his grandma.

"Nobody get on the elevator," said his mom. "Take the stairs." Clutching Boots, she led them to the far end of the hall and yanked open the door to the stairwell.

At the top of the stairs, his dad had to set his grandma on her feet. "I'm going to need your help, Gregor. I can't get her down myself."

Gregor thrust the coats into Lizzie's arms. "You carry these." Lizzie stared back at him, her pupils huge, her breath coming in short, painful pants. "It's okay, Lizzie. It's okay. Listen, you can't even hear them out here."

You couldn't hear anything. The stairwell didn't border anyone's apartment. It was sandwiched between the outside wall of the complex and the elevator shaft. It was quiet at night where they lived, anyway. Most people in the building had small kids or were elderly. Even on a Saturday night it seemed like everybody went to bed by ten.

Lizzie clutched the coats against her chest. "I — can — carry — them," she got out.

Gregor locked forearms with his dad behind his grandma's back and legs, and they lifted her in a sitting position. They had carried her this way before around the apartment, when her arthritis was particularly bad.

"Stay right with us, honey," his dad said to Lizzie. "Hold on to my arm so I know you're there."

His family moved in a tight clump down the stairs. They had gone down about two floors when the rat noise started up again. It wasn't much at first. But it increased in volume at every step until they had to raise their voices to be heard.

"Hurry!" said his mom. "It's not far now!"

Finally, the door to the lobby came into view. His mom backed into the door, holding it open as Gregor and his dad stumbled by. "When we get outside, we go straight to the avenue. Get a cab. Then the bus station. Come on, Lizzie! Come on, baby!" said his mom.

Tears were coursing down Lizzie's cheeks now. She had stopped at the bottom of the steps and was gasping so hard she couldn't speak. Shifting Boots to one hip, his mom got an arm protectively around Lizzie's shoulders and they fled for the entrance.

The clamor of the rats was worse than ever. The rodents' squeaks had evolved into horrible shrieks. Claws were scratching now with purpose, trying to dig through the plaster.

Gregor and his dad reached the entrance first. It was a double door made of thick, warped glass. They set his grandma's feet on the ground, and Gregor's dad reached for the handle. He had opened it only a crack when Gregor saw something. Gregor let go of his grandma and threw his shoulder against the glass, slamming the door shut.

His dad fell to his knees as he caught his grandma. Gregor could see his mom yelling at him, but he couldn't really hear her over the din of the rats. Knowing he couldn't be heard, either, Gregor pounded his fist into the glass near his knees, drawing everyone's focus to the base of the door.

Pressed against the outside, smearing the glass with saliva as they tried to gnaw through it, were hundreds of rats.

CHAPTER 5

Gregor's family staggered back from the front door and huddled in a knot at the center of the lobby. Lizzie was crouched down in a ball, panting, her palms shining with sweat. Gregor's mom kneeled on the floor, one arm wrapped tightly around Lizzie, the other around Boots, who had started to wake. The toddler rubbed her sleepy face in her mother's shoulder and blinked into the fluorescent lights of the lobby. His dad had gotten back to his feet, holding his grandma, who had her eyes squeezed shut and had her hands over her ears.

Gregor was afraid to leave the door to join them. Afraid the bolt would give way under the pressure of the rats. He braced his back against the door and looked at his family helplessly. There was no leaving the building. What were they going to do?

Something caught his mom's attention and she seemed to stop breathing. Gregor followed her eyes to the wall off to his right. At first he didn't see anything. Then a puff of plaster dust floated out near the baseboard. A small clawed paw broke through the wall and a rat's nose poked through.

"All right!" screamed his mother. "All right, they can go!"

It was like someone had thrown a switch. The rat noise stopped instantly. Gregor could hear only Lizzie's ragged gasps, the hum of the fluorescent lights, and the distant sound of traffic from the street. He looked down at the glass door. Not a rat in sight. But he knew they were there, in the walls, in the bushes, waiting and watching.

"We can go?" asked Gregor.

"You can go," said his mother in a hoarse voice. "But this time, I'm going with you."

"Come on. Let's get back upstairs and talk about this," said his dad.

Gregor went over to Lizzie and helped her up. "You okay, Liz?"

"My — fingers — got — pins and — needles," she choked out.

"I think you're having a panic attack, honey," Gregor's dad said softly. "And no wonder. When we get upstairs, I'll get you a paper bag to breathe in. Fix you right up." He jabbed the elevator button with his elbow and the doors to it opened at once. Like it had been waiting.

His family stepped inside.

"I can do button," said Boots. His mom

held her out so she could press the number for their floor.

"See?" said Boots proudly.

"Good girl," said Gregor's mom dully, and the doors closed.

Back in the apartment, the clock on the wall said eleven-thirty. "We've got a half hour," said Gregor.

His dad settled his grandma back in her bed. Then he sat Lizzie on the couch and taught her to breathe into a small paper bag. "Too much oxygen getting into you, pumpkin. Just take it slow."

Lizzie nodded and tried to follow his instructions. But she looked miserable. "I don't — want Mom — to go."

"I think she's right," said Gregor's dad. "We need you up here. I'll go down with Boots and Gregor."

"No," said his mom. "I have to go."

"Why can't dad go?" said Gregor, a little too forcefully. His mom shot him a look and he began to backpedal. "I mean, he's been before. People know him."

This was true, but it was not the real reason Gregor wanted his dad instead of his mom. For starters, she was furious. No telling what she'd say to the Underlanders. There was something else, too. Down in the Underland, Gregor had an identity. He was the warrior. Even if he didn't always buy into that himself, it was important that everybody else did. And somehow, he didn't think it was going to look so hot for the warrior to be showing up with his mom. Especially when he knew she'd have no problem saying stuff like, "Now go wash your hands and find your manners while you're at it," or sending him to bed even if there was a bunch of people around.

"I can't be the one waiting and wondering what's happening to the rest of you. Not this time." His mom set Boots down and wrapped her arms around Lizzie. "You know what I'm talking about, don't you, Lizzie?"

Lizzie nodded. "I could — go — too," she said bravely. But the very notion was so scary, it caused her to start panting again.

"No, I need you to stay up here and keep an eye on your dad and grandma. We won't be gone long. There's just one meeting, and we're coming straight back," said Gregor's mom, stroking Lizzie's hair.

"And then — can we go — away?" said Lizzie.

"That's right," said his mom. "How'd you like to move down to your uncle's farm in Virginia?"

"Good," said Lizzie, looking a little

better. "That'd be — good."

"Well, you better start packing while I'm gone. Okay, baby?" said his mom.

"Okay," said Lizzie. And she actually smiled.

Gregor felt like a jerk. Here he'd been worried about how cool he'd look having his mom around in the Underland. He wasn't thinking about her at all. Or about the rest of his family. He reached out and gave Lizzie a pat. "We'll be back in a couple hours, Liz," he said.

"That's right." His mom kissed Lizzie and gave her a squeeze, then turned to him. "So, what do we need to take?"

"Light," said Gregor. "That's the main thing. I'll get it, Mom."

While his dad took the crowbar down to the laundry room to pry open the grate, Gregor dug around the apartment for a couple of flashlights and all the batteries he could find. His mom just sat on the couch, an arm around each of his sisters, talking in a soothing voice about what their new life would be like in Virginia.

Gregor went into the bedroom and saw that his grandma wasn't asleep.

"You need to go back down to that place," she said to him. It wasn't a question.

"I'm in another prophecy, Grandma,"

Gregor said, and showed it to her.

"Then you got to go. You can run away, but the prophecy will find you somehow," she said.

"That's how it seems to be working out," said Gregor. He straightened her quilts. "You take care of yourself, okay?"

"You, too. See you soon, Gregor," she said.

"See you soon," he said. He kissed her on the forehead and she gave him a smile.

They had to risk leaving his grandma alone for a short time, while they went to the laundry room. But it was doubtful she would try and get out of bed, anyway. And the rats weren't coming back. They had what they wanted.

His dad had pushed the dryer over. Now there was some space in front of the grate, which was propped open. Wisps of white vapor were curling out of the darkness inside the wall. "Looks like the currents are active," said his dad. "You could probably ride them right down to the Underland. But Ripred said there would be a bat."

The words were not out of his mouth when a large, furry face appeared in the opening. The bat was extraordinary looking — white with dramatic black stripes radiating out from its nose to its ears.

His mother gasped, and Lizzie let out a sharp cry. It was the first Underland creature either of them had ever seen.

But Boots immediately put out her little hand to stroke the bat's fur. "Oh, you look like zebra. Z is for zebra. Hi, you!"

"Greetings," purred the bat. "I am she called Nike. Are you ready to depart?"

Gregor's family looked at one another, then wordlessly exchanged hugs.

"How do we . . . get on you?" his mother asked the bat.

"You must fall. But do not worry. The current is such that you will ride safely to the ground with or without a flier. I am only here for your ease of mind," said Nike.

The bat dropped out of sight. Boots started eagerly for the grate. "Me next!"

Gregor grabbed her and almost laughed at her excitement. "I think I'm going to hold on to you this time. Ready, Mom?"

His mom kneeled down by the grate and stuck her head into it. "We're just . . . supposed to jump?" She pulled her head out, looking bewildered.

"Wait a sec," said Gregor. He set Boots on the floor and climbed out into the mist, hanging from the edge of the grate opening by one hand. "Now pass down Boots," he said. His dad swung Boots into his free arm.

She latched on to him like a baby koala bear. "Come on, Mom. You jump, grab on to us, and we'll all go down together."

His mother bit her lip, gave one look back at his dad and Lizzie, and scooted herself, feet first, out of the laundry room. As she came through, her hand latched on to the wrist that was supporting Gregor, and he released the grate.

Within seconds, the swirling mist blotted out the light from the laundry room. He locked his fingers around his mom's wrist and could feel her pulse going a mile a minute. He tried to block out the terror he felt of heights, of falling, but it wasn't really something he could control. The first time he'd taken this trip he had calmed himself down by telling himself this was just a bad dream.

But the little voice squealing delightedly in his ear was all too real. "Gre-go! Mama! Boots! We all go wheeeeee!"

CHAPTER 6

"Gregor! We're going to be killed!" cried his mother.

"No, Mom, we'll be fine," said Gregor, sounding calmer than he felt. "Hey, Nike?" he called. "Do you think we could ride down?"

He didn't know if the bat had heard him, or if she was even still around, but suddenly he was sitting on her back. Nike gave a twist and his mom was riding behind him.

"Certainly you may ride," said Nike. "Whatever manner is most comfortable." Her voice had a pleasant, cheerful quality that seemed unusual for a bat. Of course, the main bat Gregor talked to was Ares, and he was usually pretty depressed. Not that his friend didn't have good reason to be.

"Thanks," said Gregor. He settled Boots in front of him and clicked on a flashlight. The beam caught the swirls of mist. It gave the impression that they were surrounded by a beautiful, spooky white forest. But through the vapors, Gregor could make out the walls of the wide, stone tube they were descending.

"I can ride bat," said Boots, rubbing her hands on Nike's striped neck. "Z is for zebra. Z is for zoo. And zip!" She'd been a little obsessed with the alphabet lately.

"I expected only yourself and your sister, Gregor the Overlander. Could it be that this third human is your mother?" asked Nike.

"Yeah, she wanted to come see the Underland," Gregor said. To himself he added, "like she wanted a hole in the head."

"Oh, there has been much speculation in the Underland as to the greatness of she who is mother to both the warrior and the princess," said Nike. "What an honor to meet you, Warrior's Mother!"

"You, too," said his mom stiffly. "And you can just call me Grace."

Gregor grinned into the mist. He could tell his mom was thrown by both the friend-liness of the bat and how complimentary she was. "So, I don't think I met you before, Nike," he said.

"Oh, no. We did not meet. But I saw you in my homeland when you were fulfilling 'The Prophecy of Gray,' " she said.

"When we went to see Queen Athena?" asked Gregor. That was the only time he had visited the bats' land. There had been hundreds, maybe thousands hanging from

68

the ceiling of the cavernous place. He could only remember the queen.

"Yes, my mother," said Nike.

"Your mother? Then you must be a princess," said Gregor, a little surprised. She had not introduced herself as Princess Nike.

"I am, yes. But I hope you will not hold it against me." Nike laughed.

When they finally landed, they had to climb off Nike's back so that they could squeeze through the crack in the side of the tube to the tunnel.

"It won't be far now to Regalia," said Gregor, as they all climbed back on Nike.

"Good. The sooner we get this meeting over with, the better," said his mom.

It had taken Gregor about twenty minutes to jog to Regalia after his first fall, but the trip was much shorter on a bat. Before he knew it, Nike was waved through a guarded entrance and there beneath them was Regalia. It was morning, and the city was just stirring to life.

"Oh!" he heard his mom exclaim under her breath. The gorgeous stone city with its ornate towers and intricate carvings could impress even her.

Nike flew them into the High Hall of the palace where Vikus was waiting for them.

The old man's face was careworn, and his eyes had lost their brightness. Luxa's disappearance and probable death had taken their toll. But when Vikus saw Gregor, he smiled with relief.

"Gregor the Overlander. I knew you would not forsake us," he said. "And here is Boots as well!"

"Hi, you!" said Boots.

Gregor and Boots slid off Nike's back, revealing their mother. She got off Nike and grabbed Boots before she could run off. "You stay right here with me."

"If my eyes do not deceive me, this must be the woman to whom the Underland owes its very life," said Vikus. He gave a low bow to Gregor's mother. "Welcome, and deepest gratitude, Mother of Our Light."

"You can just call me Grace," said his mom tersely.

"Grace," Vikus said, as if savoring the word. "A fitting name for one who has so aided us. I am Vikus."

"Uh-huh. So, where's this meeting?" said his mom, shifting Boots to her other hip.

"Now that you have landed, the preparations may begin. The delegates' blood must be screened for the plague. Forgive the intrusion, but we must examine your blood as well," said Vikus.

"But we don't have the plague!" said his mom, visibly alarmed at the idea.

"This is my hope. But our doctors have put forth the theory that Ares contracted the plague when he was attacked by mites on the journey to the Labyrinth. As both your children were present when he was bitten, and Gregor was in close contact with him for several days that followed, it is essential that we test their blood," said Vikus. "We must also rule out that the children may have passed it on to you."

It had not crossed Gregor's mind that he and Boots could have been exposed to the plague. Now, he remembered examining Ares's skin with Luxa so they could dab medicine on the spots where the mites had eaten away the bat's flesh. His fingers had been covered in Ares's blood. And, at the time, open sores from a squid-sucker attack had covered his forearm. The bat's blood could have gotten into his wounds.

WARMBLOOD NOW
A BLOODBORNE DEATH . . .

His mother's free arm reached for him and pulled him close. "But . . . if they'd been exposed to the plague, they'd have it by now, right?" she said. "I mean, they'd be showing symptoms, wouldn't they?"

"I cannot say," said Vikus. "Some creatures fall ill within days, others seem to show no symptoms for months. It is an insidious and clever thing."

His mother kept her arm tightly around him as they followed Vikus down a hall and into a brightly lit room. A small woman was leaning over a table filled with medical equipment. There were glass vials of liquids, an oil lamp with a blue flame, and an oddly designed piece of equipment that Gregor guessed was a microscope.

"Doctor Neveeve —" began Vikus, and the woman literally jumped. A glass slide flew from her hand and shattered on the floor.

"Oh," said Dr. Neveeve in a breathy voice. "There goes yet another slide. Do not worry yourselves, it was free of contagion."

"Forgive me for startling you," said Vikus. "The outbreak of 'The Curse of the Warmbloods' has us all on edge. This is Doctor Neveeve, our foremost physician in the study of the plague. Neveeve, may I present Gregor the Overlander, his sister Boots, and their most honorable mother, Grace."

Neveeve's intense, pale-violet eyes darted over them. "Greetings. You cannot imagine how welcome a sight you are."

"They must be cleared for the meeting," said Vikus.

"Yes, yes, let us proceed with all haste," said Neveeve, pulling a pair of skintight gloves over her hands. She pricked each of their fingers with a needle and examined their blood under a microscope. With one glance, she pronounced his mom and Boots plague-free. But when the doctor peered at Gregor's slide, she frowned and adjusted the microscope several times.

"Just say it," Gregor thought. "I've got the plague. I know I do."

To his relief, Neveeve lifted her head and gave them her first smile. "All clear."

Gregor let out his breath in a huff. "Now what?"

"Now if you sit, I will check your scalp for fleas," said Neveeve.

"Fleas? That boy doesn't have fleas," said his mother indignantly.

Gregor couldn't help laughing. "We don't even have a pet."

"I am sorry, but it is essential we do this," said Vikus. "The fleas carry the plague from creature to creature. Neveeve's early recognition of this explains why we have only three cases in Regalia, and hundreds of rats have been stricken."

Suddenly, being checked for fleas wasn't so funny.

When they had all been pronounced flealess, Vikus invited them to rest before the meeting. "It will be at least another hour before all those attending are tested. Come and refresh yourselves."

Vikus led them to a beautiful room. The walls were carved with soft, swirling patterns. Elegant furniture circled a roaring fireplace. There were even potted plants dripping with pink flowers. Underlanders appeared with trays of pretty food and a couple of musicians came in with stringed instruments and asked if Gregor's mom desired music. Gregor figured all the hoopla must have been for her benefit. He and Boots had never received this kind of attention.

"You didn't tell me it was this nice," said his mother.

"It's not, usually. I think somebody's trying to impress you . . . Mother of Our Light," said Gregor. She rolled her eyes but he could tell she was a little pleased.

Gregor looked at her sitting on the couch, still in her waitress uniform, and thought that if anyone deserved a little star treatment, if was his mom. He would have liked to stay himself — the music was unlike any he'd ever heard — but there was something he had to do.

"I'm going to run down to the bathroom," he told his mom.

Once he rounded the door, he did run, but not for the bathroom. He took the first flight of stairs and started down it, two steps at a time. The hospital was on one of the lower levels. That must be where they were keeping Ares.

Either he was getting better at navigating the palace, or he was just lucky, because he made it to the hospital quickly. The Underland doctors were surprised to see him, and even more surprised by his request.

"Yes," said one doctor doubtfully. "It is possible to see him. But you will not be able to converse. He is quarantined behind thick walls of glass."

"Okay, well then, I'll just, you know, wave or whatever. I just want him to see I'm here," said Gregor. If Ripred was right and Ares was hanging on only because he thought Gregor was coming, then he had to make contact.

The doctor led him to a long corridor. "There. He is to the passage on your right. You do know . . . he is very ill."

"I know," said Gregor. "I won't do anything to get him worked up or anything." He knew you were supposed to be quiet around people in hospitals. Before the doctor could change his mind, Gregor hurried down the corridor. He was suddenly excited at the prospect of seeing his friend after all these months. He wanted Ares to know that it would be okay now. He was here. A cure would be found. They would fly together again. His feet picked up speed, and he had to suppress the impulse to run. He whipped around the corner into another hall. On one side was a long glass wall.

Gregor looked through the glass and saw his bat.

Then he leaned over and threw up.

CHAPTER 7

Gregor crouched over as his dinner spewed onto the stone floor, splattering into the glass wall and onto his boots. Another wave of nausea hit him and he retched again. And again.

A cool hand touched the back of his neck, and a woman's sympathetic voice said, "Come, Overlander. Come with me." She led him to a nearby bathroom. He found himself gripping the sides of one of the toilets. A stream of continuous water ran through the basin, immediately washing away its contents. For a minute, Gregor thought he was done, but then the image of Ares filled his brain and he began vomiting again.

Ares had been lying stretched out on his back, his wings awkwardly extended. Large clumps of his glossy black fur were missing. In their place were purple bumps the size of cantaloupes. Several of the bumps had burst and were oozing blood and pus from the ruptures. The bat's tongue, which was coated in white, hung out the side of his mouth. His head was tilted back at an odd angle as he struggled for air. Gregor had never seen anything so frightening in his life.

He got rid of lunch and probably breakfast, too, and then he just heaved for a while, until nothing else came up. His body was bathed in sweat and his limbs were shaky. Finally, he pushed back from the toilet.

"I'm sorry. I'm so sorry," he said. He felt embarrassed and ashamed of his reaction to seeing Ares.

"Do not be. Many people have the same response when they first see a plague victim. My husband, a great soldier, fainted dead away. Others face it stoically, then wake up screaming from nightmares. It is a very fearful thing," said the woman.

"Ares didn't see me, did he?" asked Gregor. It would be awful if his bat had seen him throw up just from looking at him.

"No, he was asleep. Do not punish yourself with thoughts that you have wounded him," said the woman. "Here, rinse your mouth." She pressed a stone cup into his hand and he rinsed and spat into the toilet.

"I'd be okay if I saw him now. It was just the shock," said Gregor.

"I know this," said the woman.

Gregor looked up and saw her face for the

first time. There was something familiar about it but he was sure he didn't know her. "Are you a doctor here?"

"No, I am a visitor like yourself. I come from the Fount. My name is Susannah," said the woman.

"Oh, you're Howard's mom," said Gregor. That's why she looked familiar. She was the mother of one of the guys who had gone with Gregor to find the Bane. That also made her Solovet's and Vikus's daughter. And Luxa's aunt. Was everyone here related, or what?

"Yes, my son speaks very highly of you," said Susannah. "He credits you with saving his life when he was on trial for treason."

"They should have given him a medal or something. He was amazing that whole trip," said Gregor.

"Thank you," said the woman. Then her eyes welled up with tears.

"Are you okay?" said Gregor. Had he said something to upset her?

"As well as one may be under the circumstances," she said. She dampened a towel in a basin and wiped Gregor's face with it. He didn't resist. Howard was one of five children. His mom had probably seen plenty of kids throw up.

"How is Howard? Is he in Regalia, too?" asked Gregor.

Susannah stared at him a moment. "Of course, you do not know. Yes, he is in Regalia. In fact, he is but a few paces from us."

"He's in the hospital? He's not sick, is he?" The truth began to dawn on Gregor. "Oh, no, you don't mean he's . . . he doesn't have . . . ?"

"The plague, yes," said Susannah. "But he has only recently been diagnosed. The flier, Andromeda, also. So we are very hopeful that you have arrived in time. That the cure may be found and they will not —" She bit her lip.

So Howard was infected. And Andromeda, too. She was the bat who was bonded to Mareth, the soldier who had led the quest to find the Bane. During that trip, Howard's bat, Pandora, had been stripped to the bone by a swarm of mites on an island. Then the mites had attacked Ares, who had barely escaped with his life. Howard had tended Ares's wounds. Andromeda had slept pressed up against him. No wonder Vikus had had Gregor's family's blood tested the second they landed in Regalia. Boots hadn't been in contact with Ares much, but it must be a miracle that Gregor's blood was clear.

"I can't believe I don't have it, too," he mumbled.

"Perhaps, as an Overlander, you have some immunity that Underlanders do not," said Susannah.

"Maybe," said Gregor. His mom was always really careful about them being up-to-date on their vaccinations. But he didn't think he'd had a shot for anything like what Ares had.

He took the damp towel and did his best to clean his boots. "Can I see them? All three of them? If I promise not to throw up?" said Gregor.

"Of course. I am sure the sight of you will be as good as light itself," said Susannah.

She took Gregor back to the corridor lined with glass walls. Someone had already cleaned up the vomit and the floor and glass were pristine.

Gregor braced himself and took another look at Ares. This time, all he felt was agony for what his bat — his friend — must be suffering. "Oh, geez," he said. "How long can he go on like that?"

"We do not know. But his strength is almost legendary," said Susannah.

Gregor nodded but he wondered if that was a good thing. What if it just meant that Ares would suffer longer than most crea-

81

tures before he died?

A shudder ran down one of Ares's wings and he opened his eyes. His gaze was unfocused at first, but when it landed on Gregor the bat came to attention. Gregor mustered every ounce of strength he had and gave Ares what he hoped was an encouraging smile. He pressed his right hand onto the glass and saw Ares lift his left claw a few inches. It was as close as they could get to the locking of hand and claw that signified they were bonds.

Ares's eyes drifted shut and Susannah placed her hand on Gregor's arm. "Howard and Andromeda are not nearly so ill. Come," she said.

Gregor followed her farther down the corridor to another glass-enclosed room. Howard and Andromeda were sitting across from each other on the floor with a chessboard between them. Howard had only one visible purple bump about the size of a walnut on his neck. Andromeda's gold-and-black-speckled coat appeared as healthy as ever. Susannah rapped on the glass and the two looked up. The expression on Howard's face when he saw them was so elated that Gregor didn't have to force his smile. Howard and Andromeda hurried to the wall. They couldn't hear each other through the thick glass, but Gregor was sure Howard said, "Gregor! You are here!"

"Yeah, I'm here," said Gregor.

Howard turned his head to listen to Andromeda for a moment, then mouthed to Gregor. "Boots?"

Gregor nodded. "Boots is here, too."

Just then, a door at the back of the room opened. A woman, swathed in protective clothing, entered carrying a tray of medicines. She ordered Howard and Andromeda into their beds.

"Is that Neveeve?" asked Gregor. "She tested my blood."

"Yes, she personally treats all the plague cases," said Susannah.

"Wow. That's not a job for wimps," said Gregor. When he saw Susannah didn't understand, he said, "You've got to be brave to do that."

"Oh, yes. Neveeve is extremely dedicated," said Susannah. "She is determined that we will cure 'The Curse of the Warmbloods.' "

Howard stripped off his shirt and Gregor thought he should give his friends some privacy. And his mom was probably wondering where he was by now. He had to get back before she started getting worried.

As he made his way back through the hospital hallways, Gregor heard a familiar voice as he passed a room. "Overlander!"

Inside, he saw Mareth sitting up on a bed.

"Hey, Mareth!" said Gregor. "Man, it's good to see you!" He didn't add "alive" but that was what he was thinking. The last time he'd seen Mareth, the soldier had been unconscious, bleeding heavily from a bite a sea serpent had given his leg, and a long way from home.

Mareth grabbed something, swung off the side of the bed, and came to meet him. It was only then that Gregor saw that his injured leg had been amputated. All that remained was a few inches of his thigh.

"Your leg." The words were out of his mouth before he could stop them.

"Yes," said Mareth, leaning on his crutch. "I am working hard to be like Temp, and grow a new one."

"Yeah," said Gregor weakly. "That's a neat trick." The cockroach had lost two legs in a squid attack, but Ripred said he had grown them back in the Dead Land.

"They could not save it. The infection spread too deep. But what need have I for a leg when I have Andromeda to ride upon?" said Mareth. As if he had suddenly remembered about his bat, Mareth passed a hand across his eyes.

"She's going to be okay, Mareth," said Gregor. "The meeting's going to start any minute. There's got to be a cure. They'll find it."

"This is what I believe," said Mareth, pulling himself together. "They tested you? Your blood is clear?"

"I'm fine. So is Boots. And I guess you're okay, too, since you're not behind glass," said Gregor.

"Yes, somehow. It does not entirely make sense to me," said Mareth. "How some of us escaped it."

"I know. It's weird," said Gregor.

"Everyone was so afraid you would not come. But I knew you would," said Mareth.

"Of course I came. I mean, it's only for a few hours," said Gregor.

Mareth looked confused. "A few hours? Did Vikus tell you this?" he asked.

"Yeah, he said you guys just needed us for the meeting. Then we can go home," said Gregor. "Someone else is going to find the cure."

"Vikus said this? That you are not to go on a quest to find the cure with the gnawers? You are certain?" said Mareth.

"That's what he said." Gregor thought for a moment, and hesitated. "Well . . . no, I guess Vikus didn't tell me that himself. He sent Ripred to tell me," said Gregor. "But Ripred wouldn't lie about . . ."

A terrible realization came over Gregor. Yes, Ripred would. He would lie. If he thought it was the only way to get Gregor and Boots to the Underland, Ripred would lie in a second.

CHAPTER 8

Gregor hurried back up through the palace and ran into Vikus, his mom, and Boots outside the luxury room. He needed to talk to Vikus about this whole cure thing, but he couldn't do it in front of his mom. Maybe Mareth was wrong and Ripred was right. Maybe they were supposed to find the cure in a lab, not on some dangerous quest somewhere. Maybe it was all a misunderstanding.

"Where on earth have you been?" said his mother. "I thought you just went to the bathroom."

"I did but . . . I threw up," said Gregor. "And it took some time for my stomach to settle."

"You sick?" His mom's hand was instantly on his forehead.

"No, Mom, I feel fine now," said Gregor.

"Well, that stew was pretty rich. And then all this flying around. You never did have a strong stomach," she said. "He gets carsick on long trips, too," she told Vikus. "We have to travel with a plastic bag."

Okay, this was one of those mom-things Gregor had been worried about. His dad would never tell people how the warrior had to travel with a plastic bag. And she didn't even know what she was talking about because flying on bats didn't upset his stomach. Still, this was better than telling her about seeing Ares. "I'm fine, Mom. So, is it time for the meeting?"

"Yes, let us proceed to the arena," said Vikus.

Nike and Euripedes, Vikus's big gray bat, flew them all to the oval-shaped arena used for sports events and military training. The playing field was covered in a soft, springy moss and seating for a large crowd topped the high walls. The arena was on the edge of Regalia and shut off from the city by towering, stone doors. Across the field from the doors were a few tunnels, some flush with the ground, others high in the air, which led away from the city.

When they flew into the arena, the stands were empty. Most of the creatures attending the meeting were down on the field. All three species — the bats, the cockroaches, and the rats — stood in their own clump. There was no interaction between them. It reminded Gregor of the beginning of a track meet, when the teams were assembled around the field warming up, each in a different-colored jersey.

"Ready to make some new friends?" Gregor said to his mom, trying to sound positive.

She simply pressed her lips together in distaste as she stared down at the menagerie of giant Underland creatures. "Tell me again, who's on whose side?"

Gregor shook his head. "It's kind of complicated. The main thing is that most of the humans and rats hate each other. The bats are tight with the humans. The cockroaches just wish everybody would leave them alone. But they love Boots. So, if she shows up, they show up. The prophecy says they need everybody here to find the cure."

Nike and Euripedes dropped them on the field and joined a group of four bats, including Queen Athena, who perched on short, squat stone cylinders.

Ripred and two other rats sat about ten yards away. All three seemed preoccupied with trying to comb some kind of yellow powder out of their coats with their claws.

"What's that in their fur?" his mom asked Vikus, eyeing the rats with revulsion.

"A powder to kill fleas. Just as a precaution. Their blood was clear of plague, but they all had fleas, and we cannot risk the insects entering the city," said Vikus.

Waiting patiently, a little off to one side,

were a half-dozen roaches. The leader had a bent antenna.

"Temp!" Boots cried out. "I see Temp!" She wriggled out of Gregor's arms and ran for the roaches.

"Boots!" His mother started after her but Gregor caught her arm and urgently spoke in her ear in a hushed voice.

"No, Mom, don't! That's Temp! She wouldn't be alive without him! The roaches adore her. Don't mess it up!" said Gregor.

"Excuse me?" said his mother, raising her eyebrows.

"I mean, just be polite," said Gregor sheepishly. He never bossed his mom around that way at home. "Please."

His mother looked back at the roaches and hesitated. She flinched as Temp sat back on his hind legs, and Boots ran straight into his six-leg hug.

"Hi, you! Hi, Temp! You waked up!" she said.

"Temp waked up, Temp did," said the roach.

Boots stepped back and surveyed him curiously. Then she began to count his legs. "One — two — three — four — five — six! All there!"

"Like you, my new legs, like you?" said Temp.

"Ye-es! You give Boots a ride? We go for a ride now?" said Boots.

Temp dropped to his belly, and Boots climbed right up on his back and they took off running around the field.

"Come on and meet the roaches. They're nice," said Gregor.

His mother gave him a look like he was insane but allowed him to lead her over to the insects. Temp ran up with Boots.

"See? This is Mama!" said Boots, sliding off Temp and running over to swing on her mom's hand.

The roaches seemed rattled by the news. Gregor could hear them whispering to one another. "Be she the swatter, be she? Be she the swatter?" They all bowed low to the ground.

"Welcome, Maker of the Princess and Most Fearsome Swatter," said Temp.

"What is it calling me?" Gregor's mom said to him.

"Um, I think he said 'Maker of the Princess and Most Fearsome Swatter,' " said Gregor.

"What's that mean?" said his mom.

"That you're Boots's mom and . . . let's face it, Mom, you swat a lot of roaches," said Gregor.

"Well, I'm not planning to swat these

giant things!" said his mom, scowling at him.

"Hey, I didn't make up the name!" said Gregor.

"All right, listen up, you roaches," said his mom.

The roaches all sank flatter on the ground, as if being swatted by his mom was inevitable. "Yes, Maker of the Princess and Most Fearsome Swatter," Temp could barely hiss out.

"From now on, you just call me Grace. Okay?" she said. Then she turned to the rest of the creatures in the arena. "Everybody here, just call me Grace!"

She took Boots's hand and stomped back across toward the bats, muttering, "Most Fearsome Swatter. Please."

While Vikus introduced his mother to the bats, Gregor crossed to Ripred. "Oh, look who's here! I guess your mommy let you come visit after all," said the rat.

"You better not have lied to me about how long we have to stay, Ripred," said Gregor under his breath.

"You better not be planning to take me and Boots on some road trip to find the cure."

"You've read the prophecy. All it says is to bring you from above," said Ripred.

"Now you've made an appearance, it's fine with *me* if you go home. Trust me, I could do without another quest with your chatty little sister and her six-legged friends."

"Is that what everybody thinks?" asked Gregor. "That I'm just here for the meeting?"

"Well, you'll have to ask around, won't you? I can hardly answer for what goes on in the crawlers' pea brains." Ripred dug at the powder behind his ear and called out, "Can we get this fiasco started, Vikus? Some of us have lives to live. However briefly."

"But where are the nibblers?" Vikus asked.

"I don't know. Lapblood and Mange were supposed to get word to them," said Ripred, indicating the other rats with two flicks of his tail.

"Well, we didn't," snapped Lapblood. "Why would we?"

"She's right," said Mange. "We didn't spend all that effort driving the nibblers out of our land to join up with them now. If they die of the plague, good riddance."

"Who needs them, anyway?" said Lapblood. "The prophecy doesn't even mention the nibblers." She began to scratch frantically at her shoulder. "What is this poison? Does it kill the fleas or just make them extra hungry?!"

"You had very specific orders!" said Ripred, grinding his back into the moss to relieve the itching.

"Well, if you hadn't noticed, we don't take orders from you!" said Mange.

Ripred sprang to his feet and turned on the two rats. They crouched into defensive positions, waiting for his attack, but he only said, "We'll finish this discussion in the tunnels."

"This is not ideal, but if the nibblers are not to be present, then we lack only Doctor Neveeve and Solovet," said Vikus. "Ah, here they are now."

A bat flew in from Regalia and Neveeve and Solovet climbed off its back.

Solovet called the meeting to order and asked Neveeve to speak about the plague. The doctor hoisted a large leather book off the back of the bat. She laid it on the moss and knelt before it. The book was only about a foot tall, but it was at least three feet wide and very thick. When Neveeve opened it, Gregor could hear the crackling of parchment.

"I have been scouring the old records in an attempt to find any similarity between this current plague and one in the past," said Neveeve. "Some two and a half centuries ago there was an epidemic markedly like 'The Curse of the Warmbloods.' Another just over eighty years ago. In both cases, a pestilence brought fever, painful breathing, and large violet buboes on the skin. Thousands died in the Underland."

"Lovely. Do they happen to mention a cure?" said Ripred.

Neveeve turned a page in the book and revealed an ink drawing of a plant that had distinctive star-shaped leaves. "This plant. It is called starshade. Only a single field of it exists."

"I've never seen it," said Lapblood. "It must grow in the Overland."

"No, according to the records, it grows in the same place from which the plague first emerged," said Neveeve.

" 'In the cradle find the cure,' " said Vikus, quoting from the prophecy.

"On the island with the mites?" asked Gregor. He didn't see how they'd ever get the cure from there. The mites would devour them in seconds.

"No, Gregor. That is a new island and, as Neveeve said, the plague has been cropping up for centuries. The mites may have carried the plague to the island, but it is not the cradle," said Vikus.

"So, where is it?" said Mange.

"It seems the cradle lies on the floor of the valley in . . . the Vineyard of Eyes," said Neveeve.

There was dead silence. Finally, Lapblood spoke, "We may as well just slit our throats now, as enter the Vineyard."

"Yet you had no trouble driving the nibblers into it," said Queen Athena.

"The nibblers had the whole of the Underland to choose from," said Mange.

"Where? The Dead Land? The Fire Points?" retorted Solovet.

"You're a fine one to talk, Solovet, given the current circumstances," said Lapblood.

"Please!" said Vikus, cutting off their bickering.

"Remember all of our lives are now at stake. This plant, Neveeve, it grows nowhere else?"

"They attempted to transplant it to the fields of Regalia, but it died almost immediately. We have no choice but to harvest great quantities of it from the Vineyard and distill it into a medicine."

"You want us to go into the Vineyard and help you find this cure, but what guarantee do we have that we'll ever see it?" said Lapblood. "We gnawers starve now! At your hand! The plague runs like wildfire through our tunnels! Today we learn you have yellow powder to stop the fleas that spread it! But do you send it?"

"You attacked us," said Solovet in a steely voice. "And now whimper when you must suffer the consequences."

"Whimper?" snarled Lapblood. She and Mange crouched to attack. Solovet's hand flew to the hilt of her sword.

Gregor didn't understand exactly what was going on, but he could tell things were about to get ugly.

Ripred stepped between the seething rats and Solovet.

"Tides turn, Solovet," said Ripred quietly. "Remember this moment when your own pups cry with hunger and the plague stills their hearts. Even now, your grandson lies behind glass in the hospital."

"And what of my granddaughter, Luxa? Where lies she, Ripred?" spat out Solovet.

"I don't know! But you must set it aside, Solovet, or go back and tell your people to make their graves. At this moment, we have great mutual need!" said Ripred.

Gregor never knew how Solovet would have responded, because at that moment the horns began to blow. The warning came from the tunnels leading away from Regalia. A dozen humans on bats appeared and headed across the arena for the tunnels.

"What are they blowing that for? No rats are invading," said Ripred in a puzzled tone.

"There must be some threat, or they would not give the signal," said Solovet.

"But who would be attacking Regalia now?" said Vikus.

The answer came out of the tunnels. It was a bat with a bright orange coat that Gregor had never seen before. Something was wrong with it — its wings beat erratically and it was careening around in a bizarre fashion.

"It is Icarus! But what ails him?" said Nike.

As Icarus swooped down over them, Gregor saw the purple bumps oozing fresh blood into his orange fur, the white tongue wagging from his mouth, the delirious look in his eyes.

"It's the plague!" he cried. "He looks just like Ares does!"

Icarus twisted in the air, his wings fluttering out of sync, and then lost control. A general cry of alarm went up as the bat plummeted straight down at them.

CHAPTER 9

As Icarus hit the ground, Gregor could hear the crack as the bones in his neck broke. He died instantly. There was no movement except the leaking of blood from the purple bumps.

"Do not touch him!" warned Neveeve. But this was unnecessary since almost everybody was instinctively scrambling away from the bat's ravaged body. Gregor backed into a roach, lost his footing, and fell over it onto his rear end. Two bats collided on takeoff. Only his mother, who was within a few feet of the ghastly creature when it landed, hadn't moved. She was clutching Boots in her arms, rooted to the ground in terror. Gregor got to his feet and ran for her.

"Torch the body!" ordered Solovet.

"No!" shouted Ripred, but three torches had already left the hands of the soldiers above. "No!" Ripred was literally gnashing his teeth in frustration.

"Get out of here! Everyone! Run!" he screamed.

When the torches hit Icarus, Gregor understood Ripred's frantic reaction. The flames had only rested on the fur a moment when a wave of small, black specks began to abandon the dead bat's body.

"Fleas!" cried Vikus. "Get you gone!"

Gregor grabbed Boots, caught his mother's arm, and pulled her onto the back of the nearest bat, who happened to be Queen Athena. Probably you weren't supposed to hop on a queen without asking permission, but this was no time for polite small talk. As they rose into the air, Gregor could see the rats and cockroaches disappearing into the tunnels leading to the Underland. All the humans on the ground had been picked up by bats and were airborne.

The fleas were hopping madly away from the burning bat.

"To the royal box!" called Vikus. "No one enters the city!"

Queen Athena swerved in the air and carried them toward a large, curved section of seats high in the arena. It reminded Gregor of the boxes where the rich people sat in Yankee Stadium. This must be where the royal family watched the sporting events.

As soon as they landed, Neveeve made them spread out. "Put as much distance as you can between one another." Gregor moved away from his mother and Queen

Athena, but didn't feel like he could set Boots down. She'd just run off, maybe to the railing of the box, and they were up really high.

His mom started to follow Gregor and Boots but Neveeve waved her back. "No! Move into a space by yourself!"

The doctor opened a pouch at her belt and pulled out what looked like a fancy perfume bottle. It had one of those bulbs on the side so you could spray it. She closed her eyes, pointed the nozzle at herself, and squeezed the bulb. Puffs of yellow powder settled on her skin and clothing. It looked like the same stuff the rats had been scratching from their coats. The flea powder.

Neveeve moved rapidly around the box spraying everyone. "Rub it into your skin, your hair. Cover every inch of your being," she instructed.

When she got to Gregor, he covered Boots's eyes with his hands while he shut his own. He could feel the powder coating his skin. It had a sharp, bitter smell. As Neveeve moved on to his mother, Boots sneezed and gave him a surprised look. "You yellow," she said.

"You, too," Gregor said, working the powder through her hair. "And what letter does yellow begin with?"

"*Y!*" Boots said. "*Y* is for yellow!"

"And what else?" said Gregor, trying to distract her as he rubbed the stuff over her skin.

"*Y* is for yo-yo! *Y* is for yak!" said Boots. She had never seen a yak, except in her *ABC* book. Neither had Gregor, for that matter. Probably no one would have ever even heard of a yak if it hadn't been about the only animal that began with a *Y*.

In a matter of minutes, the entire party of six bats and six humans had been treated with the pesticide.

"I think it is safe now to gather," said Neveeve.

Everyone came together in the center of the box. Below on the field, the charred body of the bat lay in a puddle of water. The fire had been extinguished.

"Bat sick. Bat needs juice," said Boots. Whenever she had a cold the first thing she got was a cup of juice.

"He's asleep now. He can have some when he wakes up," said Gregor. He could never manage to work out how to tell Boots someone had died.

"Apple juice." Boots squatted down and began to draw squiggles in the fine coat of yellow powder that covered the floor.

"Give orders to disinfect the entire field," Solovet called out to a guard who hovered on his bat near the box. "Wait!" The guard stayed as she turned to the doctor. "Will that be sufficient, Neveeve?"

"They must also spray the tunnels that lead away from the arena," said Neveeve. "The fleas will not be able to enter Regalia with the stone doors shut, nor jump so high as the seats. But some may already have escaped down the tunnels and into the rest of the Underland. Any who guard there must be recalled and their skin examined for bites."

"Do as she says," Solovet told the guard.

"What of the gnawers and the crawlers?" asked Vikus.

"No flea could penetrate the coat of poison on the gnawers, and they will not bite the crawlers. They are all quite safe," said Neveeve.

"And those of us here assembled?" said Vikus.

"If any flea reached us, which is doubtful, it is now dead. We must each be stripped and checked for bites by physicians in Regalia," said Neveeve.

"We are not . . ." choked out Gregor's mother. "We are never returning to Regalia!"

"Please, Grace, I know this to be very un-expected and distressing —" began Vikus.

"We're going home! We came to your meeting! That's all you said we had to do! So you tell that bat to take us home now!" said his mother as she pointed wildly at Nike.

"Who told you this? That you were only expected for the meeting?" asked Vikus with concern.

"Ripred," said Gregor. "He said we just had to come for a couple of hours. That you didn't need us to find the cure. Then he sent a swarm of rats to scare us out of the apart-ment."

Gregor could tell by the look Vikus ex-changed with Solovet that this was the first they had heard of any of this.

"I am afraid he was not forthcoming," said Vikus.

"What do you mean?" asked Gregor's mom.

"He means Ripred lied," said Solovet.

"He may in fact have thought their pres-ence was unnecessary for the —" said Vikus weakly.

"He lied!" repeated Solovet. "Do not defend him. He knows perfectly well there will be no quest for the cure without the Overlanders! He obviously thought there was no other means of bringing them below.

I would have done the same, Vikus, if you would not have."

Gregor bet she would have, too. Solovet would not have cared what Gregor or his family wanted. Not at Regalia's expense.

"We will not force them to stay, Solovet!" said Vikus. Gregor had never seen him so angry. "They have been brought here under false pretenses. We will not force them to stay!"

Gregor's mother clutched Vikus's arm as if it were a lifeline. "You'll send us home now, then? We can leave?"

"No!" said Solovet.

"Yes!" said Vikus. "Nike! Prepare to take the Overlanders home!"

"Guards!" barked Solovet.

Gregor was bewildered at the power struggle playing out before them He had never seen Vikus and Solovet fight like this, and it rattled him. Who could actually make this decision? What would happen if his family tried to leave? What was he supposed to do?

"Wait!" Gregor took his mom's hand. "Look, Mom, I've been to see Ares. He's really bad. He's dying, Mom. I can't leave him like this. So, how about you take Boots back and I stay and try to help? Okay? You take Boots and Lizzie and Grandma to Virginia. Dad will wait for me to come back up. Then we'll come to Virginia, too."

"That might be an acceptable compromise," said Vikus, eyeing his wife.

"We could put it to the council," said Solovet, although she did not sound convinced.

"I can't leave you down here, Gregor," said his mom. "I'm sorry about your friend. I really am. But I can't leave you here."

"Look, Mom, I don't think all three of us are going to be allowed out of here," said Gregor. "Please, take Boots and go home." He squeezed her hand tightly. It took him only a few seconds to register that something was wrong.

His mom was talking back to him now, but her words weren't reaching his brain. He moved his fingers over the skin on the back of her hand. No, he hadn't imagined it. It was there.

"Gregor, are you listening to me?" pleaded his mom.

He wasn't. He was trying to make sense of what his fingers were telling him. And trying to wish it away. But he couldn't.

Gregor slowly lifted his mom's hand into the light of a nearby torch and wiped off the yellow powder. A small red bite was swelling up on her skin.

PART 2
THE JUNGLE

CHAPTER 10

His mom stared at her hand and became very still. As the rest of the group saw the bite, all movement and sound stopped. There was not a whisper, not a rustling of a wing or robe.

Curious, Boots climbed up on a seat to see what everyone was looking at. "You need pink," she said when she saw the bite.

Gregor knew she meant the pink calamine lotion they put on bug bites in the summer.

"I need to go home," his mother whispered.

"We cannot let you," said Vikus with a sad shake of his head. "Not now."

"If the plague were unleashed in the Overland, it could mean the annihilation of the warmbloods there as well," said Solovet.

"We must place you in quarantine at once," said Neveeve.

Solovet touched his mother's shoulder. "We are so deeply sorry this happened." She sighed. "Nike, take her in and report to be inspected for bites."

Gregor was still holding his mom's hand. He couldn't let go. "Mom . . ."

She gently pried his fingers loose and stepped back from him. "You take your sister home."

Did he nod? Gregor wasn't sure. But his mom got on Nike's back and disappeared.

"We must all be checked for bites immediately," said Neveeve.

Somehow they were all on bats. They did not go through the city, but took some tunnels that opened out over the white seething river that ran by Regalia. At the dock, no one assisted them. The yellow powder was enough to keep people at bay.

They were sent to bathe and then had to stand naked while no less than seven teams of doctors inspected their skin for flea bites in bright light. Boots, who was exceptionally ticklish, giggled through the whole thing. Gregor submitted to the inspection without objecting, but he was almost certain he and Boots had not been bitten.

"You can run away, but the prophecy will find you somehow," he heard his grandma saying.

Oh, it had found him, all right. And dug its teeth into him. Into Boots, too. And it would not let them go until the whole terrifying episode had been played out. Their mom was infected with the plague. Now the warrior . . . the princess . . . they had to go try and find the cure.

Gregor wanted to scream out to no one in particular that it had been enough for Ares and Howard and Andromeda to be sick. He would have found a way to go on the quest. But his mother would never have let Boots go to the . . . what was it? The Vineyard of Eyes? For the prophecy to be fulfilled, his mother had to be taken out of commission. Quarantined. Made a victim. Yes, prophetically speaking, everything was right on schedule.

He felt exhausted by the responsibility that lay ahead. He was so sick of being dragged into the Underland. Of being expected to solve its problems. Of having the rest of his family suffer for causes that did not even really involve them.

After he and Boots had been pronounced free of flea bites, they were given new silky Underlander clothes. Gregor managed to talk them into letting him have his boots back, but they had to be inspected for fleas and disinfected first. While they sat on a bench in the hospital waiting to hear about the others, Boots nodded off on his shoulder. No wonder, she'd only had a couple of hours of sleep. Vikus sent for Dulcet, the nanny who had looked after Boots on earlier visits.

Dulcet took the sleeping little girl from Gregor's arms and then touched his shoulder. "I am very sorry to hear about your mother. But do not lose heart. You will find the cure. Of this, I am certain."

Her tone was so kind that Gregor almost broke down and told her about how he *had* to find the cure. How his mom just *had* to live. How his whole family would break apart into splinters if she wasn't there to hold it together. How she could not die because he could not imagine the world without her. And how it would be Gregor's fault . . . her horrible death . . . the purple bumps . . . the struggle for air . . . because he had wanted to make this trip to the Underland . . . and she had not.

But all he said was, "Thanks, Dulcet."

When everyone who had been at the meeting had been scrupulously checked, a total of three were sent into quarantine: Gregor's mom and two bats named Cassiopeia and Pollux.

Gregor saw Neveeve at the end of the hallway, writing something on a clipboard. He walked over and touched her arm.

"Oh!" she exclaimed. Her arm jerked to the side and the quill pen she'd been writing with left a large blot on her parchment.

"Sorry," said Gregor. Boy, she sure was

jumpy. Of course, spending your days treating plague patients was not exactly a vacation.

"Can you tell me where my mom is?" asked Gregor.

"We have her isolated," said Neveeve. "Come, she sleeps, but you can see her."

The doctor led Gregor through the hospital.

"Does she know Boots and I didn't get bitten?" asked Gregor.

"Yes. But she was still highly agitated," said Neveeve, her fingers rubbing her eyelid, which seemed to be twitching. "I gave her a medicine to calm her." Gregor thought Neveeve might benefit from a little of that medicine herself, but he didn't say so.

His mom was in a private room on the same hall as Ares, Howard, and Andromeda. Gregor looked through the glass wall and saw that all the yellow powder had been washed off her and she was dressed in fresh white pajamas. She looked small and vulnerable in the hospital bed. It was good she was asleep. If she could speak, she would order Gregor home and he would have to tell her that he and Boots couldn't go back now and she'd go crazy. So he fixed the picture of his mom in his head. What if this was the last time he ever saw her?

He shook the thought from his head and turned to Neveeve. "I need your help. I really need to know everything you know about the plague," he said.

"I am now headed to my laboratory where I study this sickness. Would you like to ac-company me?" asked the doctor. "It is out-side of Regalia, but it will take some time for them to resume the meeting to discuss the cure."

Nike flew them out of the palace, over the city, and high above the arena. The body of the bat had been removed and the moss of the playing field had a yellow coating of flea powder. They went down a tunnel, picking up a few torches from the holders on the walls. As the tunnel began to fork, Gregor knew he'd been this way before.

"Isn't Ares's cave out this way?" he asked.

"I believe it is. I have never visited it," said Neveeve. "It is said to be well hidden. This is why it took Howard and Andromeda several days to find Ares and bring him into the hospital."

"He didn't come in because he felt sick?" asked Gregor.

"No, Vikus had not heard from him for weeks. So Howard and Andromeda flew out to search for his cave. He was so ill already, they had to carry him in," said Neveeve.

Gregor thought of Ares, alone and sick in his cave. His few close friends were dead or missing. And Gregor, his bond, was unreachable. "Poor Ares."

"Yes," said Neveeve. "Ares has been greatly persecuted through no fault of his own, and this is the result."

This surprised Gregor because there was not much sympathy for Ares in the Underland. He was deeply mistrusted and most people and bats wanted him dead. He felt a surge of warmth toward Neveeve for her compassionate view of his bond.

"Did you know him well?" asked Gregor.

"Not well. After you left Regalia, Ares would not return to the city, fearing they would imprison him again. On Vikus's instructions, I continued to care for the mite wounds on his back at my lab. Even then, Ares would only come very late at night when I was the only one present."

"I appreciate you doing that," said Gregor.

"As I said, I believe his treatment has been unjust," said Neveeve.

Her laboratory was housed in a series of large connecting caves. Long stone counters were covered with a variety of lab equipment. A stream had been diverted into a narrow channel that ran through the back of one of the caves. A handful of people in gloves moved about their duties. A few bats were there as well, peering into microscopes, consulting with the humans.

Neveeve guided Gregor into a room that was separated from the rest of the lab by a heavy stone door. "This is where I conduct my research," she said, carefully shutting the door behind her.

There were test tubes and beakers and several microscopes. Along one wall were four large glass containers that fitted into stone cubes. They reminded him of water coolers. Gregor moved in to examine one. Little black specks were crawling around inside it. Fleas. His torchlight reflected off a shiny red pool at the bottom of the container. Gregor realized it was blood and gave a little jump backward. His arm caught the adjacent container, causing it to tip sideways, but he managed to catch it. Fortunately, this one was empty.

"Sorry! Man, I'm sorry," said Gregor, steadying the container.

"That was well caught," said Neveeve with a high-pitched laugh. "Thank goodness, as these are made specially for the plague and not easily replaced. It took me several months to receive this one when its predecessor was broken. I am about to use this new one to test out a most promising antidote."

Gregor put the torch in a holder and stuck his hands in his pockets so he wouldn't bump into anything else. All he needed now was to be busting up some experiment that could save everybody's life.

The doctor told him what she knew about the plague. It was bloodborne, not airborne, which meant you couldn't get it if somebody just sneezed on you, only if their blood got in your veins. That was where the fleas came in. They transmitted the disease from warmblood to warmblood.

"In many plagues, the insects would die as well. Not as the warmbloods do, but the germs would multiply in their bodies and kill them. Not so with this one. We believe that no insect has died. No fish or scaled creature, either. That is why it is called 'The Curse of the Warmbloods' and not 'The Curse of the Underland,' " said Neveeve.

"Ripred said you could treat the symptoms in Regalia,' " said Gregor.

"Yes, we can ease discomfort, lower fever, give medicines to induce sleep, but these do not kill the plague," said Neveeve. "We are attempting to come up with our own cure in the event that your search is not successful. Although almost no one really believes we can do it," said Neveeve with a weak smile. "I have faith that we can, but it will take time."

Time. It was all going to come down to time. "How long do you have after you're bitten?" he asked.

"It varies greatly. Ares, for instance, was the first Underlander to fall ill, but he shows remarkable resistance. It seems the fliers do not sicken as quickly as the humans do. Howard and Andromeda have only become symptomatic in the past few days. But then, we do not know if they contracted the disease from the mites or when they brought Ares into the hospital. Your mother . . . as a human who has had a flea bite from Icarus, clearly an advanced case . . ." Neveeve hesitated.

"I need the truth. How long would you give her?" said Gregor.

Neveeve lowered her gaze and massaged her forehead with a trembling hand. "If things go badly . . . we could lose her in two weeks."

CHAPTER 11

The stone floor was cold. Gregor lay on his side, holding a small mirror by the handle. He was trying to read "The Prophecy of Blood" but it wasn't easy.

"You know, I've already got this thing memorized," he said.

"We know, Gregor, but Nerissa and I feel it is important for you to examine the original," said Vikus. "There are clues you may pick up from the way it is written."

So Gregor peered back into the mirror.

The first two prophecies that had involved him had been carved in big letters right in the middle of the walls of the stone room that held all of Sandwich's visions. This third one was almost impossible to decipher.

In the first place, "The Prophecy of Blood" was on the floor, which might have been okay if it wasn't crammed into a corner. Secondly, the letters were very tiny and had a lot of confusing curlicues and junk coming off them. Then, of course, the thing was written backward.

No matter how he twisted and turned his

body or positioned the light or squinted to make out the letters, Gregor could never really get a clear shot of it. He seemed to spend more time looking at his own face than at the prophecy. When his mirror arm began to cramp, he finally gave up.

"What's the deal with this thing? It's like Sandwich didn't even want us to be able to read it," said Gregor.

"He did want us to read it, Gregor. Or he never would have written it," said Vikus. The old man knelt down and rubbed his hand over the prophecy. "But Nerissa believes he purposely made it difficult to read."

"Yeah? Why's that, Nerissa?" asked Gregor, sitting up to look at her.

When Luxa had disappeared in the rats' tunnels, Nerissa, as the last living member of the royal family, had been crowned queen. Many people had opposed her coronation because she had visions of the future that made her seem crazy. Others simply doubted if she had the physical strength for the job. At present, she was curled up in a cloak on the floor, leaning against the wall for support. Now that she was queen, she was better dressed and her hair was neatly pinned on top of her head. But she was as bony and tremulous as ever.

"Because the prophecy itself is difficult to read. Its meaning — it is hard to understand," said Nerissa.

"There's only one part of it that really seems confusing to me," said Gregor. The first stanza said there would be a plague. Okay, it was here. The third stanza said to bring Gregor and Boots. Okay, they were here. The fifth stanza said the warmbloods had to find the cure. Okay, they were going to try. The seventh stanza said you do it or you die. Okay, they knew that.

But those words that appeared in the second, fourth, sixth, and eighth stanzas. The repeating stanza. That was the confusing part.

TURN AND TURN AND TURN AGAIN.
YOU SEE THE WHAT
BUT NOT THE WHEN.
REMEDY AND CURE ENTWINE,
AND SO THEY FORM A SINGLE VINE.

" 'Turn and turn and turn again,' " said Gregor. "What's that about?"

"Before I burden you with several centuries of scholarly opinion, what is your interpretation of it, Gregor?" said Vikus.

Gregor considered the stanza again, rolling the words around in his mind. "Well, it sounds to me like Sandwich is trying to tell us . . . we're wrong. Like whatever we think is happening . . . it's not."

"Yes. Not only wrong now. But as we 'turn and turn,' we are still not seeing the truth," said Nerissa.

"So . . . if we're wrong . . . then why are we doing anything?" said Gregor. "Why are we even going to the Vineyard of Eyeballs or whatever it's called?"

"Because the alternative is to do nothing," said Vikus. "And a journey is indicated. We must go to the cradle to find the cure. It seems likely that the 'single vine' would grow in a vineyard, does it not? So we go, and perhaps along the way we will unravel this stanza as well."

"When you say 'we' do you mean 'you and me'? Because you're coming with me this time?" asked Gregor hopefully.

Vikus smiled. "No, Gregor. I confess, I was using a more general 'we.' I cannot go. But if it is any consolation, Solovet is planning to travel with you."

"Well, that's something," said Gregor. He'd rather have Vikus to help unravel the prophecy, but he knew Solovet would be better at fighting. And if this place were as dangerous as everybody thought, he would need her. "And Ripred. Is he coming?"

"He says he would not miss it for all the world," said Vikus.

Gregor felt his heart lift a little. With both Ripred and Solovet along, they might just make it.

An Underlander knocked on the door and announced that they were needed.

"The rats and crawlers must have returned," said Vikus. "We are going to continue the meeting within the walls of the palace. Come, let us go."

As they started down the hallway Gregor tried to give the hand mirror back to Nerissa. "Keep it," she said. "You may have need of it again." He stuck the mirror in his back pocket absent-mindedly.

The moment they crossed the threshold, he recognized the place. How could he forget it? He took in the stone bleachers that rose up around a stage that sat right in the middle of the circular room. On that stage — that was where he and Ares had made the vows that bonded them together. Now the stage was empty, but the bleachers held clusters of creatures. The human council occupied one section of seats. The bats sat to their right, the roaches to their left, and the rats were milling around the benches directly across the stage from them.

Vikus and Nerissa went to join the

humans but Gregor had that odd feeling he'd had in the cafeteria one day when both Angelina and Larry had been sick and missed school. He did not know where to sit. Not with the rats, that was for sure. But he didn't much like the Regalian council, which was probably still thinking about tossing him off a cliff for treason. The bats had made Ares's life miserable by shunning him. Finally, Gregor went over and sat with the roaches. They were the only ones he really felt comfortable with.

Vikus opened the meeting by greeting everyone formally. Then he got right down to business. "So, it seems the journey to the Vineyard of Eyes becomes more urgent with each passing minute. We must begin at once. The proposed members of the quest are currently Gregor and Boots, as the warrior and the princess are called for. Nike will be their flier, also providing us with a backup princess in case we have misinterpreted Boots's role. Solovet and her bond, Ajax, complete the humans and fliers. Ripred, Mange, and Lapblood will represent the gnawers. And as Sandwich specifically mentions the crawlers, Temp has valiantly offered his services."

"We don't really have to drag that crawler along with us, do we?" said Mange.

"I suppose we can always eat him if the supplies run low," said Lapblood.

There was laughter from some of the bats and humans at the comment. They were always making fun of the roaches.

Temp said nothing, but gave a slight tremor of fear at Lapblood's comment.

Gregor locked eyes with the rat. "Or maybe we'll eat you. I've never had rat. But with the right sauce, who knows?"

Only one creature was laughing now. Ripred. "Well, at least the trip isn't going to be dull!"

"At present," hissed Lapblood, "there is no trip. We have yet to be convinced that it is to our advantage."

"The council has agreed to open the fishing grounds to the west," said Vikus. "That should provide the gnawers with enough food."

"And the yellow powder?" asked Mange. "To kill the fleas?"

There was only silence from the humans. Then Gregor thought he heard Vikus sigh.

"No powder, no deal," said Lapblood.

What? Was the whole quest going to fall through because the humans wouldn't send the rats flea powder? Was it really so much to ask? Gregor thought of the purple bumps bursting, oozing out pus and blood. . . .

He sprang to his feet and shouted at the council. "Send them the powder! Geez! Have you seen Ares? Have you seen what the plague does? No matter how much you hate the rats, do you really want them to die like that?"

His question hung in the air a long time before anyone answered.

"You have a very forgiving heart, Gregor the Overlander," said Solovet.

It wasn't true. Maybe Gregor didn't want the rats to die such a gruesome death. He thought of the expression "I wouldn't wish it on my worst enemy." But he had not forgiven them for his father, for Tick, for Twitchtip, for Aurora, or for Luxa. He had a whole list of things he would never forgive them for.

"No, I don't," said Gregor bitterly. "But I've got a mom and a bond with the plague. Your hospital is starting to fill up. We need the rats to find the cure. So, what's it going to be, Solovet?"

CHAPTER 12

There was no choice, ultimately. They had to agree to send the rats the flea powder. Gregor did not think this was much of a concession, given they were all supposed to be on the same side, fighting the plague. But it was obviously a wrenching decision for the humans, who whispered furiously among themselves for several minutes before Solovet announced they had given in. By that point, three people were crying and one had left the meeting in protest.

The way they hated the rats — the degree to which they would sacrifice to have them dead — was beyond anything in Gregor's experience. That guy who had left the meeting, would he really rather see everybody dead than help some rats survive? Apparently, the answer was yes.

The next point of contention was the execution of the journey to the Vineyard of Eyes. For the first time, Gregor saw a map of the Underland. Four Underlanders unrolled the enormous scroll flat on the stage and secured the corners with marble pyramids. You could see it clearly even from the bleachers. The map was divided into many sections, each painted a different color and labeled in black. Gregor found Regalia in the north. The gnawers had a region in the south, although part of it had been painted over and had the word "occupied" spread across it. The Waterway took up a large portion of the center of the scroll. To the southwest of Regalia, Gregor picked out the lands belonging to the fliers and the crawlers, but there were many names on the map Gregor didn't recognize.

Gregor's eyes lingered on the portion of the map labeled "occupied." He could see a large river curving through it. By the different paint colors, he could tell it had belonged to the rats, but now the humans controlled it. A river that size would supply a lot of fish. This must be the river that Ripred had talked about when he said the humans were trying to starve out the rats. No river, no fish. But now the humans had agreed to give back the fishing grounds so that the rats would go on the quest.

Solovet came to the stage with a pointer and drew everyone's attention to a large triangle of green that extended from the rats' current territory halfway up the eastern side of the Waterway. "By our best estimates, the Vineyard lies in this general area." She tapped a spot that was so deep in the jungle it was almost off the map. "It is very near the Firelands, but any entry from the east would be blocked by the cutters."

"Who are the cutters?" Gregor asked Temp. The roach consulted with a few of his friends in clicking sounds.

"Ants, some call them we think, ants," said Temp.

"Why would the ants block our way?" asked Gregor.

"Hate warmbloods, the cutters do, hate warmbloods," said Temp.

Gregor would have liked to ask more about the ants, but he didn't want to miss what was going on in the meeting.

"That jungle goes on for days," said Mange. "How are we supposed to find the Vineyard in a sea of vines?"

Nerissa cleared her throat and spoke for the first time. "I have arranged a guide for you."

"You . . . have?" said Ripred, and looked to Vikus for confirmation. But the old man looked as surprised as Ripred sounded.

"When did you do this, Nerissa?" asked Vikus.

"Quite a long time ago. But I have every confidence he will be there," said Nerissa. "I have seen him with the Overlander in a vision."

Uh-oh. Vision talk was never good. While everybody seemed to take Sandwich's prophecies very seriously, Nerissa's visions were not given much respect.

If the humans refrained from doubting her to her face, the rats did not.

"A vision?" said Lapblood, over-enunciating as if she were speaking to a very small child. "I thought I had a vision once but it was only some very bad mushrooms. Have they been feeding you mushrooms lately, Your Majesty?"

"Nerissa has no taste for mushrooms, and while her visions may not always be complete, we have gained much of value from them," said Vikus sharply.

"Who is this guide?" said Solovet.

"I cannot tell you. On my word. Only that you are to meet him some eight hours hence at the Arch of Tantalus," said Nerissa.

"Are we? Now don't get me wrong, my dear, I love the Arch of Tantalus. Always a bone or two to gnaw on there," said Ripred. "But what if you actually dreamed up this guide?"

"If I dreamed up this guide, then you will be none the worse than you are at present," said Nerissa. "The Arch of Tantalus is as good a place to enter the jungle as any."

"Yes, if you ignore the piles of skeletons

that seem to collect in the vicinity, it's top-notch!" said Ripred.

Throughout the room came murmurs of agreement.

"It is where your guide will be awaiting you, Ripred," said Nerissa. "Whether or not you choose to meet him is your own doing."

Gregor had to give Nerissa credit. It couldn't be easy to stand up to the rats' mockery, especially when none of the humans was backing her up except Vikus. Maybe Gregor was wrong, and there was a queen inside her after all. Besides, she had saved his life at the trial after "The Prophecy of Bane" mess. He owed her.

"Well, that's where I'm going," said Gregor loudly. "To the Arch of Tantalus. Nerissa's word is good enough for me."

"That's that, then," said Ripred. But he shot Gregor a look that seemed to add, "You idiot."

The rats, who were making the journey to the jungle on foot, had to leave immediately to make the rendezvous in eight hours. It would take the bats less time to cover the same distance, so Gregor found himself with a few hours to prepare.

Gregor went back up to the luxury room, since no other room had been set up for him, and asked an Underlander for something to write a letter on. He was provided with three fresh scrolls, a bottle of ink, and a quill pen. Getting the hang of the quill pen and bottle of ink took some doing. In fact, the first two scrolls turned into practice sheets, and when he finally did get around to his letter, it was so full of ink blots and smears that he could only hope it was legible.

As for the contents . . . well, he had agonized over what to write, but this was all he managed:

Dear Mom,
I'm doing what I think you would do if I were the one with the plague. Trying to find the cure. Please don't be mad.
I love you,
Gregor

He had initially thought about writing to his dad as well, but somehow the short note to his mom had drained him. Besides, it would take pages to explain how all this disaster had fallen on his family. He would ask Vikus to write and leave the scroll in the grate in the laundry room.

Mareth came to the doorway. He had a pack slung over the arm that was not using his crutch. His face was flushed and his breathing audible. The exertion of moving around the palace had taken its toll on him.

"Hey, Mareth. Here, sit down," said Gregor. He made a space on the couch for the soldier.

"Perhaps for just a moment," said Mareth. He sat down gratefully on the couch, leaning his crutch against the arm. "I am supposed to be gaining strength every day by moving around the palace. But the stairs are still a challenge for me."

Gregor felt a twinge of sadness as he remembered training with Mareth. How fast he could run, how strong he was. That was before they had gone to find the Bane and Mareth had lost his leg. He wondered what Mareth would do now. He could probably still fly on Andromeda, if she survived the plague, but surely he couldn't be a soldier anymore.

"What's in the pack?" asked Gregor.

"Oh, I have taken the liberty of choosing some supplies from the museum for you. You may go yourself as well, of course. But having been with you on the last two quests, I have some idea of what you need," said Mareth.

Gregor opened the pack and found several flashlights and a bunch of batteries.

"Yep, this is exactly what I'd have picked out myself."

"Here in the side, I placed a roll of this gray sticking strip," said Mareth. He pulled a brand-new roll of duct tape from the side pocket. "Howard said you used this both for securing bandages and making the raft after I had lost consciousness."

"Great. Yeah, that's duct tape. It really came in handy," said Gregor. He looked in the other side pocket and found a quart bottle of water with a classy label. "Water's always good to have."

"It says it comes from glaciers," said Mareth, tapping the label. "What exactly are glaciers?"

"They're, like, these gigantic pieces of ice," said Gregor.

"I have heard of ice. Water that is hard as stone. So, this glacier water . . . does it have special benefits?" asked Mareth.

What did Gregor know? His family drank water from the tap. His mom made them let it run for a full minute in case there was any lead from the pipes in it. They sure didn't go out and spend four bucks on a bottle of glacier water! Gregor ran his thumb over the price tag on the bottle uncertainly. "Um, I don't know. I mean, I think it's just water," said Gregor. But Mareth looked a little disappointed so he added, "But I bet it's really clean, because it was frozen a while ago, before there was so much pollution. Yeah, look right here on the label, 'extra pure.' "

"Ah," said Mareth, gratified. "Pure water is not always easy to find, especially where you are going. I brought one more thing, although I am not sure exactly what it is. But it has a sense of happiness about it. I thought carrying it might remind you of home."

Mareth pulled a packet of bubble gum from the pocket. The paper was bright pink and had cartoon pictures of pop-eyed kids blowing giant bubbles.

Gregor laughed. "All right, bubble gum. My sister Lizzie loves this stuff. You know, it does remind me of home. Thanks, Mareth."

Underlanders showed up with trays of food and began to place them on the table in front of the couch. Mareth rose to go.

"Don't go. There's tons of food. Stay and eat with me," Gregor said.

Mareth hesitated. Gregor was pretty sure he was worried about breaking some kind of rule. Soldiers probably never ate in the luxury room.

"Come on, Mareth. You must be hungry. Everybody knows that hospital food is lousy," said Gregor. Actually, when Gregor would go to visit his friend Larry in the hospital when he had bad asthma attacks, the food usually looked pretty decent to him. But the patients were always complaining about it. Lying around a hospital, especially if you felt bad, probably gave you a lot of opportunity to dislike the food.

Mareth grinned. "It is somewhat bland," he admitted. "Although one has only to think of eating raw fish on our last journey to appreciate a simple meal."

"So stay. I don't want to eat alone," said Gregor. "Please."

Mareth sat back on the couch and put his crutch aside. "This is quite a feast."

It was. It ranked right up there with the food that had been prepared for Nerissa's coronation. There was a savory egg-and-cheese pie, stuffed mushrooms, steak, tiny raw vegetables with a dip, and a dish Gregor had come across a few times before, shrimp in cream sauce.

Gregor pointed to the shrimp. "That's Ripred's favorite. Last time I was here he stuck his whole face in a pot of it and scarfed it down."

"I do not blame him," said Mareth, taking a small serving of shrimp.

"Shoot, you can eat more than that," said

Gregor, dumping another large ladle of the stuff on Mareth's plate. He took a piece of egg-and-cheese pie for himself. His stomach was still rocky and acidic from throwing up, but he knew he had to eat if he were heading out on the road. It helped that the pie tasted amazing.

"Hey, Mareth, what was the deal with you guys starving out the rats?" he said.

Mareth took a few moments before he answered. "It was Solovet's way to show them that whenever they attack us, there will be consequences."

"But that means the pups are starving to death, too. Not just the big rats," said Gregor. "Doesn't that bother you?"

"Of course it bothers me!" Mareth shook his head and sighed. "It is so hard for you to know what it is like for us here, Gregor. We are raised in a world where one must kill or be killed. Sometimes I try to imagine what it would be like if we did not always have to devote ourselves to the possibility of war. Who would we be? What would we do?"

"Well, what would you do?" asked Gregor.

"I do not know . . . to live without war. It seems like . . . a fairy story," said Mareth. "Do you have those in the Overland?"

"Fairy tales, yeah," said Gregor.

137

"It seems like that," said Mareth.

When the Underlander came back to clear away the dishes at the end of the meal, Gregor pointed to the rest of the shrimp. "Can I take that with me?"

The Underlander looked confused. "Take it with you . . . to where?"

"On the trip. Can you stick it in a bag or something?" Gregor asked.

The Underlander stood holding the dish, staring down into the creamy sauce. "Stick it in a bag?" Doggie bags must be a new idea down here.

"Perhaps you could put it in a wineskin, Lucent, and then it would not leak out," Mareth said helpfully. "The seals are airtight."

"Oh, yes," said Lucent, relieved. "A wineskin."

Gregor walked Mareth back to the hospital and asked him to make sure his mom got the letter. A doctor told him he was wanted on the dock. And when he arrived, he saw that everyone was waiting on him to leave.

Vikus, Solovet, and two male guards were mounted on bats.

"I thought you weren't coming," Gregor said to Vikus.

"For safety's sake, the guards and I will

escort you as far as the Arch of Tantalus. Then only the designated party will enter the jungle," said Vikus.

Nike, who was without a rider, was grooming her black-and-white-striped fur. Dulcet stood next to her, holding a sleeping Boots in her arms. Temp sat at her feet. Gregor almost said, "Where's Ares?" before reality clicked in.

Gregor crossed over to Nike. "So, I guess we're flying together this trip?" he asked.

"If you have no objections," said Nike. "I am not as strong or large as Ares, but I have a certain agility."

"You're perfect," said Gregor. She didn't have to sell herself to him. No one could replace Ares, but Nike seemed like a good bat. Suddenly, Gregor felt exhausted. He hadn't slept at all Saturday night; it must have been Sunday evening by now. "Hey, Nike, is it okay if I sleep for a while?"

"Certainly," said Nike. Gregor slid the pack on his back for safekeeping and lay on his side on Nike's back. The wineskin of shrimp in cream sauce didn't make a bad pillow. He reached out his arms and Dulcet settled Boots down next to him. Temp scampered up by their feet.

"If we're still flying, wake me up if Boots wakes up, okay, Temp?" Gregor said.

"Wake you, I will; if wake she, wake you," said Temp, which Gregor took to mean "yes."

"Fly you high, Gregor the Overlander," said Dulcet.

"Fly you high, Dulcet," said Gregor and, as Nike lifted into the air, he locked his arms around Boots and fell asleep.

When he awoke, he was lying on stone. The wineskin was still under his head. A blanket had been spread over him although he didn't really need it; the air was warm. His arms were empty but he could hear Boots chattering away to Temp.

Gregor could smell food cooking, too. He rolled over and saw a fire with several large fish grilling on it. The bats were clustered together, sleeping. The humans and rats were spread out in small groups, talking. Boots was riding around on Temp, playing some simple game where she'd throw a ball and they'd run after it.

They were in a big clearing with a dense jungle looming up all around. Gregor got a flashlight from his pack and shone it through the trees. No, they weren't trees. They were vines. Thick, ropy vines that wove in and out of one another and towered high above his head. From them issued a humming sound that was vaguely mechan-

140

ical. There were clicks and whirrs and taps. The whole jungle buzzed with life.

Gregor sat up and saw a stack of stark white bones piled a few feet from his head. At first, he thought this was some kind of sick joke on Ripred's part, but as he moved the flashlight beam around he realized there were skeletons everywhere. They must have reached the Arch of Tantalus. Yes, there, at the edge of the jungle, Gregor spotted a pile of boulders whose shape suggested an arch. The rocks looked unstable, as if they might easily fall on the head of anyone foolish enough to pass through them. No wonder nobody had wanted to come here. Gregor hoped Nerissa knew what she was talking about.

"The whole thing is ridiculous," he heard Lapblood snarl. "We're just sitting here asking to get eaten, and for what? To humor some lunatic girl's fancy."

"She is not a lunatic," said Vikus.

"Well, you have to at least credit her with a certain instability. Remember when she told you I was plotting to take over the Fount with an army of lobsters?" said Ripred.

"You did try and take over the Fount with an army of lobsters," said Vikus.

"Yes, yes, but it was several years before

141

Nerissa was even born. The point is, she flip-flops in and out of time like a fish in the shallows. Who's to say that this guide, whoever he may be, didn't show up three days ago? Or three years ago for that matter?" said Ripred.

"They are right, Vikus. We invite trouble stopping in this place," said Solovet. "And how, in your mind, did Nerissa arrange a guide for us? She scarcely sees a soul."

Gregor wondered what was up with Vikus and Solovet. They really weren't seeing eye to eye.

"Only a few more minutes," said Vikus firmly. "Then we will part ways."

"I throw up to sky!" Boots squealed.

Gregor turned and saw her wing the ball high into the air. "Well, that's the last we'll see of that ball," he thought. He caught it in his flashlight beam as it flew into the jungle.

He was right. The ball disappeared. But not in the twisted vines, as he had anticipated. Instead, it landed squarely in the mouth of a colossal lizard.

CHAPTER 13

All he could really see was the creature's head, a scaly iridescent blue-green face fifteen feet above him. It swallowed and Gregor caught a glimpse of rippling neck muscles.

"My ball!" said Boots.

Temp was already chasing after the ball but he put on the brakes when he became aware of the enormous reptile in the jungle.

Boots was not so easily deterred. She slid from the cockroach's back and ran forward, pointing at the lizard. "You eated my ball!"

"No, Boots!" Gregor cried. He scrambled to his feet and tripped over a skeleton. "No!"

"You eated my ball!" repeated Boots. She smacked her hands into the vines at the edge of the clearing, sending a vibration through the jungle. The lizard dipped its head in her direction.

Temp opened his wings and flew straight at the lizard's face. But the cockroaches rarely used their wings, and he ended up hopelessly tangled in the vines several feet from his target.

Gregor tried desperately to free his feet

from something's rib cage. "Boots! Get back!" He could see the other members of the party springing into rescue mode, but how could they reach her in time?

"You give Temp my ball!" Boots howled at the lizard. "Yooooouuuuu!"

The lizard glared at Boots and opened its jaw wide. A frightful hiss issued from its mouth as a rainbow-colored ruff shot out around its neck, making its head look five times bigger.

"Oh!" said Boots in surprise. Her own arms shot up over her head as if she had a ruff as well. "Oh!"

For a moment, the towering lizard and the tiny girl were mirror images of each other. Mouths open, ruffs up, eyes wide.

And then someone started laughing. The sound came from the direction of the lizard, and seemed to be coming from its mouth. But it was a distinctly human laugh, so Gregor knew it must have some other source.

The blue-green lizard's tail flopped out of the jungle, its tip resting on the ground near Boots. The vines rustled and someone slid down the tail. A pale, violet-eyed Underlander landed easily on his feet next to Boots. He was still laughing as he bent on one knee next to her.

"So, are you a hisser, too?" he asked.

"No, I'm Boots," she replied, dropping her arms. "Who you?"

"I am Hamnet. And this is my friend, Frill," said Hamnet. He indicated the lizard, whose ruff was slowly folding down.

Boots considered Frill for a moment. "*I* is for ig-ig-aguana," she said. She meant "iguana." It was another one of those animals like a yak. If the *ABC* books didn't have an ibex for the letter *I,* they were sure to have an iguana.

"Yes, I suppose it is," said Hamnet. "Whatever an ig-ig-aguana is."

"It eated my ball," said Boots in an injured tone.

"She did not mean to. Let us see if we can retrieve it. Frill, any way to have the ball back?" asked Hamnet.

The lizard's neck convulsed and the ball shot out of its mouth and straight down into Hamnet's hand. He wiped it on his shirt and Gregor noticed it was not the woven fabric generally worn by the Underlanders. Hamnet's clothes seemed to be made of reptile skin.

"Good as new, if you do not mind a little hisser spit," said Hamnet. He held out the ball to Boots.

What was that thing called? When you

thought something was happening that had happened before? Déjà vu? Gregor was experiencing a very big one now. He flashed back to Luxa, down on one knee, holding out a ball to Boots in the arena, that very same half smile on her face . . . the first time they had met. The similarity was so striking Gregor almost said her name. Who was he? Her dad? No, her dad was dead. But they must have been related. And what was he doing here in the middle of the jungle? Could this guy with the lizard be their guide?

Gregor looked over to the rest of the party for an explanation and found another puzzling scene. The humans were all standing like statues, as if they had seen a ghost. Vikus had his arm around Solovet, and for the first time, Gregor thought they actually looked like a married couple.

Boots reached happily for her ball. Gregor remembered how Luxa's fingers had held that first ball tightly, challenging Boots to take it away. "You will have to be stronger or smarter than I am." But Hamnet's fingers opened readily as Boots took the ball.

"*B* is for ball," she said with a grin.

"And for bright. Like you," said Hamnet, and gently poked her in the stomach. She giggled and looked up at Temp, who was still struggling to get free from the vines.

"Temp! You come down! Ball is back!" called Boots.

"Ohhhh . . ." Temp gave a moan. Hamnet reached up and untangled the vines from Temp's wings. He set the crawler on the ground.

"And what bold crawler is it who flies in the face of a hisser?" asked Hamnet.

"I be Temp, I be," said Temp, rearranging his wings so that they lay flat against his body. Boots scampered up on his back and tossed the ball. Off they ran, as if no stranger, no giant lizard had appeared out of the blue.

Hamnet turned back and surveyed the group. The half smile still played on his lips. There was a long silence.

"Oh, look. It's Hamnet. He's not dead," said Ripred finally. The rat picked up what appeared to be a human skull and started to gnaw on it.

"The skull is a nice touch, Ripred," said Hamnet.

"I thought so. How've you been?" said Ripred.

"Remarkably well, all things considered," said Hamnet. He looked back over his shoulder at the lizard. "It is safe. You may come down."

The leaves stirred and a small boy slid off the end of the lizard's tail. He did not land so easily as Hamnet had, but had to take a few hops to keep from falling over. Something was wrong about the boy. "No, not wrong, just different," Gregor thought. Then it struck him. The kid had that superpale Underlander skin, but his head was covered with jet-black curls, and his eyes were the green of a lime lollipop. Who was he? He didn't look like he came from either the Underland or Gregor's world.

The boy intertwined his fingers in Hamnet's and took in the group one by one with those strange green eyes. "This is my son, Hazard," Hamnet said.

"Not only alive but with a Halflander child," said Ripred. "You do know how to make an entrance."

Halflander. Did that mean half Overlander and half Underlander? That would explain how he didn't seem to come from either place.

Vikus slowly released Solovet and crossed over to the newcomers. He knelt down in front of the boy and took his free hand. "Greetings, Hazard. I am your grandfather, Vikus."

"My grandfather lives in New York City," said Hazard simply. "My mother was going to take me to see him, but she died." His accent was somewhere between Gregor's own and the clipped formal speech of the Underlanders.

"You have two grandfathers. I am your father's father," said Vikus.

Hazard looked up at Hamnet questioningly. Hamnet gave a small, noncommittal nod. "I didn't know I had two," said Hazard. "Where do you live?"

"I live in Regalia," said Vikus.

"I don't know where that is," said the boy. "Are we going to visit you?"

"You . . . are always . . . welcome. . . ." Vikus had to let go of the boy's hand because he was starting to cry now. He walked back to Solovet and stayed facing away from Hamnet and Hazard, his face buried in a handkerchief. Gregor had seen him cry a couple times before — but this time he didn't understand what was going on. If Hamnet was Vikus's son, why had Gregor never even heard his name? Where had he met an Overlander woman and had a son with her? What was he doing way out here in the middle of nowhere? How come Nerissa had known about him, but everybody else had . . . what? Thought he was dead? It occurred to him that maybe Hamnet had been banished, and that's why the whole thing

149

was such a big secret. People only got banished for really terrible things. Of course, since Ares was almost constantly about to be banished and Gregor had been on trial for his life a few short months ago, he couldn't make any snap judgments about that.

"Why come you here, Hamnet?" said Solovet hoarsely. "You have done well enough without us for ten years. Ran off and cared so little for us you let us believe you dead. Why come you here now?"

Ran off? Gregor didn't know anyone "ran off" from Regalia. It was generally considered to be a death sentence to be outside the city's protection. But here was someone who had run off and appeared to be doing okay. Why had he left? Gregor was dying to know, but this seemed like a really bad time to ask. In fact, it was sort of embarrassing being here at all, during such a personal moment.

"I am here because I promised I would be," said Hamnet. "Ten years ago when I was leaving Regalia, a little girl crept after me and made me swear to be at this spot at this time. She told me I would be in the company of a hisser and a Halflander child. Thinking she was mad, I agreed only to quiet her. But ten years later, still alive and

150

indeed finding myself in the company of a hisser and a Halflander child, I thought she might have true vision. Where is Nerissa? Does she still live?" said Hamnet.

"Not only lives, but reigns, Hamnet," said Ripred.

"Reigns?" said Hamnet. "But what of . . ."

"Your sister, Judith, and her husband were killed by rats. Your niece, Luxa, vanished battling in the Labyrinth some months ago. She is presumed dead," said Solovet. "But you have lost your right to mourn them, Hamnet. Your twin, Judith; her husband; your niece — you forsook them when you turned your back on us."

Whoa. Now Gregor really didn't want to be here. There was a whole lot of bad family stuff going on.

"You do not command me, Mother," said Hamnet. "Not what I do, not what I think, and never what I mourn."

"So, are you our guide?" broke in Lapblood, impatiently whipping a pile of bones aside with her tail.

"I do not know. Am I?" said Hamnet.

"According to your crazy queen," Mange said. "She said you're going to get us to the Vineyard of Eyes."

"Did she? And what business could a

mixed pack like yourselves have there?" said Hamnet.

" 'The Prophecy of Blood' has reared its ugly head," said Ripred. "Supposedly the Vineyard is the cradle." His teeth broke through the top of the skull he was gnawing on and protruded through the eye sockets.

" 'The Prophecy of Blood' . . . well, I have been gone a long time. So, where's your warrior?" asked Hamnet.

"Over there, with his boots in the bones," said Ripred.

Gregor, who was still trying to quietly work his feet out of the rib cage, stopped under Hamnet's gaze. Leave it to Ripred to introduce him when he looked like a complete fool.

"That is the warrior? Are you sure?" asked Hamnet.

"Quite sure. Been through two prophecies already. Don't worry, he's a lot more competent than he seems. A bit cocky, though. He's even spreading rumors that he's a rager," said Ripred.

"A warrior and a rager. My mother's dream come true," said Hamnet, eyeing Gregor with positive loathing.

Gregor kicked angrily at the rib cage and finally managed to get his feet free. He hated Ripred for bringing up the rager thing. What was it Twitchtip had said a rager was . . . a natural-born killer? Who wanted to be that? Not Gregor! And he certainly wasn't going around talking it up!

"Well, in the jungle, being a rager will only triple your difficulties," said Hamnet. "I hope you have gotten your 'powers' under control." He said this last part sarcastically.

"Yeah? Well, I hope you know where you're going, because I don't have a lot of time," Gregor shot back. He really didn't need this right now.

"I do not remember agreeing to take you anywhere," said Hamnet.

"And I don't remember asking you to," said Gregor. Man! He felt like he'd spent about half this trip mouthing off to somebody, but everybody just kept messing with him.

"Then it's settled. We have no use for each other," said Hamnet. "Come, Hazard." He began to lead the child back toward the lizard.

Mange gave a growl of fury and turned on Solovet. "You're worthless! All of you! You drag us out to this ridiculous spot and for what? Your own son will not help you find a cure for this plague!"

"We do not need his help," said Solovet dismissively.

"You don't think you need anyone's help. It would serve you right if we all left you here to rot in the jungle, Solovet," said Lapblood.

"Go, then. Return to your caves. We will find the cure without you," said Solovet. "But do not come whining to our doors that your pups are dying!"

"That's a promise. And here's another. They will not die alone!" hissed Mange and he crouched to attack.

The next moment was a blur. The guard nearest Solovet drew his blade as the second guard jumped on a bat and shot in the air. Lapblood sprang into place beside Mange.

Gregor knew that in a matter of seconds somebody was going to be dead.

Suddenly, the guard on the ground flipped onto his back, and Hamnet stood in place, the guard's sword in his hand. As Mange lunged, Hamnet threw the sword so that the tip of the blade plunged into a crack in the stone, directly in the rat's path. Mange sheared off all his whiskers on one side of his face as he veered sideways to avoid running straight into the blade. Then he plowed into Lapblood, knocking her off balance. The two rats slammed into a heap. As the guard on the bat swept down at the rats, Hamnet leaped in the air, grabbing his sword arm, and yanked him to the ground. The guard landed on his stomach with a grunt and his sword blade snapped in two on the stone. It all happened so fast. Nobody knew what had hit them. The rats and the guards slowly sat up, looking dazed.

Gregor's mouth fell open. He wasn't sure exactly how, but Hamnet had stopped the fight and no one had lost anything but some whiskers. Gregor looked over at Ripred, who was still crunching on his skull, unimpressed by the scene.

"I knew he'd take care of it," Ripred said with a shrug, and popped the rest of the skull in his mouth.

Hamnet plucked the sword from the crack and examined it. "Nothing ever changes, does it?"

"You changed," said Solovet softly. "Or why does that gnawer live?"

Hamnet placed the lower end of the blade across his wrist and offered her the hilt of the sword. "Why do you, for that matter?" he said.

"Because I never cease fighting," said Solovet, taking the sword.

"Stop," said Vikus. "Stop this, please." He mopped his face with the handkerchief and turned to his son. "Hamnet, the plague is upon us. Our hospital fills with victims. The gnawers are nearing an epidemic. We must get to the Vineyard of Eyes. Can you not do this one thing for us?"

Hamnet, his head already shaking, was on the verge of replying when Hazard tugged on his hand. "You know where that is. The Vineyard of Eyes."

"Hazard, you do not understand the —" Hamnet began.

"We could take them. I could talk to the bats. And the crawler," Hazard said. "Is he really your father? Like you're my father?"

The question pulled Hamnet up short. He just stood there, holding Hazard's hand, his face pained.

"Is he?" insisted Hazard.

"Yes, yes, he is," said Hamnet. "All right. All right, then. Who am I taking? Not this entire mob."

"No, just a handful. We three rats, the two Overlanders, the crawler, a couple fliers, and your mother," said Ripred.

"Not my mother, nor her flier," said Hamnet flatly.

"We might actually need her, boy, if we run into any trouble," said Ripred.

"No! Not if you want my help!" said Hamnet. Now he turned to Solovet and addressed her directly. "Not if you want my help."

"Is that lady your mother?" asked Hazard, wide-eyed.

"Clear out! The rest of you clear out, you have drawn half the jungle here as it is!" shouted Hamnet, waving his arms as if to brush them aside. "Kill that fire and be on your way!"

The human guards looked to Solovet, who gave them a nod. The fire was quenched; the guards and Solovet mounted their bats. Vikus was about to follow suit when he suddenly moved to Hamnet and locked him in an embrace. Hamnet's arms stuck out awkwardly, not returning the gesture but not resisting it.

"You may come home at any time. Know this. There are many ways to occupy yourself. You would not have to fight!" said Vikus.

"Vikus, I cannot —" stammered Hamnet.

"You can! Only think about it. Think of the child. If something should happen to you." Vikus pulled back, almost shaking Hamnet by his shoulders. "What do you do here that you could not do there?"

"I do no harm," said Hamnet. "I do no more harm."

Vikus slowly released Hamnet and nodded. He crossed and mounted his bat. "Fly you high," he said to no one in particular.

Solovet gave a signal and the party of bats and humans left.

"Bye! Bye, you!" called Boots, waving good-bye.

"Glad that's over," said Ripred. "Always some big scene with your family. You're miserable to have dinner with."

"I know," said Hamnet. "Is Susannah dead, too?"

"No, she's fine. Whole castle of children now. The Overlander knows one of them," said Ripred. "What's his name?"

"Howard," said Gregor. He was a little overwhelmed by everything he had just witnessed.

"I know Howard. He was about Hazard's age when I left," said Hamnet. "So how is he, Rager?" The last word was heavy with disdain.

The admiration Gregor had felt when Hamnet stopped the violence faded. "He's in quarantine," said Gregor. "But I'll tell him you said 'hi' if I get back. You know, if he's still alive."

Ripred's tail smacked Gregor on the back of the head. Not hard enough to knock him over, but hard enough to hurt. "Watch it," the rat said.

Gregor rubbed his head and scowled at Ripred, but he shut up. After all, he really didn't know what was up with Hamnet. He obviously didn't get along with Solovet. She obviously was mad he'd left Regalia. But maybe he had a good reason for leaving. Maybe Gregor should find out what had happened. Or maybe — now here was an idea — maybe he should just mind his own business and get on with finding the cure.

Hamnet called them all together. They made three distinct groups. Gregor, Boots, Temp, and Nike, that was one group. Hamnet, Hazard, and Frill were another. The rats were the third.

"So, who's in charge of this thing, anyway?" asked Gregor. Hamnet was their guide, but it was hard to imagine anyone bossing Ripred around.

"Not you, and that's all you need to know," said Ripred, which made Hamnet and the other rats laugh. "You had something to say, Hamnet?"

"Thank you, Ripred. Now before we enter the jungle, let me make one thing clear. It is not a place for swords and claws. Eat only what you carry. Take care your flame singes nothing. Crush no berry, bruise no leaf, tread as gently as possible on the roots," said Hamnet.

"What? I can't even eat a vine?" said Mange.

"You can," said Hamnet. "If you wish to risk your life."

"They're just plants," said Lapblood.

"Some are just plants. But the ones that are harmless mimic the ones that are poisonous or constrictive or hungry," said Hamnet. "Look like them, smell like them, act like them. Can you tell the difference between what you can eat and what can eat you?"

"They can't really eat us," said Gregor uneasily. "Can they?"

Hamnet just gave him that half smile. "Ask the skeletons."

CHAPTER 14

While Gregor was wondering if he had enough nerve to walk into a jungle full of deadly plants, Hamnet organized the more mundane aspects of the trip. Light was the first order of business. Instead of the usual open-flame torches, the Regalians had provided glass lanterns with handles. They were half-filled with a pale, slightly sweet-smelling oil and had wicks. Unless one of them broke on the ground, the fire inside would not damage the plants.

Gregor's flashlight batteries died just as he was getting his lantern lit. Much to his surprise, he could still see! Not very well, not as if he were in daylight. But well enough to make out the silhouettes of the individual vines around him. Although the campfire had been extinguished, his flashlight was off, and the lanterns were unlit, the entire jungle was visible. He set the lanterns down and went to investigate. What was the source of light? It seemed to emanate from the ground itself. It grew fainter higher up, then dissolved into blackness about twelve feet in the air.

He moved to a spot where the light seemed strongest and found a narrow but deep stream. Along the bed, flashes of light came and went. He had seen something like this before in the crawlers' land — a stream with small volcanic eruptions on the bottom — but the bursts weren't as large or explosive as the ones before him. Gregor dipped his fingers in the stream and felt the warm water roll over them.

"There are hundreds of those streams crisscrossing the jungle," he heard Ripred say behind him. "Don't step in them, don't drink from them, and try not to use your fingers for bait."

Gregor jerked his hand out of the water as a set of spiky teeth snapped together in the space his fingers had just occupied. "What was that?" he asked, stepping back from the stream.

"Something that thinks you're yummy," said Ripred.

"Is that why we can't drink from them? It's too dangerous to get water?" asked Gregor.

"No, the water's tainted. Drink it and you die," said Ripred.

Gregor immediately went back and explained to Temp how scary the streams were so the cockroach would know to keep

Boots clear of them. "Stream bad," agreed Temp.

But when Gregor told Boots to stay out of the water, she looked around eagerly and took off for the stream squealing, "Water? We go swimming?"

He chased after her and caught her by the arm. "No! No swimming! Bad water, Boots! You-don't-touch-water!" He said this so sharply that the sides of her mouth pointed down and her eyes filled with tears. "Hey, hey, it's okay. Don't cry." He hugged her. "Just stay away from the water here, okay? It's . . . it's too hot," he said. "Like in the bath?"

This seemed to make more sense to her. When the oil heater worked in their building, sometimes scalding water came from the tap.

"Ow?" she said.

"Right. Ow." He picked her up and carried her back to the others. "You going to ride Temp?" said Gregor.

"Ye-es!" said Boots. She wiggled out of Gregor's arms and onto the cockroach's back. "You don't touch water, Temp!"

That made Gregor feel a little better. "Or plants!" he added.

"Or plants!" Boots told Temp severely.

The humans had also left behind several

packs of supplies. One contained first aid supplies and fuel for Gregor to carry. Three larger packs of food were designed for the rats to haul. They had straps for the rodents' forelegs and a belt that fastened under their bellies. Nike was in charge of several heavy leather water bags.

Gregor surveyed the dense tangle of vines doubtfully. "How are you going to get along in there, Nike?" She would not be able to fly much, and travel on foot was very taxing on the bats.

"Up higher, there are places where the foliage is not so heavy," said Nike. "I will fly above the vines when I must, and join the party when I can. Will you and your sister ride?"

Gregor didn't think it would be fair to ask her to carry him and Boots along with all the water bags. Besides, Temp wouldn't want to be left on the ground without them. "We'll just walk," he said.

He lit a lamp and prepared to travel. As a backup to the lamp, he hung a flashlight from a belt loop at his waist. The big pack with the first aid supplies and oil went on his back. The smaller backpack that Mareth had filled with flashlights and stuff, he wore on his chest. It also contained some items Dulcet had included for Boots — a change of clothes, a blanket, some toys, some cookies, a hairbrush. Gregor took the mirror Nerissa had given him from his pocket and put it in the backpack, too. He didn't even have a copy of the prophecy with him, but Boots liked to play with mirrors, and she might need a distraction. He slung the wineskin full of shrimp and cream sauce around his neck. Initially, he'd asked for the shrimp as a treat for Ripred. He still intended to give it to the rat, but now he thought it might make a good bargaining tool. It would be nice to pull out the rat's favorite dish if he needed a favor in the jungle.

Gregor thought he was done when he felt Temp nudging him. He turned to see the cockroach holding a sheathed sword in his mouth. "Not this, forget, not this," said Temp.

Where had that come from? Gregor hadn't even seen it until this moment. Solovet must have left it for him. He clumsily buckled the wide leather belt around his hips and tried to slide the sword around to the most accessible position. Somehow he ended up with it on his right hip, the tip angled forward. That seemed wrong. He finally wriggled it around to his left hip with the tip pointing behind him. Now he could grab the hilt and pull the blade out with his right hand easily.

"Worked that out, have you, Warrior?"

Gregor looked up to find Hamnet watching him. He wasn't wearing a sword, just a short knife in a sheath on his leg.

"Guess I'll find out if I have to use it," said Gregor, hitching up the belt like he knew what he was doing. The sword banged awkwardly against his leg.

"How old are you, anyway?" said Hamnet.

Gregor thought of saying thirteen or fourteen. He was tall even if he was on the skinny side. If he were older, maybe Hamnet would treat him with more respect. No, probably not.

"Eleven," said Gregor.

"Eleven," said Hamnet, and the expression on his face changed. He looked almost sad.

"I'll be twelve real soon," said Gregor. He said that as if it had some significance, but what did it mean, really? The only thing he could think of was he'd have to start paying full price at the movies. And that wasn't a very warrior-like thought. "Why?"

"I was just thinking, it did not take long for my mother to get her claws into you," said Hamnet.

Gregor felt himself bristling again.

"Look, I don't know what's going on with you and Solovet. But I'm not here for your mother. I'm here for mine. She's got the plague." Mentioning his mom made him feel upset. To his surprise, he felt his eyes filling with tears. Blinking them back, he looked down and adjusted his belt again. He did not want Hamnet to see. "So, maybe you could just back off, okay?" he said gruffly.

There was a pause. "I will back off, if you keep that sword in your belt," said Hamnet. "Agreed?"

Gregor nodded. He took another few moments to compose himself. When he looked up, Hamnet had moved away to fix a strap on Ripred's shoulder. Gregor actually felt a little better. He did not want to head into the jungle at odds with Hamnet. It was enough to have three rats picking on him. And he had no plans to draw his sword, anyway.

It wasn't until everyone was loaded up that Frill slid out of her spot in the vines to join them in the open circle. She wasn't fifteen feet tall, as she had seemed at first. In fact, she just about looked Gregor in the eye. He realized she must have been standing up on her hind legs. Even on all fours, she was still an impressive creature. Twenty feet long from nose to tail, with that shimmery blue-green skin covering every inch of her. The ruff had had several other colors in it, but you couldn't see it much now that it had folded down. Frill had wonderful feet, too, each with five long toes that could wrap around anything.

"You've got a good-looking lizard," Gregor said to Hazard. The boy looked up at him with surprise.

"Thaaaaank yoooouuuuu," said Frill in a long breathy hiss.

Gregor should have known better than to treat Frill like she was some kind of pet. He had made the same mistake with the bats on his first visit. Frill was no more a pet than Ares was. She knew what was being said. Hadn't she spit back the ball when Hamnet had asked her to?

"Sorry," said Gregor, "I didn't know you could . . ."

"Thiiiink?" hissed Frill.

Hazard turned to Frill and made a long, freaky series of hissing sounds. Frill hissed back unintelligibly, and the two laughed. Gregor had never seen a human speak anything but English in the Underland.

Frill dipped her head and Hazard hung a large, reptile-skin pack around her neck. They continued hissing back and forth as

168

Hazard adjusted the pack under Frill's ruff.

"What's he doing?" Ripred asked Hamnet with a frown. "Can he speak to that hisser?"

"Hazard can speak to anything. Well, at least he will try, if it will give him a chance," said Hamnet with a gleam of pride. "Go ahead, squeak at him."

"What?" said Ripred.

"Greet him in Rat," said Hamnet.

Ripred eyed the little boy and then let out a high-pitched squeak. Almost immediately, Hazard parroted back a sound that was indistinguishable from Ripred's own.

"What's that mean? Does that mean hello? I've talked to mice sometimes, but they say hello like this. . . ." Hazard let out an even higher-pitched squeak that caused all three rats to grimace.

"Well, it's about time one of you made a little effort to communicate outside your own tongue," said Ripred. "Gets a little tedious for the rest of us, having to learn Human if we want to talk with you. Can you do it, too?"

"I can get by in Hisser," said Hamnet. "A word here and there of other creatures. I do not have Hazard's ear."

"You learned too late. See, this one, start her off now, and she'll be fluent in Crawler by the end of the trip," said Ripred, poking Boots with the tip of his tail. "Even the warrior — no, forget the warrior. He's been trying to master basic echolocation for months with no result. Just keep knocking your head against that one, okay, boy? Don't want to overload your massive brain with too many tasks at once."

Gregor said nothing but decided he would dump the shrimp in the stream before Ripred would get one bite. Stupid rat.

"So, shall we get going?" said Ripred.

"Yes, we have lingered here too long," said Hamnet. "Frill will lead and I will go last. We will take the path that begins at the Arch of Tantalus, but eventually the jungle overcomes it. Remember, step lightly and hurt nothing. And keep a close eye on your provisions. The fliers did not name the Arch of Tantalus frivolously."

"What's Tantalus?" Gregor asked Nike, as he adjusted the water bags on her back.

"He was a who. An Overlander from long ago. He had committed a great crime. As punishment, he had to stand in a pool of water beneath a tree of luscious fruit. He had great thirst and hunger. But when he bent to drink, the water receded. When he reached for the fruit, the branches rose out of his reach."

"Is that how he died?" asked Gregor.

"He was already dead," said Nike. "The punishment was for eternity."

Gregor was trying to wrap his mind around that and exactly what it had to do with going into the jungle as the party began to move through the archway. Frill went first, with Hazard perched on her back. Mange and Lapblood went next. Gregor fell into step with Temp and Boots. Ripred brought up the rear with Hamnet. Nike disappeared up into the vines above.

Everything changed the instant he was through the Arch of Tantalus, as if he had stepped through some portal into another dimension. The ground beneath his feet turned from stone to moss. The air became thick and pungent with the smell of decaying plants. He couldn't prove it, but he would've sworn the temperature rose twenty degrees. And the jungle sounds, which had seemed a healthy distance away, now clamored in his ears.

Within a few minutes his skin was damp with sweat and he was thinking of chopping his pants off into shorts. The straps of the packs cut into his shoulders. His nose began to run in the warm, moist air. He had never been hot in the Underland, and only cold when he was wet. Usually the temperature was comfortable if you wore short sleeves.

The smooth carpet of moss transformed into a tricky web of roots. They popped up at various heights, and the flickering light of the streams made it difficult to judge how high to lift his foot. Gregor had pretty big feet, too, for an eleven-year-old. His parents always laughed about that and told him he'd grow into them. But they felt clunky in the hiking boots Mrs. Cormaci had given him. The boots were hand-me-downs from one of her grown-up sons and a size too large — he had toilet paper stuffed in the toes to make them fit right — so he had that extra half inch to deal with. Everyone else seemed to walk so easily — Frill, the rats, Temp with his delicate roach feet. Gregor glanced over his shoulder to see how Hamnet walked, and he tripped over a root, smacking into Mange.

"Why don't you take those ridiculous things off your feet?" snapped Mange.

But Gregor didn't dare. Who knew what kind of creature might be lying in wait? He thought of fangs and stingers, thorns and spikes, and kept his shoes on.

Boots, riding comfortably on Temp's back, was having a fine time teaching him "The Alphabet Song." The roach held his own up to about the letter *L,* but that whole

L-M-N-O-P run kept throwing him off track. In all fairness, this part of the song was fast and easy to garble, anyway. "Elemenopee!" sang Boots, as if it were one long letter.

"Elenenemopeeo," sang Temp, off-key as usual.

For a while, Hazard just perched up on Frill, watching Boots and Temp with great absorption. Finally, he slid off Frill's back and ran back to them. "What are you singing?"

"I sing *A-B-C*," said Boots. "Who you?"

"I'm Hazard," said the boy, skipping lightly over a root. "Will you teach me that song?"

Would she? Boots loved to teach anything! Soon there were three voices weaving through the song. Gregor thought it was going to drive the rats crazy but Mange and Lapblood were whispering intently between themselves, and Ripred was filling Hamnet in on what had happened in his ten-year absence. No, the one who was feeling a little crazy was Gregor, as the three conversations joined the jungle chatter already assaulting his ears. He would've liked a quiet moment to think, to catch up his brain to where his body was, to examine "The Prophecy of Blood" in light of everything that had happened, but he wasn't going to get it anytime soon.

By the time Hamnet called a break, Gregor's clothes were soaked with sweat. Inside his boots, his socks felt squishy. A sharp pain jabbed between his shoulder blades from the heavy packs. He could've drunk the glacier water in three big gulps, but he'd decided to save the fancy bottle Mareth had put in his pack. He wanted to have some water with him, in case Boots needed it or he got separated from the group.

For their resting spot, Hamnet had chosen a small clearing lined on one side by a strip of mossy rocks. Gregor could hear the gurgle of water nearby, but no stream was visible through the vines. The rats dumped the packs of food by the rocks and stretched out. After carefully examining a spot, Gregor unloaded his stuff and sank onto the ground across from them. Nike swished down from the trees and shook off her water bags next to him. Hamnet opened one and went around, letting everyone drink their fill.

Hazard helped Hamnet pass out bread, meat, and some raw carrotlike vegetable. Gregor was not all that hungry, probably because of the heat, but he ate what was given to him. Boots munched down all her food and some of Temp's bread, which was standard. The cockroach always let her have whatever she wanted. Then Boots and Temp and Hazard began to play on the rocks.

"*R* is for rock," said Boots and soon a chorus of "The Alphabet Song" was in progress.

Lapblood and Mange, who were gnawing on bones they'd brought from the Arch of Tantalus, winced at the singing.

"They're off again!" said Lapblood.

"It'd be one thing if they could stay on key, but that's just painful," said Mange.

"It's no worse than listening to you guys gnaw on stuff," said Gregor.

"There must be some way to muzzle them," said Lapblood.

"None I can think of," said Gregor.

"Well, I'll think of one, if they keep on like this!" said Mange.

"You rats . . . you've got a problem with little kids, don't you?" said Gregor. Ripred had never taken to Boots and had been openly hostile to the baby Bane. "Bet you don't even like your own pups."

What? What had he said? Something really bad by the way Mange's and Lapblood's eyes were burning into him. Were they actually going to attack him? As tense as everyone had been today, it wasn't hard to imagine.

"Speaking of needing a muzzle," said Ripred pointedly to Gregor. "Not making many friends with that mouth of yours, are you?"

Gregor had not taken his eyes off Mange and Lapblood. He could see the muscles in their forelegs tightening. His fingers instinctively found the hilt of his sword.

"Overlander," said Hamnet. Gregor remembered his agreement with Hamnet and slowly released his sword. "That is better. Remember where you are, all of you. And that you need each other, Warmbloods."

The sounds of the jungle took over as everyone remembered, but no one relaxed.

Then a little voice piped up, "*F* is for fog! Oh, Gre-go! *F* is for fog!"

Gregor didn't want to look away from the rats, but something was wrong. There was no fog in the jungle. What was she talking about?

When he turned his head, Gregor felt a whole new coat of sweat break out over the one that had never dried from the hike. Boots was sitting up on the highest of the rocks, clapping her hands in delight. Temp and Hazard were frozen in the act of climbing after her. Dotting the rocks like brightly colored jewels were about fifty little frogs. Green and black, sunset orange, grape-soda purple. Poison arrow frogs. Gregor recognized them from the Central Park Zoo. Only there, you had to view them from behind a thick pane of glass.

There was a good reason for that. If you touched one of them, you could die.

CHAPTER 15

As if to illustrate Gregor's worst fear, a hapless lizard slithered onto the rocks. Not a big lizard, like Frill, just a foot-long one like you might see in the Overland. It shot out its tongue toward one of the frogs. The instant it made contact with the orange frog skin, the lizard went stiff as a board. Paralyzed by poison. Dead.

"Don't touch, Boots! Don't touch!" cried Gregor. Oh, this was bad. Really bad. Gregor had once bought her a tube filled with plastic poison arrow frogs that looked very much like the ones around her. She spent hours lining them up on the arm of the couch. The frog set was one of her favorite toys.

Boots giggled and clasped her hands together. But she was so excited that her little feet drummed on the mossy rock. "*F* is for fog! I see red, I see yellow, I see blue!"

The frogs were hopping around, not wildly, but still, it was only a matter of time before one landed on Boots, Hazard, or Temp.

"Hazard, can you jump clear?" said

Hamnet in a ragged voice.

The boy flexed his legs and sprang out over the packs of foods. He landed unevenly and tumbled into Ripred, but the rat didn't even seem to notice.

"You can't help her up there, Crawler. Clear out of the way so the rest of us stand a chance," said Ripred.

Temp hesitated, as if trying to take in what Ripred had said. Gregor knew Temp would sacrifice his life for Boots, but how could he protect her from that tiny army of amphibians?

"He's right, Temp, just get out of there," said Gregor.

Gregor's words seemed to decide him. Temp spread his wings and flew off the rock onto the path. Now it was just Boots, sitting happily among the frogs.

"Rib-bit! Rib-bit! Fog says rib-bit!" she said. "And tongue goes like this!" Boots's tongue darted in and out of her mouth and she imitated a frog catching flies. Gregor had shown her that. "Rib-bit!"

A red-and-black spotted frog leaped into the air and landed right by her hip.

"Ooh!" said Boots. "Red fog says 'hi!' "

"Don't touch it, Boots! Do not touch!" ordered Gregor. He was slowly moving in toward her.

Another frog, a salmon-pink color, hopped over her shoe. "Hop! Hop!" Unable to contain herself, Boots scooted her feet under her and assumed the classic frog position, knees bent, hands between her feet. "Hop! Hop! I am fog, too!" She bounced up and down. The vibration of her movement seemed to stir up the creatures. They began to spring around with more energy. "Hop! Hop!"

"No, Boots . . . no hopping!" pleaded Gregor.

He was at the base of the food packs now. The frogs had spread out from the rocks onto the packs. Two orange frogs and a green one were within inches of his stomach. Boots was about a foot above him, five feet away. His arms reached out for her. "Just jump out to me. Like at the swimming pool? You jump, and I'll catch you. Okay?"

"Ye-es!" Boots agreed. She straightened her legs and bent her knees to jump into Gregor's arms, but at that moment, a particularly dazzling sapphire-blue frog leaped right for her arm.

The next few moments seemed to happen in slow motion. The sapphire frog sailing at Boots's arm, Lapblood's body twisting into the air, her tail catching Boots on the behind and catapulting her up over Gregor's head,

Hamnet's voice as he caught her, the frog landing, leaping again directly for Lapblood's face, Gregor's arm in motion, his sword skewering the sapphire skin inches from Lapblood's ear.

"Get back!" Ripred's sharp command reached his brain. "Get out of there!"

The whole party staggered backward as the frogs began to invade the path.

"Stay together!" he heard Hamnet's voice, but it was too chaotic. Everyone was crashing into the jungle, forgetting about the path as they fled the tiny, fatal frogs.

Gregor was some twenty yards into the vines before he realized he was stampeding over the plants like a buffalo. He looked around the gloomy jungle and could spot no one. "Hey!" he yelled.

"Stay where you are!" he heard Ripred call. "Everyone hold your position!"

It took fifteen minutes for Hamnet and Ripred to reassemble the group.

Gregor could hear Boots and Hamnet talking about the "fogs," so he knew she was okay. He stood very still, holding the dead frog out in front of him on his sword. His blood was still buzzing in his veins. His vision was oddly fragmented. It had happened again. The rager thing. Somehow, he had drawn his sword and stabbed this frog with deadly accuracy without even thinking about it. He couldn't have stopped himself if he had tried, because he didn't even know what he was doing. His "powers," as Hamnet had called them, were not under control. And he had no idea how to master them.

When Ripred's nose scooted aside the vines, Gregor had still not moved a muscle. "I need help, Ripred," he said weakly.

"You seem to be managing yourself all right," said the rat.

"I can't control it," said Gregor. "Being a rager!" His arm jerked up, and Ripred jumped out of the way of the frog on the tip of his sword.

"Whoa! Watch where you're swinging that thing!" said the rat. "Get rid of it. Go on, wipe it on that rock over there." Gregor dragged the tip of his sword along the rock and scraped off the tiny carcass of the frog. "And rinse it in the water," said Ripred so Gregor held the point in a nearby stream. "Now sheath your blade but remember its touch may still have poison on it. So, don't be pulling it out without thinking," Ripred said.

Gregor stuck the sword back in its sheath. "How do I know when I'll pull it out? I don't plan these things!" he said, agitated.

"I know, I know. Look, just calm down. Ragers feel insane at first. I did myself. The more it happens, the more you'll get used to it," said Ripred.

"But I don't know when it happens!" Gregor almost screamed. Wasn't the rat even listening to him?

"Yes, you do. You can feel it in your blood, your eyesight alters, your focus sharpens to exclude anything of unimportance. You're aware of these things?" said Ripred.

Gregor nodded. "Sometimes. When Ares and I were fighting rats in the maze, I knew it was happening."

"All right, good. That's good. That's a start. Now when you're in danger, when you feel you might be attacked, pay attention. Eventually, you'll be able to turn it on and off. But it takes time," said Ripred.

"How long did it take you?" asked Gregor.

"It's different. I battled so frequently. I had more opportunity to master it quickly," said Ripred.

"How long?" repeated Gregor.

"A few years," said the rat.

A few years! When Ripred probably fought almost every day! Gregor shook his head, already feeling defeated.

"It's not that bad, Gregor. Believe me, at times you'll see it as a gift," said Ripred.

"I don't want this gift, Ripred," said Gregor.

"Well, it's yours," said Ripred. "Come on now, before your sister makes any more friends."

As Gregor followed Ripred back through the jungle, it struck him how nice the rat had been. Usually, he was needling Gregor or knocking him around. But Ripred seemed to know when he could push him and when he genuinely needed help. Like the time Gregor had cried after Tick died. Or when he had tried to tell him about how he had lost Boots to the serpents. And here, now.

They rejoined the group some distance up the path from the frog incident. Gregor felt embarrassed, like everybody was staring at him. He particularly didn't want to meet Hamnet's eyes.

"Don't jump down his throat, Hamnet. He couldn't help it," said Ripred.

"I could see that, but it is not reassuring," said Hamnet.

"Well, at least Lapblood's still alive to fight," said Ripred.

Gregor knew he should probably thank Lapblood for saving Boots's life, but the rats were so hostile, he let it lie.

Boots was still geared up about her encounter with the frogs, hopping around and making "rib-bit" sounds.

"She says you have the same kind of frogs at home. She says they sleep in her bed," said Hazard to Gregor.

"They're fake, Hazard. They're just toys," said Gregor.

"Strange playthings you choose in the Overland," Hamnet commented.

It must seem strange to them. Making a toy out of something so deadly. Encouraging a little kid to want to pick one up. But then again, poison arrow frogs weren't exactly hopping down Broadway.

"What'd we lose?" said Ripred.

"All the food, I'm afraid," said Hamnet. "The frogs swarmed the packs, and now they're too dangerous to touch, let alone risk eating from. Nike got the water, though. And Frill saved your packs." Hamnet dropped Gregor's two backpacks and the wineskin on the ground at his feet. "Any food?"

"Just some cookies for Boots. Oh, and this," said Gregor, holding up the wineskin. "It's shrimp in cream sauce. I brought it for Ripred."

"Now who's my favorite little rager?" said

185

Ripred, running his twitching nose up the bag. "Did you really bring this for me?"

"Sorry, Ripred. You know it goes to the pups," said Hamnet, swinging the wineskin over his shoulder.

Ripred sighed. "First that greedy Bane and now these brats. They'll be the death of me, pups."

"Oh, you will live." Hamnet laughed. "Long after the rest of us."

They lined up again and continued down the path. Gregor tried to stress the importance of avoiding pretty frogs to Boots, but she didn't really seem to be getting it. In fact, she started snoozing on Temp's shell right in the middle of Gregor's lecture so he had no choice but to let it go.

There was not much discussion after that. The heat was becoming more oppressive and the loss of the food was troubling. They marched forward until Gregor's feet were so heavy he seemed to be tripping over every root. Then at last Hamnet called for them to set up camp.

They all gathered in a circle around a lantern. Everyone got a generous drink of water, but there was only food for the "pups." Gregor gave Hamnet the cookies, and he gave a few each to Boots and Hazard. Then, to Gregor's surprise,

Hamnet held two out to him.

"No, no, thanks," said Gregor.

"You are only eleven, boy, you still qualify as a pup yourself," said Hamnet.

"No, give it to them," said Gregor. He didn't feel like a pup. Somehow having the responsibility of saving his mother, Ares, and every warmblood in the Underland knocked that feeling right out of him.

When Hamnet unscrewed the top to the wineskin, the mouthwatering aroma of shrimp in cream sauce made Gregor gulp.

"Do you think it wise giving that to the pups?" said Ripred. "Cream has a bad reputation for spoiling in the heat."

"The only thing spoiled is you. You can smell perfectly well that it's fine," said Lapblood.

"You can never be too careful," said Ripred as he grumpily watched Boots and Hazard dipping their cookies in the sauce.

When the kids had eaten, everyone settled down to sleep. Frill volunteered for the first watch. Gregor spread a blanket on the ground and lay down with Boots. She snuggled up on his arm and drifted off. He had to wait until she was asleep so he could free his arm from under her sweaty head of curls. Man, it was hot!

He was exhausted, but the jungle sounds made it difficult to sleep. Plus the heat. Plus the fact that he'd had another rager experience. All of which seemed inconsequential when his mind rolled around to the images of the hospital. His mom lying in that white bed, Ares's heaving chest, the hope in Howard's eyes when he'd seen Gregor's face.

So he was still awake, staring into the dimly lit vines, when they began talking. Lapblood and Mange.

"Do you think there's any chance they're still alive?" whispered Lapblood. "Not the two little ones. I know they were dying when we left. But Flyfur and Sixclaw?"

"Yes, yes, I do," said Mange soothingly. "The yellow powder is on its way and they had no signs of the plague when we left. And you know Makemince will manage to feed them somehow."

"The two little ones . . . do you think they suffered much?" said Lapblood. "I can't bear to think of them, calling me, and no one answering. My pups."

"No, I'm sure they went quickly," said Mange in a choked voice. "But we can't think of that. We have to think of Flyfur and Sixclaw. They still have a chance."

"Yes. Yes, I know. I will," said Lapblood. "I am."

"Now go to sleep, Lapblood," said Mange. "Please."

It was quiet then, but now Gregor knew he was not the only one awake. He knew someone else was lying across the lantern, staring into the jungle, and wondering how long someone they loved had to live.

CHAPTER 16

Gregor dozed in and out of sleep until Hamnet woke him up to continue the next leg of the journey. As he rolled up his blanket, his mind went back to the conversation he'd overheard between Lapblood and Mange. So, two of their pups were dead and two might well be dead soon. He thought of the crack he'd made about rats not even liking their own pups, and his face turned hot with shame. Especially since Lapblood had risked her life for Boots. Whether she had done it because she thought Boots was necessary to find the cure or done it simply to save the little girl, he didn't know but the result was the same. Maybe he could talk to Lapblood privately. . . . No. His dad said if you did something wrong to someone in public, you ought to admit it in public, too.

"Hey, Lapblood," he called. It was hard to apologize. Especially to a rat. He started with the easy part first. "I just wanted to say . . . thanks for getting Boots away from those frogs yesterday."

"Forget it," said Lapblood.

She had not thanked him back for saving

her from the blue frog, but maybe she thought he just owed her that as a matter of course. He forced himself to continue. "And what I said . . . that thing about rats not liking their own pups . . ." Everybody had stopped what they were doing to listen to him now. "I'm sorry. That was stupid." He crammed the blanket roll in his pack.

Lapblood didn't respond. Neither did Mange. Oh, well. He had said it, anyway.

While Hamnet fed Boots and Hazard, the rats and Nike groomed themselves. Even Temp seemed to be tidying himself up with his legs. Gregor wiped Boots down with a damp cloth and ran her brush through her hair. His mom would want him to keep her neat. He wasn't much concerned with his own appearance, but he wished there were a safe stream to wash in, just so he didn't feel so hot and sticky. At least he didn't have fur.

When it was his turn to drink, Gregor lifted the water bag and gulped down as much as his stomach could hold. It helped to fill the hollow, empty feeling.

They fell into their lineup and headed deeper into the jungle. The path was noticeably narrower, so much so that he could not walk beside Temp. Frill offered to carry Boots and Temp along with Hazard, and

Gregor agreed, figuring they could entertain one another.

He was a little concerned they'd take off on another marathon *A-B-C* sing-along, but Hazard came up with another diversion. Learning to speak Cockroach. Hazard had only exchanged a few sets of clicks with Temp when Boots tugged on his arm. "Me, too! I can talk like beeg bug, too!" she insisted. The three settled down on Frill's back and were occupied for hours with the game. It was just as Ripred had predicted. Boots learned the clicks and absorbed their meaning quickly. And Hazard was an amazing mimic. As for Temp, after his initial shyness, it turned out he was a natural teacher. He was endlessly patient and never critical. By the time they broke for lunch, the three were conversing in a strange mixture of English and Cockroach without thinking anything of it.

At lunch, the water did little to affect the gnawing hunger that had settled in Gregor's stomach. He hadn't eaten in a day, and they'd been hiking for most of that time. When he was digging through the backpack for a toy top Dulcet had packed for Boots, he made a welcome discovery. "Hey, the bubble gum!" he said. He held up the bright pink package to the others.

"I want bubba gum!" said Boots, hanging on his arm.

"No, Boots. You're too little," said Gregor. His mom wouldn't let them give her gum because she might choke on it. "But, here, you can have the paper." He carefully shook out the gum and gave her the shiny pink wrapper, which she ran to show her friends.

"Is that food?" asked Mange.

"Not food exactly. You chew it, but you don't swallow it," said Gregor.

"What's the point in that?" said Lapblood.

What was the point in bubble gum? "I don't know . . . it tastes good. You want some or not?" said Gregor.

There were five individually wrapped squares of gum. The kids had just eaten, and Temp could go a month without food. Nike and Frill were managing to catch enough bugs as they traveled, so that just left Gregor, Hamnet, and the rats.

"Okay, perfect, that's one piece each," said Gregor. He tossed the rats and Hamnet each a square. "Remember, chew it. Don't swallow it."

He peeled the waxed paper off his gum and stuffed it in his mouth. The burst of sugar was fantastic. He saw the others watching him. "Go on! Try it!"

Hamnet slowly opened his piece and sniffed it. He tentatively put it in his mouth and chewed. A perplexed look crossed his face. "It is very sweet . . . and it does not diminish when you chew it."

"No, it's gum. You can chew the same piece for days. Years probably!" said Gregor.

One by one, without bothering to remove the paper, the rats took the gum into their mouths. Gregor had to bite his lip not to laugh as they snapped their jaws open and shut, trying to make sense of the stuff.

Ripred made a slight gagging sound. "Uh. I swallowed mine."

"It's okay, it won't hurt you," said Gregor.

"I don't know where mine went," said Mange, running his tongue around his mouth. "Just gone." He opened his jaws wide and Gregor could see the wad of gum wedged up between two of his long teeth.

Lapblood seemed to be the only rat capable of sustained gum chewing. "It's not bad. Not as good as gnawing, but it gives you something to do with your teeth."

"Why is it called bubble gum?" asked Hamnet, taking his piece out of his mouth to examine it.

"Because of this." Gregor blew a bubble and popped it with a loud crack. Everyone jumped.

"Don't do that! We're edgy enough in here as it is!" said Ripred.

"Hey, just answering a question," said Gregor.

His craving for food got worse as they walked along. While the sugar from the bubble gum had given him a brief lift, it had also stirred up the juices in his stomach, making him more aware of his hunger than ever. He wanted cold, icy foods . . . Popsicles, watermelon, ice cream. And salt . . . he was losing enough of it sweating.

He had not taken his boots off the whole trip and his socks were sodden. Unfortunately, he had neglected to pack any extra clothes, even socks, so he couldn't change them. And he couldn't borrow any from Hamnet, since he and Hazard didn't wear socks, just shoes made of reptile skin like the rest of their clothes.

The lack of food combined with the heat was beginning to drain his energy. Hamnet had taken over the wineskin of shrimp, but Gregor still had the big pack of fuel and medical supplies and his backpack. His knees were buckling every few yards when he felt a hand on his shoulder.

"I will take the pack, Gregor," said Hamnet.

Gregor let him slide it off his back without objecting. He wished he had the strength not to accept, but frankly, he was just glad for the help.

"Thanks," he muttered.

Hamnet stayed directly behind him and left Ripred at the back of the line. "Ripred tells me you caused quite an upheaval by not killing the Bane."

"I guess I did. But it was just a baby," said Gregor warily. Most of the humans were pretty mad at him about that.

"It was a good decision. Else the rats would never have agreed to this journey. Plague or no plague," said Hamnet.

Gregor had never thought of that, but it was hard to imagine the rats traveling with the Bane's killer. It felt good, too, to have Hamnet approve of his choice, especially when so few others did. "It didn't win me a lot of points with the Regalians. Now everybody hates me. Rats and humans."

Hamnet laughed. "Not everybody. Ripred clearly adores you."

"Oh, yeah, I'm a big favorite of his," said Gregor. "Probably wondering right now how I'll taste for dinner."

"Might be, if you were something besides

196

skin and bones," called Ripred.

Gregor blew a bubble and gave it a loud pop.

"Cut that out!" snarled Ripred.

"Sorry," said Gregor, but he was grinning. This bubble gum was coming in handy.

Hours later, when they came upon a small clearing that would allow them to camp safely, the grin had been completely wiped off Gregor's face. His feet had been rising and falling out of habit, but he had lost the sensation of walking miles ago. Utterly exhausted, he lay right down on the ground without bothering to put down a blanket or even remove his backpack or sword belt. The air was so hot and steamy he was having trouble breathing. He wondered if there was enough oxygen, then he wondered if there was too much oxygen. Something was wrong, because his mind felt gluey and confused.

As Hamnet fed the last of the cookies and shrimp to Boots and Hazard, Ripred went over to him. "We've got to get some food, Hamnet. Not just for the pups, although the little one will be squawking her head off in a few hours if we can't feed her. But for the rest of us, too. Look at the warrior."

Gregor thought about raising his head to

tell them he was okay, but he became preoccupied with the pattern on a small, green leaf and couldn't take his eyes off it. Possibly he had stopped breathing entirely and the heavy air was just drifting in and out of his lungs whenever it felt like it.

"Yes, you and I will forage. I do not see any choice," said Hamnet. He lifted Gregor's head and held the water bag to his lips, urging him to drink more than he really wanted. "Try and rest, Gregor. We will be back soon. And drink as much water as you can." Hamnet laid his hand on Gregor's forehead for a moment, and Gregor felt oddly comforted. It was something his mom or dad might do. It was almost like having a parent around.

The water revived him a little. After a while he sat up. Hamnet and Ripred were gone. Boots and Hazard had fallen asleep in the curve of Frill's tail. Temp stood next to them, cleaning himself. Nike was in a deep slumber a few feet from Gregor — he hadn't even known she had landed. Most of the water bags were still on her back — like Gregor she must have been too tired to care. Across the lantern, Gregor saw that Mange and Lapblood were stirring. They looked haggard. They'd probably been near starvation even before they came on the trip. At least Gregor had been eating regularly.

"You guys want some more water?" asked Gregor. He had noticed the rats, even Ripred, had to rely on Hamnet to open the tops of the water bags to drink. Gregor picked up the bag Hamnet had left by his side and removed the stopper. He went over and kneeled next to Mange. "Come on, Hamnet said we should drink a lot."

Mange allowed him to pour the water into his mouth. Then Gregor did the same for Lapblood, being careful not to wash her bubble gum down her throat. Where was his gum? His tongue found it tucked up between his molars and his cheek and he began to chew it again.

"Water's all very well, but if we do not have food soon, none of us will be reaching the Vineyard of Eyes," said Lapblood.

"I can't believe that everything in this jungle is inedible," said Mange.

"I don't think it is," said Gregor. "Probably some of it's fine, but Hamnet didn't think we would be able to tell the good stuff from the bad."

"Hamnet," spat out Mange. "What does he know? He's human! Of course his nose can't tell the difference between what's poisonous and what's safe. My nose can, though. Even now I can smell a potential meal. I don't know what it is, but believe me, we can eat it."

Gregor sniffed the swampy air. "I don't smell anything."

"I do," said Lapblood. "Something sweet."

"Yes, that's it," said Mange. "I'm going to find it. Anyone else coming?"

"I'll come," said Lapblood. "Better than lying here dying of hunger."

"I don't know, I don't think Hamnet would want us looking around the jungle for food," said Gregor doubtfully.

"Why not? Isn't that exactly what he and Ripred are doing now? The more of us look, the more likely we are to find something," said Mange. "Don't come if you don't want to, but don't expect us to share what we find. Not even with your sister."

Gregor thought about Boots waking up hungry, not understanding about there being no food and why she couldn't eat, especially if the rats were. She would start to cry and then what would he do?

"Hamnet said something about the plants attacking us," said Gregor.

"We've been trampling through this jungle for days," said Mange. "Your sister beat the vines with her hands when she wanted her ball, you've been snapping every

200

other root with those boots, all of us caused damage when we ran from the frogs. Have you even seen one plant make any kind of move to stop us?"

"No, I haven't," Gregor admitted. "Okay, I'm in." He took another pull on the water and stood up. He took off his backpack to let his shirt dry out. "Hey, Temp, we're going to look for some food. Mange and Lapblood smell something."

"Not go, I would, not go," said Temp, shifting uncomfortably.

"Don't worry, we'll be back soon," said Gregor. "Just give a yell if you need us." He did not intend to get very far from the campsite. Even with Frill and Temp on guard, he wanted to be close to Boots in case there was any danger. But the biggest danger right now was starvation.

Following his nose, Mange led the way into the jungle. Lapblood went next and Gregor last. He wished he had some bread crumbs or something to leave a trail. Of course, if he had bread crumbs, he wouldn't be looking for food. Just sitting around eating bread crumbs. Whatever.

They were moving farther away from the campsite than he wanted to go, but since Mange was walking in a fairly straight line, Gregor hoped they could get back okay.

After a few minutes, he was heartened by a whiff of something sweet. "Hey, I can smell it, too!"

"About time," said Mange. "We're nearly on top of it."

They came out into a small glade. The air was permeated with a strong, sweet odor that reminded Gregor of ripe peaches. He shone his flashlight around the grove of plants. These were different than the vines that lined the path. There were long leafy stems curling high above their heads, but these plants also had big graceful yellow pods dangling horizontally from the greenery. They were at least six feet across and tilted up at the edges like huge, sunny smiles. Along the upper lips of the pods hung round, rosy fruit. Without further examination, Gregor knew that they were the source of the delicious smell. A thin stream of drool slid out of the corner of his mouth and ran down his chin. Out of some vague sense of manners, his hand reached up to wipe away the spit before he grabbed one.

That same moment, Mange leaned his front paws on the lower lip of a pod and raised his head toward the delectable fruit. The instant his muzzle brushed the rosy skin of one of the spheres, the pod lunged forward, engulfed the rat, and snapped shut.

All that was visible of Mange, poking out from between the yellow lips, was the tip of his tail.

CHAPTER 17

Lapblood gave a screech and leaped for the pod that had trapped Mange. When she was in midair, a long vine whipped out from another plant and wrapped around her waist. Her claws slashed at the vine, severing it, and the entire grove of plants went wild.

Gregor felt bewildered as the jungle sprang into action. His fingers fumbled with the hilt of his sword but it was much too late. Vines twisted around his body and limbs. Roots arched out of the ground and clamped around his boots. He tried to squirm free but the plants were far too powerful.

Where was his rager reaction? He scanned his body for any sign that he was transforming into a deadly adversary but nothing was happening. No shift in his vision, no rush in his blood. All he felt was extreme fear.

Mange was still in the pod, as far as he could tell. He could see Lapblood about ten feet away, struggling in a net of greenery.

A thick vine that had wrapped itself around his stomach began to tighten. It was like he had a giant anaconda squeezing the life out of him. "Help!" he tried to call out, but the sound was pitiful. "Help!" But who would come to help? Ripred and Hamnet were gone. He and Mange and Lapblood were immobilized. For all Temp's courage . . . well, what could the cockroach do except die along with them?

Gregor was aware of being drawn forward. The plant was pulling him toward one of the gaping yellow mouths. He thrashed helplessly, feeling his strength waning. He couldn't breathe. . . . The vine was so tight. . . . He could see the inside of the pod about a foot away now. A slimy clear liquid was oozing down the yellow walls.

Gregor could feel himself beginning to lose consciousness. Black specks swam around in front of his eyes. As the vine tightened one final notch he coughed. His bubble gum flew out of his mouth and into the pod.

Stretchy, sticky lines of pink spun up in his vision. He was vaguely aware that the gum was doing something in the pod. Mixing with the clear ooze . . . creating a whole new bubbly pink goo. The vine around his stomach began to loosen enough for him to get a few good breaths.

Lapblood's teeth were still weakly snapping as she was about to enter another pod.

"Spit!" Gregor croaked out. "Spit your gum into it!"

Lapblood gave her head a little shake. Did she register what he was saying?

"Spit your bubble gum in it, Lapblood!" Gregor yelled.

Rats probably couldn't spit like humans did, but she managed to thrust her gum out of her mouth. Since her snout was hanging over the edge of the pod, it landed squarely in the middle. The slimy pink bubbly reaction began in her pod as well.

Unfortunately, the plants did not free them. The pods with the gum were going into a frenzy. Pouring more clear ooze down their walls, chomping up and down, frothing pale pink bubbles. Temporarily out of order. But there were more pods turning toward them, hungry mouths open.

"Help!" hollered Gregor, and at least this time his voice carried. Lapblood was giving off high-pitched shrieks, too. Surely somebody would come!

Gregor saw a zebra-striped flash above his head and the pods tilted upward. Nike, still encumbered with her water bags, was flitting in and out of the vines, raking through the plants with her claws. She held her own for a bit, but there were too many plants shooting tendrils at her. He saw one lasso her back claw and knew it was over.

The vines started to tighten again; the pods turned back. Gregor was about to abandon hope when a voice reached his ears. "Now what have you done?" Out of the corner of his eye he saw half a dozen vines fall lifelessly to the ground.

"Ripred," he whispered and felt himself smile.

The air filled with shreds of plant matter as Ripred went into one of his spinning attacks. Gregor couldn't help thinking of those gadgets they sold on TV that chopped up vegetables at the press of a button.

His vines loosened; the roots withdrew. Gregor fell to the ground and just lay there trying to fill his lungs as a shower of green rained down on him. One of the giant yellow pods fell at his feet and oozed clear liquid onto the toes of his boots. He watched, a little fascinated as it ate through the leather and began to work on the reinforced steel toes.

Someone yanked him up and slung him over his shoulder like a sack of potatoes. Hamnet. His face bounced against the reptile skin shirt as Hamnet ran. They were back to the campsite in a minute. Gregor could feel his boots being tugged from his feet. His socks stripped off. Water gushed on his toes.

"Hazard! Hold this water bag!" said Hamnet.

There was a pause while the bag changed hands and then more water running over his feet.

Gregor saw Nike a few yards away. "I am all right. I am fine," she was telling Hamnet, who was examining her leg.

"The bone to your claw has been snapped in two. I do not call that fine," said Hamnet.

Someone was crashing through the vines, no longer worried about what he damaged. Ripred dragged Lapblood into the camp by the scruff of her neck. The minute he released her, she tried to crawl back in the direction they'd come.

"Mange . . ." she said.

"He's dead, Lapblood!" snarled Ripred.

Lapblood kept moving until Ripred flipped her over on her back and pinned her to the ground.

"He's dead! I killed the plant that did it! The pod opened and what was left of his carcass fell out! Believe me, he's dead! And the rest of you should be as well!" shouted Ripred. "Who started this? Whose brilliant idea was it to leave the camp?"

The rat turned his focus on Nike, perhaps because she seemed best able to answer, but she remained silent.

"Not Nike," said Gregor. "She only came to rescue us."

"So, was it you?" Ripred's muzzle poked in Gregor's face.

"Mange smelled food. Lapblood and I went to help him look. We didn't know . . ." Gregor got out.

"Didn't know what? That the plants here could kill? You'd been told! You'd been warned! How can I keep you alive if you won't even listen! All you had to do was lie here and drink water! And you couldn't even do that!" fumed the rat.

"Enough, Ripred. Let me patch them up," said Hamnet.

"Oh, yes, patch them up. So they can hatch some stunning new plan to save the day. Worthless pack of fools," said Ripred. "You could have gotten us all killed, you know! Following one stupid idea like that, that's all it takes! Good-bye us, good-bye cure, good-bye Underland!"

"Enough!" said Hamnet. "Just sit over there and calm down."

Ripred moved off by himself but did not calm down much. He would mutter to himself for a while and then unleash a volley of insults at Gregor and Lapblood. Mutter, unleash, mutter, unleash. It went on for quite a while.

Hamnet sent Hazard over to pour water on Lapblood's eye. It had been splashed with pod acid. He got the medical pack and daubed Gregor's toes with a blue ointment and then bandaged them with white fabric.

"Does it hurt?" asked Hamnet.

"Not really," said Gregor. There was a strange, almost electric sensation on the tops of his toes. That was all.

"Well, it will," said Hamnet, shaking his head.

"The water's almost gone," said Hazard.

"I will get another bag," said Hamnet. He stood up and looked around. "Nike, where are the water bags?"

"With the plants. The vines ripped them from my back," said Nike.

"Stop!" Hamnet whipped around and caught Hazard's wrist, but it was too late. The last trickle of water was drizzling out of the bag.

"What is it, Father?" asked Hazard, puzzled. "Did I do something wrong?"

"No. No, you did what I asked," said Hamnet, running his hand over Hazard's curls. "It is just . . . the water. This was our last bag."

CHAPTER 18

"What?" said Ripred.

"Nike lost the water bags when she went to help the others. We used the remainder of this one on the acid burns," said Hamnet.

"No water. Just exactly how long do you thin we'll last without that?" asked Ripred.

Hamnet shook his head. "Not long. It will take another couple of days before we will near fresh spring water. We will simply have to do our best."

"I have some water." Gregor pushed himself up to a sitting position and reached for his backpack. He pulled out the quart of glacier water. "It's not much, I know."

"It is a great deal, Gregor, if it keeps the pups from dying of thirst. They will be most vulnerable as they will dehydrate the fastest," said Hamnet, taking the bottle. "The rest of us will have to do without."

Gregor nodded. Of course the water should go to Boots and Hazard. He was okay, anyway. He'd chugged down a lot before they'd left in search of food. He could get by.

"Did you two find any food?" he asked hopefully.

"No, nothing wholesome," said Hamnet.

"Mange said the fruit we found was edible. He could smell it was okay," said Gregor.

"Oh, why don't I just pop back and grab us a bushel or two?" said Ripred in disgust.

"Well, at least we have your water," Hamnet said almost kindly. "That may make all the difference. It was good thinking, to pack it."

"Mareth put it in. He said pure water wouldn't be easy to find," said Gregor.

"Mareth?" said Hamnet. "Has he managed to stay alive all these years?"

"Yeah, he lost his leg, though. On the trip to get the Bane," said Gregor. He realized Mareth and Hamnet must be about the same age. "Were you guys friends?"

"Yes," said Hamnet. He turned the bottle of water over in his hands, but didn't elaborate.

It was on the tip of Gregor's tongue to ask why Hamnet had left Regalia, where he had family, where he had friends, to live out in this dangerous, lonely place. What was it he had said when Vikus had asked him what he could do here that he couldn't do in Regalia? "I do no harm. I do no more harm."

Gregor hadn't paid much attention to that at the moment. But the words had been enough to send Vikus back to his bat without further discussion. What harm had Hamnet done? It was hard to imagine.

Hamnet rose and put the water with the medical supplies. "I know everyone is spent, but I believe we must keep moving if we are to reach water in time. Can you manage?" he asked Gregor.

"He can manage," hissed Ripred. "So can Lapblood. And I better not hear any complaints out of either of them."

Hamnet anointed Lapblood's eye with medicine. For Nike's leg he made a splint with strips of stone and fabric. But when he tried to give her a dose of pain medicine from a large green bottle, she refused. "I do not want to muddy my thoughts. Not in here."

Hamnet tried to talk her into it, but she was adamant. "All right. We may need your head clear. But you will ride on Frill," he instructed the bat.

"I can fly," said Nike.

"You can fly, but you cannot land well. The foliage is getting too thick for easy access to the ground. Ride, Nike. And try to sleep," said Hamnet.

Gregor helped Hamnet position Nike

lying flat on her back atop Frill. They had to secure her with strips of bandages so she wouldn't roll off.

"I'm sorry about all this," Gregor told her.

"But why?" said the bat cheerfully. "Now I get to take a lovely nap while the rest of you walk. I should be thanking you."

Somehow, her being such a great bat made Gregor feel even guiltier about her injury.

Hazard climbed up in front of her onto Frill's neck and curled up in the folds on the ruff to go back to sleep. When Gregor laid Boots on her stomach on Temp's back she didn't even stir. He hoped she would sleep for a good long time. With no food and precious little water, he didn't know how he'd handle her.

His boots had been ruined by the acid. As Gregor was looking down at his bare feet, his bandaged toes, and wondering how he'd walk, Hamnet peeled off his reptile-skin shoes. "Here, Gregor. You must wear these," he said.

"What will you wear?" asked Gregor.

"I will be fine. I spent many years without shoes before I came upon the idea of using shed skin. But you must take them now, or your bandages will not hold," said Hamnet.

"Thanks, Hamnet." Gregor gingerly pulled the shoes over his bandages. They were kind of like short socks really. Thin and clingy. But somehow they made him feel more protected.

Lapblood still lay where Ripred had left her, as if she had lost the power to move. The ordeal with the plants had been physically exhausting, but Gregor knew that was not what was weighing her down.

"Hey, Lapblood, are you okay?" he asked. She wasn't okay, though. Mange had just died. All her pups might be dead, too. How could she be okay? "Because we've got to keep moving. We've got to find water."

Lapblood rolled onto her feet and got in line behind Frill without a word. Gregor remembered his state of shock after he'd thought Boots had been killed by the serpents. How Luxa had been unable to speak when Henry had betrayed her and died for it. He left Lapblood alone.

The path was gone now. It had progressively narrowed until it had disappeared altogether. Now it was a matter of trying to step between plants. At first, Gregor found it a little easier since he was wearing Hamnet's fitted shoes instead of his boots. Then the pain in his toes began to register. There was a slight tingling, then itching, then he felt like his toes were on fire. He knew any mention of his wounds would only trigger another round of abuse from Ripred, so he gritted his teeth and moved forward.

Perhaps it was the knowledge that there was no water available that made him so intensely aware of his thirst. The dryness inside his mouth. The skin cracking on his lips. Thirst had never been a problem before in the Underland. Fresh water had been available even in the Dead Land. And there was always plenty of cold, clean water to drink at home. Right out of the faucet.

They walked for four straight hours, although it felt like forty to Gregor, and then they only stopped because Boots and Hazard woke up. Hazard understood there was little water to be had, but Boots kept tugging on Gregor's shirt saying, "Thirsty! I'm thirsty, Gre-go!" As if he must not be understanding her because he wasn't getting her anything to drink.

She was so fretful and sweaty. Gregor stripped her down to just her underpants and sandals so she wouldn't perspire any more than was necessary.

When Hamnet finally held the bottle of glacier water to her lips, Boots gulped down about a third of the bottle before he could stop her. "Slowly, Boots, we must make this water last," he said, gently disengaging her from the bottle.

"More," said Boots, pointing to the water.

"You may have more in a little while," said Hamnet, and gave Hazard a drink.

Boots was confused. She pulled on Gregor. "Apple juice?"

"No apple juice, Boots. Try and go back to sleep, okay?" he said. Of course, she didn't. After a short rest, Hamnet had them moving again. Boots rode on Temp's back and kept up a steady stream of requests for a drink. After answering with patience for about the first three hundred times, Gregor finally snapped at her. "I don't have any, Boots! No juice! No water! Okay?"

It was exactly the wrong thing to do. Boots burst into tears at a time when any loss of fluids was critical and wailed inconsolably for at least twenty minutes before Hamnet reluctantly gave her another few swallows of water. Finally, she fell back asleep, much to everyone's great relief.

Gregor's toes were raw, searing, swollen lumps at the end of his feet. Roots stabbed at them through the shoes. Salt from his sweat ate into the wounds.

And then there was Ripred's voice,

taunting him from behind. "It didn't happen this time, did it, rager boy?"

Gregor knew what he meant but he didn't answer.

" 'Oh, I don't want this gift, Ripred,' " the rat imitated him in a whiny voice. "You thought you could go anywhere and do anything and be safe. You thought you were invincible. Because you're a rager. Well, you're finding out now just how weak you really are."

"Cease, Ripred, the boy has enough to bear," Gregor heard Hamnet say.

"He needs to understand how close to death he came!" snapped Ripred.

"And so he does," said Hamnet firmly. "He knows he did not think well before he acted. Who among us has not been guilty of that? Certainly not you. Certainly not me."

Thankfully, Ripred stopped. But Gregor knew there was a certain amount of truth to what the rat had said. He had not thought he was invincible, but knowing he was a rager had made him less afraid to go into a dangerous situation. Sometimes he had trouble turning off his rager reaction. He had not known it could desert him in times of need. The knowledge shook his confidence and left him feeling defenseless.

It was hard to concentrate, but Gregor

tried to think back to the times he'd transformed and the times he hadn't. He'd been
careful not to get into any fights in the Overland so it hadn't been an issue. When
Ripred had knocked him to the ground in
the tunnel, he hadn't experienced the rager
sensation. But that had happened so fast,
and Gregor had stopped feeling threatened
as soon as Ripred had revealed who he was.
When the infected bat had fallen into the
arena, the situation had been dangerous,
but there had been no one to fight except
the fleas. Then there had been the moment
with the frogs. He had known Boots was in
peril. The threat had had time to register.
But later, the plants had attacked so
quickly. . . . Was that the answer? Could he
only become a rager if he had time to recognize a threat? No, no, because he had turned
into a rager for the first time with just wax
balls filled with red dye flying at him. Those
weren't dangerous at all.

"There's no pattern." This was the last
clear thought Gregor had for a long while.
What happened next was a haze of hours,
maybe days, filled with pain, fear, and dis-
orientation. Walking. Lying face pressed to
leaves, unrelenting pain in his feet, Hamnet
rubbing oil on his bleeding lips, bandaging
his toes. Boots crying, whimpering, then fi-

nally making no sound at all, just lying limp on Temp's back, with no way to help her. Intense thirst, dreams of water, of frosty white glaciers he could never reach. Walking . . . walking again . . . tongue swollen, head aching, heart racing, stomach sick. Collapsed on the vines looking at his sister limp on Temp's back. Boots . . . asleep . . . unconscious . . . dead? Not dead, her chest rising and falling rapidly, her cracked lips, shiny with oil, tinged a faint blue. Then Ripred's voice, hoarse and weak. "I smell clean water. . . ."

He must have gotten up somehow. Followed Ripred and Lapblood into the jungle on the burning hunks of meat that were his feet. He could hear the water. . . . Not the quiet, teasing gurgle of the jungle streams that had tormented them for days . . . but a rushing, splashing sound. The rats were running now, Gregor hobbling behind them. He could see the water, bursting out of a rock, cascading into a pool, a sandy beach . . . water . . . but then . . .

Ripred gave a cry of alarm. "Get back! Get back!"

Gregor could see Ripred and Lapblood floundering as if the ground was melting under them. Robotlike, he kept coming forward, although he could hear Ripred's voice, trying to stop him, force him backward. His own feet were too heavy to lift and he realized he was up to his ankles in something. Looking down, he watched himself sink to his knees before a wave of adrenaline brought his brain back to life.

"Quicksand!" he said, and tried desperately to backtrack out of the stuff. It was impossible. He was in too deep.

"Stop struggling!" Ripred ordered. "You'll only sink faster!"

"Float!" Gregor cried. "Try and float!" He remembered that quicksand was like water. If he could get on his back he could float until help came. But it was too late. He was up to his thighs and had no way to pull himself free.

"Hamnet!" Ripred called. "Hamnet, get in here!"

Ripred was doing okay. He had managed to splay out all four legs and was precariously keeping on the surface. But Lapblood had panicked. Her thrashing paws were digging her rapidly into the quicksand.

Gregor leaned way out and caught hold of a vine. He lifted himself up about six inches before the vine snapped and the force of the weight sunk him up to his waist in the quicksand. "Nike!" he screamed. "Nike!"

There was a rustling in the vines to his

right. Help had come! But the black, shiny eyes poking through the greenery were unfamiliar. At first he thought they were rats. No, the faces were smaller, more delicately boned. Mice. They must be mice.

"Help!" cried Gregor. "Help us!" The mice didn't move.

Someone fell from high in the vines, spinning, flipping, landing neatly in the small space between two of the mice. And Gregor did recognize the newcomer. Her clothes were rags, her pale skin marred with bruises and cuts. A long, curved scar ran from her left temple to the tip of her chin. But she still wore that thin band of gold around her head. And those violet eyes . . . well, he would know them anywhere.

"Luxa!" Despite his desperate condition he felt joy spreading through him. She was alive! He smiled and felt fresh blood run out of his cracked lips. "Luxa!" He reached out his hand so she could save him.

But Luxa didn't reach back. She didn't flatten herself on the bank and stretch out her arm. She didn't even throw him a vine.

Instead, Luxa folded her arms and watched him sink up to his neck.

PART 3
THE MIRROR

CHAPTER 19

"Luxa! What are you doing?" gasped Gregor.

"What are you doing, Overlander? Here in the jungle in the company of rats?" she asked coolly.

What was she talking about? What was going on?

"We need the rats!" sputtered Gregor. "You don't understand!"

"I understand you spared the Bane's life. I understand he thrives under Ripred's protection. What more do I need to understand?" said Luxa.

So that was it! How she'd gotten here or why she had remained, Gregor had no idea. But she knew enough of what was going on outside the jungle to have heard about the Bane.

"Nerissa said I did the right thing!" said Gregor. That was all he could manage because the quicksand was now reaching his mouth.

"The plague has erupted, you self-righteous brat. We're seeking the cure! Now get us out of here!" Ripred growled at her.

"The plague?" repeated Luxa. Her brow

225

furrowed, but she did not make any move to help them. "I have not heard of any plague."

"Really? Well, with all the visitors you must get here, I can't believe someone hasn't mentioned it," said Ripred. "It's the talk of the Underland!"

"Judith!" Gregor heard Hamnet's voice. "Help them!"

Hamnet skidded to a stop before he reached the quicksand, but his attention was on Luxa. She looked back at him in shock. As they faced each other in profile, Gregor could see the resemblance was uncanny.

"I am not Judith," said Luxa, confused.

"No, you are not," said Hamnet, recovering and yanking a vine from a nearby tree. "My sister would have never stood by and watched those who had risked so much for her die!"

Gregor's fingers caught the vine just as his nose was going under. He clung to it with what little strength he had left, and Hamnet slowly pulled him from the quicksand. He lay on the ground, covered in wet sand, sick and dizzy as he watched the rest of the rescue.

Hamnet had swung another vine that was still attached by its roots out to Ripred, and the rat was managing to inch himself to safety.

It was Lapblood who looked like a goner. All that was visible of her were a few inches of snout and one paw still feebly clawing at the surface. Hamnet threw her a vine, but there was no way she could see it since her eyes had sunk under the sand.

"Lapblood!" Hamnet shouted.

"Lapblood!" hollered Ripred. "Get the vine!"

It was no use. She was going down.

The paw was gone and the last bit of her twitching nose had almost disappeared when Nike dove in from above. The claw of her sound leg dug into the quicksand and latched on something. Then her wings began to beat like crazy. Slowly, very slowly, she managed to raise Lapblood's head out of the muck by the scruff of her neck.

"I cannot lift her!" panted the bat. "You must help!"

Hamnet threw out the vine again, but Lapblood's eyes were sealed shut with sand. "Lapblood!"

"Wake up, Lapblood!" ordered Ripred. "You've got to get hold of the vine so we can pull you out!"

Lapblood's mouth began to work. "No . . . just let me go. . . . Let me go. . . ." she barely whispered.

"Let you go? After I saved your sorry hide

227

from those plants? Not likely! Now do as I say!" roared Ripred.

But Lapblood only gave her head a slight shake. "No . . . no more . . ."

Gregor realized it had all been too much. The months of starvation, watching her pups dying, this torturous trip, Mange's death. And Lapblood had decided that she no longer wanted to live.

"No!" Gregor said. "Don't give up! Lapblood!" She didn't respond. His words meant nothing. But then he thought of some words that might make a difference. Words that had never been meant for his ears. "What about Sixclaw? And Flyfur? What about them?"

At the sound of the names, Lapblood's eyes opened. She looked around frantically. "My pups!" she said.

"That's right! Your pups need you!" said Ripred. "Now pull yourself together and grab that vine!"

Lapblood swung a claw out and dug it into the vine. Ripred and Hamnet pulled from the bank and, with Nike's help, they finally dragged her from the quicksand. She lay next to Gregor, her fur coated in a thick layer of wet sand.

"So this is my niece, then?" Hamnet asked Ripred as he turned angrily on Luxa.

"You know it is. She's the spitting image of your twin," said Ripred.

"Hamnet," said Luxa. "You are Hamnet. We thought you dead."

"We thought you dead, too, Luxa. And perhaps better you were, if you can so unflinchingly watch the death of your comrades," said Hamnet.

"Oh, I can tell we're in for another lovely family reunion," said Ripred. "But it will have to wait. Take us to water, Your Majesty, or I swear I'll rip you and your nibbler friends to shreds on the spot."

Gregor felt himself being lifted and then began to move. Frill. He must have been the one on her back this time. In a few minutes he could hear water again. Ripred was nudging him in the side with his snout.

"Come on, warrior. Up you go. Get yourself a drink," said Ripred.

Gregor slid off Frill's side onto his hands and knees and crawled to the splashing sound. A spring burbled out of a rock and down into a crystal-clear pool. He stuck his whole face in the water and sucked cool mouthfuls into his body. He lifted his head for just a moment to catch a breath and plunged his face back into wetness . . . into water . . . into life . . .

When he had finally slaked his thirst, he

looked around. They were on a big stone slab of rock that stretched out beside the pool. Luxa and the mice were nowhere in sight. Ripred, Nike, Hazard, Frill, and Temp were all lined up along the side of the pool drinking with Gregor. Hamnet had filled their last water bag and was alternating between trickling water into Boots's and Lapblood's mouths.

Gregor crawled over to Boots's side. "Is she okay?" he asked.

"She will be fine, Gregor, once we get some food and water into her," said Hamnet.

Gregor pressed his nose into Boots. She opened her eyes and smiled a little. "Hi, you," he whispered.

Boots's lips moved in response. No sound came out. But she was alive.

"I can give them water," said Gregor. "You should go drink."

"I have been drinking from the bag. And I am well enough," said Hamnet. He seemed wiped out but he looked pretty good compared to the rest of them. Gregor guessed that years of jungle life combined with his natural physical strength had made him survive the trip better. "You must go wash the sand off you before it hardens, Gregor."

"He's right," Ripred said. "This stuff will

be like cement soon." With that the rat dove into the pool and began to roll over and over. Sand billowed out from his coat and into the clear water.

"Come, those of you who are still thirsty, and drink from the bag until the sand settles," said Hamnet.

When Ripred had pulled himself out of the pool and begun to groom his coat, Gregor got on his wobbly legs and made it to the pond. He thought about undressing, but his clothes were so caked with sand he wasn't even sure he could find the fasteners. So he just jumped in.

Ahhh! Nothing had ever felt so good as the cool liquid enveloping his body. The water came about chest high on him so it was plenty deep for swimming. He dove under the surface and swam across and back before he came up for air. After a few laps, most of the sand had fallen away from his clothes. He sat on the side of the pool and stripped down to his underwear. Taking off the reptile shoes was a special challenge, since his toes were about the size of walnuts and embedded with bits of sand. He had to soak his feet a while before he could peel off the bandages. Big pieces of skin came off. But, underneath, delicate new skin was beginning to grow.

Gregor swam over to the spring, stood on the rock ledge, and let the water cascade down his body. He stayed under the flow until he was sure every grain of sand, every drop of sweat, and every bit of dead skin had been washed from his body. Then he rinsed his clothes and climbed up onto the slab to lay them out to dry.

Luxa appeared, swinging several large fish by the tails and carrying something in the lower part of her shirt. When she released the hem, a bunch of round yellowish fruit fell to the ground. She tossed the fish beside them and selected the largest. "I will grill this for Boots. She will not eat it uncooked," she said to no one in particular.

It was hard not to dive on the food before Hamnet divided it up. Gregor received four pieces of yellow fruit. His teeth split the skin of the first and a delicious plum taste filled his mouth. He decided it was safe and ate it in three bites.

Propping Boots up on his lap, he tried to coax her to eat. At first, she seemed indifferent. But when he dribbled some of the sweet juice into her mouth her face lit up. She grabbed his hand and pulled the fruit to her mouth and gobbled it up. "*P* is for pum," she said, licking the juice off her fingers. "More pum?" And Gregor was happy he could give her a whole handful.

The fish was good, too. On his last trip, he'd had a little trouble adjusting to the cold, raw flesh. This time he scarfed it down without a thought. Luxa brought over some pieces of fish she had grilled over the lantern on her sword for Boots. She had squeezed the juice of one of the golden plums over the chunks to make it more appealing.

"Will you try some fish, Boots?" she asked, not even looking at Gregor.

"Ye-es!" said Boots and stuck a piece in her mouth. "Where is rat?" she asked Luxa and then pressed her hand to her nose. "Ow!"

"Who, Twitchtip?" said Luxa, and Boots nodded. Gregor realized that the last time the queen and his little sister had seen each other had been in the rats' maze. Twitchtip had been with them, with a badly damaged nose. "I do not know."

"Oh, yes, my darling Twitchtip. Where did you leave her, Your Majesty? Dead in the Labyrinth, I'll warrant," said Ripred. "It's too bad, really. I mean, it's not like anyone will miss her, but what an amazing nose."

"I'll miss her," said Gregor brusquely. He had liked Twitchtip, rat or no rat. He didn't want to hear Ripred running her down now.

"Sorry, I forgot what chums you'd become," said Ripred. "But she's just another dead rat to you, right, Your Queenliness?"

Luxa ignored him. She ignored everyone except Boots. But what was she so mad about, anyway? Gregor not killing the Bane? Yes, but he had told her Nerissa said he had done the right thing. Finding him with two rats? Well, there was no other way to get the cure for the plague. Hamnet chewing her out? Yeah, she wouldn't have liked that. Besides, she must have been living out here with the mice in semidarkness for months. When someone finally did show up, it wasn't to rescue her, it was just by chance. Maybe she was just mad at everything and everybody.

And where was her bat, Aurora? Dead, probably, or why would Luxa be hanging out in the jungle instead of flying home? Gregor started to feel sorry for Luxa until he remembered she had been prepared to watch him smother to death in the quicksand. "I don't owe her a thing," he thought. But he didn't quite believe that. There were times in the past when she had saved his life and, even more important, saved Boots. Still, he wasn't going to beg her to talk to him if that's what she was waiting for.

When Boots had finished eating, he gave her a bath. Mostly he just held her and walked around the pool. She was too weak to really play. But he could tell the water felt good to her. After she was clean, he made her a little bed out of a blanket, and she drifted off to sleep. He washed all her clothes, too, and laid them out to dry beside his on the slab. Then he stretched out beside Boots and slid into oblivion.

He was unsure how long he slept before he was awakened by Ripred's voice laying into Lapblood. She had not moved since they'd arrived at the pool. She'd let Hamnet pour water into her mouth, but sometimes it just ran out of the side. None of the food before her had been touched. And she had made no attempt to bathe, so her fur was still caked with sand. Whatever brief rally she had made to save herself from the quicksand was over. Grief and pain had consumed her again.

"Get up, Lapblood! You've got to get that sand out of your fur before it's too late!" ordered Ripred. She didn't even react to his voice. He tried a few different methods of persuasion, but got no results. Finally, he snorted in frustration. "Fine! If you're just going to lay there, I'll throw you in myself!" With that he grabbed Lapblood by the scruff of the neck and dragged her into the pool. She floundered around in a daze, as if she wasn't quite sure what was going on, until he pulled her back out. "Now groom yourself! The water doesn't get in by your skin! You've got to clean the rest of the sand out with your claws before it rubs you raw!" said Ripred. But Lapblood seemed no more inclined to groom herself than she had been to bathe. She just lay on her belly, indifferent to the world. Ripred began to threaten her, and had actually opened his jaws to bite her on the flank when Gregor intervened.

"Stop it!" Gregor said.

Ripred looked at him in surprise. "Excuse me?"

"Stop it. Just leave her alone. She feels bad, okay?" said Gregor.

"Tell you what. Later, when we're all safe and sound, I'll make a point to be extra sympathetic. But at the moment, I can't have her checking out," said Ripred. "I need her. She can fight and chances are we're going to run into at least a few more things that want to eat us in the Vineyard. And who do I have as backup? A handful of pups, a lame bat, a crawler, a couple of pacifists, and a rager who freezes up. All of you in bad shape, to boot. Oh, Lapblood will clean her fur, if I have to yank every piece out to convince her!" He opened his teeth to tear out a hunk of her fur. Gregor's fingers closed around a plum Temp had set aside for Boots, and he beaned Ripred between the eyes with it.

The rat looked at him in disbelief. It couldn't have hurt; Gregor hadn't thrown it hard. But it was so rare that anyone defied Ripred that it genuinely took him aback. "What was that?"

"I'll do her fur," said Gregor.

"What?" said Ripred.

"I'll groom her myself," said Gregor. He took out the brush Dulcet had packed for Boots and crossed over to Lapblood.

"You? You're going to groom her?" said Ripred with a laugh.

"Why not?" said Gregor. He'd brushed dogs before. How different could it be?

"This I've got to see," said Ripred, and settled himself back comfortably to watch the show.

Water was still dripping off Lapblood. She had not even given herself a shake when she'd come out of the pool. While the swim had rinsed away the big chunks of sand, her fur was still gritty to the touch. Gregor wasn't exactly sure how to start. For one thing, she was way bigger than any dog he'd ever brushed. Plus she was wet.

Still, he had to give it a shot.

Gregor got his clean shirt, which was mostly dry, and patted a patch on her back so it was at least not soaked. Then he took the brush and began to work through the fur very gently. Ripred was right. It was matted in places and the grains of sand were already beginning to rub sore spots on her skin. It took him a while to get a patch the size of his hand clean.

"Man, this will take forever!" he thought. But he didn't stop because Ripred was watching. So were a lot of other creatures. As they awoke, his traveling companions seemed fascinated by the sight of him brushing Lapblood's coat. A dozen pairs of shiny black mouse eyes peeked out from the vines. And though he could not see her, he felt certain Luxa was somewhere in the jungle watching him, too. Disapproving, no doubt.

As the fur dried, the job became easier. His arms ached but his fingers loved the feel of the silky coat. Who knew rats had such soft fur? There was something soothing about the whole thing.

When he'd finished her back, Gregor moved around so he was facing Lapblood for the first time. She seemed startled by his appearance. Confused.

"I'm going to brush out your belly now. You've got to lay on your side," said Gregor.

As if in a trance, Lapblood rolled over on her side. But she kept her eyes trained on Gregor. He wondered if at any moment she might come to her senses and bite his head off. She didn't. She was too far gone. Too weak. Too sad. And a little crazy, or why would she ever ask Gregor what she did just then?

"Do you think they're still alive?" whispered Lapblood. "Flyfur and Sixclaw?"

It was almost the same question she had asked Mange.

"Sure. Sure, I do," said Gregor. He tried hard to remember what Mange had said to her. "They'll have the yellow powder by now. And —" What was that other rat's name? "And Mincemeat will feed them." That name wasn't exactly right, but it must have been close enough.

"Yes, she will feed them," said Lapblood. "My pups."

"Now you should try and get some sleep, Lapblood," said Gregor. "Okay?"

She blinked at him a few times and then, amazingly, fell asleep.

Gregor's thoughts turned to his own mother. She must be very sick by now.

Howard as well. Neveeve said the bats didn't get sick as quickly, so maybe Andromeda was still okay. But Ares? Face it, Ares must be dead. Gregor was blindsided by pain for a few moments, and he struggled to push it away. He couldn't afford to give in to it now. Like Lapblood, he had others to save.

He brushed her coat until every inch of it was as smooth as velvet. It was funny . . . how he and Lapblood were like two sides of one coin. A mother fighting to save her kids. A kid fighting to save his mother. Despite their differences, he felt they'd had a special link from that first night, when they had lain awake together in the darkness, wondering about their loved ones. At the moment, Lapblood was past being able to bear what she had to bear. He knew what that was like and he could not watch Ripred abuse her. That's why he had stepped in. He would like to have explained that to all the spectators. But he didn't have the words.

So instead, without bothering to clean out the brush, he groomed his own hair.

CHAPTER 20

Food, water, and a good night's sleep produced a miraculous change in Boots. She woke up cheerfully and demanded breakfast. By this time, both Hamnet and Ripred had gone foraging for food and there was plenty. Dozens of fish, piles of plums, and big heaps of mushrooms.

Hamnet made a small fire on the stones using chunks of dead vines for fuel.

"Are you sure you should be building a fire?" asked Gregor, looking nervously around at the jungle.

"Take ease, Gregor, the plants are harmless in this part of the jungle," said Hamnet. He grilled several fish basted in plum juice. Gregor thought it was the best thing he'd ever tasted. Everyone packed away a huge breakfast except Lapblood, who was still dead to the world.

"Let her sleep," said Hamnet. "There will be food when she wakes."

Boots was begging to go swimming so Gregor took her in the pool. She rode on his back, jumped off the bank into his arms, and practiced blowing bubbles. When she got tired of the water she ate again and then pulled Temp and Hazard into a game with her ball.

Hamnet called Gregor over so he could examine his feet. "They are healing, but you must take care to keep them from infection," he said. He painted Gregor's toes with the blue medicine, bandaged them again, and made him put the reptile shoes back on. Then he turned his attention to Nike's leg. "How is the pain?" he said.

"Not too bad," said Nike, but she let out an involuntary squeak when Hamnet ran his fingers over the break.

"We will have to camp here at least a day, Nike," said Hamnet. "Take the painkiller. It will allow you to rest." This time Nike did not object so Gregor knew she must really be hurting.

Hamnet dug through the medical supply pack, then emptied it on the ground and ran his hand over the contents. "Where is it? Where is the medicine?" The big green bottle was not among the supplies. "Has someone taken the painkiller?"

Gregor looked around the group but no one spoke up. It was unlikely that any of them would have taken it. Boots and Hazard were just children. Temp, Nike, and Frill wouldn't have been able to even open the container. The rats might be able to break the bottle. But Lapblood was in a state of shock. And Ripred? He wasn't in pain, and he probably wouldn't be interested in something that fogged your mind. Gregor saw Hamnet looking at him and realized that he was the most likely suspect. He had fingers to open the bottle and painful toes to motivate him to want the medicine.

"You know, Gregor, if you had asked for the painkiller I would have given it to you," said Hamnet. "It is just that we usually save it for those in the greatest agony."

"I didn't take it. Honest," said Gregor. "You can look through my stuff."

Ripred crossed to where he was sitting. "Open your mouth," he said. Gregor did, not sure what was going on. The rat took a deep sniff of his breath. "He hasn't swallowed any of it."

"My apologies," Hamnet said to Gregor. "Well, that does not leave us many options."

Before Gregor could ask what he meant, Boots threw one of her long high balls into the surrounding jungle. Hazard started after it but Gregor caught his shoulder. "No, I'll get it, Hazard." He didn't want either of the kids running around out there, even if the plants were supposed to be harmless.

It took a little while to find the ball since there was no path and the vines were thick close to the ground. He finally spotted it wedged between two roots. "Heads up!" he called and winged it back into the clearing. That's when he caught a glimpse of her out of the corner of his eye. She was sitting motionless up in the vines and must have been watching him the whole time.

While he spoke, he examined a hangnail that was bugging him. "So, you were just going to stand there and watch me die."

"I thought you and Ripred were here to attack the nibblers," said Luxa. There was nothing apologetic in her tone.

"Why's that?" said Gregor.

"The rats have always hated the nibblers because they are on good terms with the humans. The nibblers fought on our side in the last war. So the rats drove them into the jungle, hoping they would starve and be eaten by predators. However, the nibblers are stronger than the rats give them credit for," said Luxa.

"That could be a reason why the rats are here. What about me?" said Gregor.

"You did not kill the Bane," said Luxa. "When I saw you and two rats in the jungle, I could only assume you had crossed over to their side."

"Okay, you got me. I've hooked up with Ripred, and we're taking over the Underland and splitting it fifty-fifty. Because, you know, I just can't get enough of the place." Gregor bit off the hangnail and spit it into the vines with disgust. "Geez, Luxa." The whole time he was down here all he ever wanted to do was get home to his family in one piece. She knew that. The idea that he had some big plan with Ripred was ridiculous.

"You may sneer, but that is not so different from what Henry tried," said Luxa.

Henry. He'd been her cousin, her best friend, and the guy who had sold her over to the rats for some crazy scheme where they would all share power. Gregor admitted Luxa had cause to be suspicious. But still.

"I'm not Henry," said Gregor. He sighed when he thought of what an impossible task it was to get Luxa to trust him. Probably the only one she trusted was her bond. If the bat was still alive. "What happened to Aurora?"

"She is injured," said Luxa.

That was a relief, anyway. To know Aurora hadn't been killed. "Injured how?" asked Gregor.

"It is her wing. It has been pulled from its socket. She cannot fly and I cannot leave her. She suffers greatly," said Luxa.

Something clicked in Gregor's head. "So, you took the painkiller?"

"I did not know Nike needed it. I will bring some back," said Luxa.

"You know, your uncle should look at Aurora. He's pretty good with medical stuff," said Gregor. Luxa didn't answer. She had not made a very good impression on Hamnet. And who knew what she thought of the guy? Showing up after ten years when everybody believed he was dead. As things stood, Gregor realized she would never be able to ask him for help. "I'll talk to him. See if there's anything he can do. But you have to come with me."

After a minute, she slid down a vine next to him. Her eyes were so sad and tired. Suddenly, it was hard to stay mad at her. "What happened here?" he asked, drawing a line from his temple to his chin to indicate her scar.

"A rat clawed me in the Labyrinth," said Luxa.

"Thanks for getting Boots out of there," said Gregor.

"It was Temp," said Luxa.

"It was Temp who ran. It was you who fought so he could," said Gregor. She just shrugged. "Come on, let's talk to Hamnet."

When Gregor told him about Aurora,

Hamnet slid the pack with the medical supplies on his back. Gregor and Hamnet followed Luxa a short distance through the jungle. She pushed aside a thick swath of vines and revealed the entrance to a cave. Inside were a few mice and Luxa's golden bat, Aurora. The poor thing was lying on her belly, probably the last position a bat would choose to rest in, with one wing extended at a grotesque angle. Her eyes had a dull, remote expression that Gregor had never seen in them. He hoped it was just from the pain medicine.

"She has dislocated the wing," said Hamnet with a frown. "How long has it been out of the socket?"

"Many weeks," said Luxa.

Hamnet shook his head. "Even if I can maneuver it back into place, the damage may be lasting. But we can do only what we can do."

Just getting Aurora into a standing position caused the bat to shriek.

"Can you not do it while she is lying down?" said Luxa, stroking Aurora's face to calm her.

"No, even this may not work," said Hamnet. He instructed Gregor to hold Aurora securely by the chest. Gregor couldn't wrap his arms around her, since her wings interfered. The best he could do was to clutch large handfuls of her fur on each side of her body.

"Sorry, Aurora," he said.

She blinked at him, dazed. "Overlander? You are here?"

"Yeah, I'm back again," said Gregor.

"And Ares? He is with you?" asked Aurora.

"No, he . . . he got the plague," said Gregor.

"The plague?" Even though Aurora was in a drug-induced stupor, he could hear the horror in her voice. Images came rushing back into Gregor's mind. Purple lumps bursting . . . white sheets stained with blood . . . his bat . . . his mother . . .

"Oh, not Ares . . ." said Luxa hollowly.

"It is time." Hamnet had moved behind Aurora and taken hold of her twisted wing near the top. "Brace yourselves!" he ordered and then gave a quick, sharp tug on the wing. Gregor lost his grip on her fur, and the bat gave a heartbreaking cry.

"Stop it!" screamed Luxa, and Gregor could see she was about to lose it. She grabbed Hamnet's arm and tried to pull him away. "Do not give her any more pain! She cannot bear it!"

Hamnet caught her by the wrists. "If you

do not want her to die here in the jungle, there is no other way, Luxa. You do not help by objecting. Go outside the cave."

But Luxa wouldn't. She pressed her back into a wall and refused to move.

"Again, Gregor," said Hamnet grimly. "And you must hold her tighter. I must have something to pull against."

Gregor wiped his sweaty hands and latched on to Aurora's fur.

"On the count of three," said Hamnet. "One — two — three!" There was another yank, another screech, but this time Gregor managed to hang on.

And this time, wonderfully, beautifully, Aurora's crooked wing popped back into place and folded neatly up against her side.

"Ohhhh!" Aurora let out a gasp of relief. "Ohhhh!"

"Good," said Hamnet. "Very good. But it is not healed. You are not well. No doubt damage has been caused by its displacement. Use it too quickly, and it may dislocate again. But the pain is much less, I believe."

"Much less," whispered Aurora. She gingerly opened and closed her wings a few times. Luxa wrapped her arms around her bat and pressed her face into the golden fur.

Gregor was sure she was crying and didn't want them to see.

"Rest now. I will come back and check on you in a few hours," said Hamnet. He picked up the green bottle of painkiller that was lying against the cave wall and returned it to the medical pack. "Come, Gregor."

As they walked back to the camp Gregor said, "I guess they've had a pretty bad time."

"It could not have been easy," replied Hamnet. He stopped to strip a vine of a dozen of the yellow plums. "You know my niece better than I. What manner of person would you say she is?"

"Luxa?" said Gregor. He tried hard to think how to describe her. "Well, when I first met her, she seemed stuck-up. That's when she was hanging out with Henry all the time. Then we sort of became friends." It seemed so weak, his impression of Luxa, when she was so strong. He thought of her killing the rat, Shed, to save his life. Flipping through the air with Aurora as they destroyed a funnel spiderweb with a move called the coiler. Secretly flying out after the boats on the Waterway so that she could help him find the Bane. How to describe Luxa? "She's brave," said Gregor finally. "Brave as anybody I've ever known. And I know this might sound crazy . . . what with the quicksand thing and all . . . but I trust her with my life."

"That does sound crazy," said Hamnet, but he smiled.

Back at the campsite, Hamnet administered the painkiller to Nike. It affected her almost immediately. "Ah, I can barely feel my leg. Well, I have not been able to unravel 'The Prophecy of Blood' with a clear head, perhaps I can do it when everything seems unreal," she murmured.

"Yes, 'The Prophecy of Blood,'" said Hamnet. "It has been many years since I studied it in Sandwich's room. How goes the repeating stanza?"

It was still so fresh in Gregor's mind that he answered automatically.

TURN AND TURN AND TURN AGAIN.
YOU SEE THE WHAT
BUT NOT THE WHEN.
REMEDY AND WRONG ENTWINE,
AND SO THEY FORM A SINGLE VINE.

Hamnet had him say it a few more times so he could commit it to memory. While he recited it for the fourth time, Gregor realized Boots was by his side, doing a little dance to the words.

" 'Turn and turn and turn again,' " she said. Every time she said "turn," she'd spin in a half circle. " 'Turn and turn and turn again.' 'Turn and turn and turn again.' " She went on until she got dizzy and tumbled over, giggling.

"Okay, it says, we 'see the what,' " said Gregor. "So, what's the what?"

"Presumably, the plague," said Ripred.

"We 'see the "plague" but not the when,' " said Gregor, swapping in the word. "Then what's the when?"

"It could be many things. When the plague began. When the cure will be found. When the last warmblood dies," said Nike dreamily.

" 'Remedy and wrong entwine, / And so they form a single vine,' " said Hamnet. "I suppose that refers to the plant that is the cure. What is it called again?"

"Starshade," said Gregor. "It looks like this." He took a piece of charred vine from the edge of the fire and drew the plant on the stone as he remembered it from Neveeve's book.

" 'Remedy and wrong entwine . . .' if the remedy is the starshade, then what is the wrong?" asked Ripred.

But no one could even venture a guess.

So instead they ate and got ready for bed.

Hamnet and Luxa helped Aurora back to the camp. The two injured bats greeted each other warmly and snuggled together to sleep.

"It will be much comfort for Aurora to have another flier to sleep with," said Luxa. But Gregor wondered if this was the only reason they had moved to the camp. Luxa could probably use some human company, too.

"Are you going with us to the Vineyard?" Gregor asked her.

"You might have need of me," said Luxa.

He thought about mentioning how dangerous it was to her, but he knew that wouldn't matter at all.

Hamnet let them sleep a full eight hours. Then they had breakfast and prepared to travel the last leg of the trip to the Vineyard of Eyes. The two bats were secured on Frill, Boots was assigned her regular seat on Temp's back, and everyone else was to go on foot.

"To the Vineyard of Eyes, then," said Hamnet, and Frill led the way into the jungle.

Gregor tried to get Boots up on Temp's back but she was still enamored with her dance. She would take a couple of steps into the jungle and then say, " 'Turn and turn

and turn again,' " and run back in the oppo-
site direction.

"No, Boots, that way leads to Regalia,"
said Gregor. Back to Regalia where everybody was counting on them. He scooped up
Boots and planted her on Temp's back.
"Come on," he said. "The cure's this way."

CHAPTER 21

There was a small path, probably worn by the mice traveling from their nests to the spring, but it quickly became overgrown, and they were just wading their way through the jungle again. It was harder here. The vines grew more thickly so that, in places, they had to separate them with their hands to get through. Then the stems snapped closed behind them. At times, Gregor couldn't even see most of his fellow travelers. He stayed right on top of Temp and Boots, making sure they didn't get lost in the foliage.

Hamnet assigned each of them a number, one through eleven, and made them sound off periodically. Boots loved this and never failed to shout out, "Nine!" with great enthusiasm. It was trickier for Temp, who had trouble remembering he was the number ten and also that it followed nine. Gregor knew math was not the roaches' strong suit; they had trouble with the simplest addition. Boots, who could now count up to twenty with just a few problems in the thirteen-fourteen area, kept jumping in to help Temp. "Temp, say 'Ten'! Temp, say

'Ten!' " she'd cry when he missed his number. Gregor hoped this wasn't embarrassing him, but if it were, he didn't show it.

At one point during the sound off, Gregor realized Luxa had fallen back in line and was walking just ahead of them. "How's Aurora doing?" he asked.

"Better, so much better, although she still has some pain," said Luxa. She waited until he had caught right up to her and asked in a puzzled voice, "Gregor . . . who is that boy? The one who speaks to the hisser?"

"His name's Hazard. He's Hamnet's son. So, I guess that makes him your cousin," said Gregor.

"How is that possible?" said Luxa with a frown. "His eyes are green."

"Yeah, his mom was an Overlander. Hamnet met her somewhere out here. He hasn't talked much about it," said Gregor.

"My cousin," said Luxa. She looked conflicted. Her experience with cousins had not always been happy.

"I think he'll be a good one. Like Nerissa or Howard," said Gregor.

"So, Nerissa is queen now?" asked Luxa.

"Yeah, but you'll be queen again when we get back, right?" asked Gregor.

"Oh, yes. I will not be relieved of this crown so easily. How fares Nerissa? Have

they been dreadful to her?" asked Luxa.

"She seems to be hanging in there. She stood up to Ripred and everybody in a meeting. You'd have been proud of her," said Gregor.

"I am always proud of Nerissa," said Luxa. "If fools wish to belittle her, it does not affect my judgment of her gifts."

"That goes double for me. You know, she's the only reason Ares and I are alive. She's the one who finally figured out what the Prophecy of Bane meant. Why it was good I didn't kill the Bane," said Gregor significantly.

"Then tell me, Gregor, why it is good that the Bane lives?" said Luxa with a sigh.

So Gregor took a deep breath and started back at the fight with the sea serpents where he had lost Luxa. He told her about sparing the Bane's life in the Labyrinth, leaving it with Ripred, the angry reaction back in Regalia and how Nerissa had saved his life by cracking the prophecy. He told her of Boots's return, and the months he'd spent waiting for word up in New York City. Then he explained everything he knew about the plague and the hardest part — the names of all who were stricken. He quickly moved on to the search for the cure, meeting Hamnet, and the treacherous trip

through the jungle that landed him in a pit of quicksand. "And that's where you came in," he said. "So, what happened to you and Aurora?"

Luxa's was a shorter story, but as loaded with trouble as Gregor's. During the battle with the sea serpent, she and Aurora had caught Boots and Temp and dove into a tunnel. Waves had soon blocked their way to their companions and they had floated for hours in the chilly water, clinging to Boots's and Temp's life jackets. Eventually, they had made their way into the Labyrinth and ran into Twitchtip, who was in the process of leading them to a safer spot when a dozen rats had attacked. Luxa had ordered Temp to run with Boots and held off the others long enough for him to get a good start. Then she had fled, following Twitchtip's directions. It took them two days to find a path out of the maze and into a network of tunnels that had led to the jungle, where almost immediately, Aurora had dislocated her wing in a fight with a giant tree snake. If the mice had not given them refuge then, they would not be alive.

"Any idea what happened to Twitchtip?" he asked.

"I do not know, Gregor. She was so weak from her injuries . . . I do not know," said Luxa.

The dense foliage ended abruptly and they came out along the stone rim of a valley. What lay below them took Gregor's breath away. The valley was covered with vines, too, but these were more slender and graceful with delicate blossoms of every shade. A light, sweet scent filled the air, which was the coolest they had encountered since they'd entered the Arch of Tantalus. The relentless chatter of the jungle was behind them now, because over the valley was a hush.

"Here lies the Vineyard of Eyes," hissed Frill.

Gregor wondered why everyone dreaded it so. It was like a magnificent garden with those multicolored blossoms and that glorious smell and . . . then he remembered the plants that had taken Mange's life. Maybe here in the jungle, beauty was synonymous with danger.

There was a smooth, wide stone path leading into the valley. The vines grew in a high arch above it, as if they'd been planted and pruned by an expert gardener.

"Who made the path?" asked Gregor.

"The Vineyard made the path itself. To

invite weary travelers in," said Ripred.

What? The Vineyard had made the path? Was this just a large-scale version of the plant that ate Mange. But instead of just one plant, a whole variety had worked out this enticing trap together? Suddenly, all the beauty became sinister, and Gregor did not want to enter the Vineyard at all.

"Courage, boy," said Ripred, who could no doubt smell the fear in Gregor's sweat. "Others must have survived it and lived to tell the tale if your Doctor Neveeve has a record of it in her books. That means it can be done. And if it can be done, then we can do it. Hamnet, what do you suggest?"

"Stay very close together. Walk in twos or even threes if possible. But avoid touching any plant. And under no circumstances, leave the path," said Hamnet.

"Boots," said Gregor weakly and then cleared his throat and tried again. "Boots, you have to stay on the path. Like . . . like . . . you know how Red Riding Hood had to stay on the path?" he asked.

"Because of wuff?" said Boots, her eyes lighting up.

"Right, these plants have bad things like wolves in them, so you stay right here on the path, okay?" said Gregor.

"You stay on the path, Temp!" said

Boots, but then she immediately began to peer into the vines, clearly hoping for a glimpse of a "wuff." Gregor would just have to keep her right next to him.

Frill and Hamnet led the party down the path with Hazard walking between them. Aurora and Nike, still secured to Frill's back, were completely vulnerable. Luxa covered them on the right and Lapblood on the left. Gregor came next, holding Boots's hand while she rode on Temp. Ripred, in the rear, walked alone.

Quiet. It was so quiet. Gregor strained his ears as the last vivid clamor of the jungle died away. Then, for the first time, he heard the sounds of his companions, stepping, sniffing, sighing. Nike coughed, Frill gave a hiss of surprise when Ripred trod on her tail, Gregor's stomach rumbled with hunger. But the Vincyard of Eyes drank in their sounds and gave them nothing in return. It was very creepy.

They had been walking for about five minutes when Gregor began to see them. The eyes. At first he mistook them for flowers or some of the enticing fruit that hung from the vines. But flowers didn't blink and fruit didn't roll around to follow your movements. Were they insects? Did the plants themselves have eyes? Was that possible? Gregor didn't know and didn't ask. He just kept one hand on Boots and one on the hilt of his sword and pretended not to notice them. Yeah, right.

They made good time. The path continued to be smooth and straight, sloping gently downward. It was easy to travel but Gregor had the sense they were descending down the throat of some horrible beast. "Just waiting for the right moment to swallow us up," he thought. He tightened his hold on Boots's hand until she complained.

Eventually, they came to a large clearing, shaped in a geometrically perfect circle. Across the path from which they had arrived, three smaller paths branched out from a single point, equal angles between them. Like they had been measured and drawn with the aid of a protractor. Gregor had never seen anything like this in the Underland. Sure, he'd run into plenty of paths that forked, but they were a variety of sizes and shapes and seemed to have formed naturally, by streams or rivers that had dried up long ago. The Vineyard of Eyes had been carefully designed and executed by someone. Or something.

"Why don't they just attack us?" he blurted out, not even knowing who "they" were.

"This part of the Vineyard must not be as hungry as others," said Hamnet. "Or perhaps they want our blood for a special purpose. To feed the young or heal an ill."

"So, this place, it has a brain or something?" said Gregor.

"Look at the paths, boy. Do you think they just happened by accident?" said Ripred. No, they hadn't. So, the answer must be "yes."

Hamnet positioned a lantern directly in the center of the circle and they all gathered tightly around it while they ate. When they were done, Hamnet rose. "I am going to take Frill and scout the paths," he said.

"Fine. The rest of us can take turns sleeping," said Ripred.

"I'm going with you," said Hazard, jumping up and clinging to Hamnet's hand.

"You will be safe here, Hazard," said Hamnet. "Ripred will look after you."

But Hazard would not let his father and Frill leave without him. After it was clear he was determined to follow them on foot down the path, Hamnet gave in and took him along. They took the path that branched off to the left and soon they were out of sight.

"Will they be all right?" Gregor asked Ripred.

"Don't worry about Hamnet. He can look after himself," said Ripred. "Survived ten years out here without any help from the rest of us."

"Why did he leave Regalia, Ripred?" said Luxa in a hushed voice. She rarely addressed the rat, so Gregor knew the question had been weighing on her.

"They never told you? Not your mother? Or Vikus?" said Ripred.

"No. Henry heard Hamnet had gone mad. But he could never find out the whole story, and Henry could find out almost anything," said Luxa.

There was no sound except their breathing while Ripred considered this. Gregor looked into the Vineyard and saw the lantern light reflecting off numerous pairs of eyes. Blinking. Blinking. He wanted to scream at them to go away, but that would only frighten Boots, and he felt sure they wouldn't go anywhere.

"You may as well know," said Ripred finally. "I expect Vikus is only waiting for you to be old enough to tell. But he would keep you young as long as possible. And then, it's hard for him to talk about Hamnet without weeping."

"Then you tell me," said Luxa. "And Vikus and I will both be in your debt."

"You in my debt, Your Highness? Well, that's an opportunity I can scarcely let pass," said Ripred. He slouched over on his side and stared into the lantern's flame. "Now where to begin? . . . You see, the thing is . . . the thing you have to understand is that the humans and the rats were not always so consumed with hatred for each other. Or at least, the hatred has ebbed and flowed, so that there have been periods when one could hope for a genuine peace. These times coincided with both the rats and the humans having leaders that were willing to place a higher priority on harmony than gain. Several hundred years ago, they say, was such a time."

Boots nudged her way onto Gregor's lap, and he wrapped his arms around her. She gave a big yawn and leaned her head against his chest.

"As a token of goodwill, the humans gave a gift to the rats. A place the bats had named the Garden of the Hesperides. Sandwich's own people had planted the garden soon after they had arrived in the Underland. There was a small plain that flooded each year when the river was high. The humans built a dike so that the plain would no longer flood, and when it dried, the land was very fertile. They planted apple trees. They were

265

small by Overland standards, but sturdy and able to grow with just the light from the river. There were sluice gates along the dike that could be opened and shut to provide water. The trees flourished and soon their branches were heavy with golden apples."

"*A* is for apple," murmured Boots.

"For the rats, it was a rare gift indeed. Unlike the humans, we can't grow crops. But the trees required little care and produced fruit almost continually. When I was a pup, I remember, it was a great treat to go to the garden," said Ripred, "to eat the apples, to sleep in the caves surrounding it, which smelled as sweet as the fruit."

"Yes," whispered Lapblood sadly. "Everyone loved the garden."

"I have never even heard of the Garden of the Hesperides," said Luxa suspiciously.

"No, because if you had heard of it, you would also have heard the story of why your uncle left. Which I will tell you now," said Ripred. "Ten or so years ago was not one of those fortunate times. While your father was a decent enough king in some respects, Your Highness, he was too rigid in others. And, of course, King Gorger was a bloodthirsty monster from the get-go."

"The same King Gorger . . ." Gregor began.

"Yes, the same King Gorger who fell to his death on your first visit, Gregor. Anyway, the humans decided they wanted the garden back. Solovet sent an army under Hamnet's command to run out the rats. Hamnet, at the time, was hands down the best warrior among the humans. Everyone assumed he would take control of the army after his mother, since he seemed just like her. But as it turned out, he was as much like Vikus as he was like Solovet. And so he was doomed."

Gregor began to get a sick feeling in his stomach. He had an impulse to tell Ripred to stop. He was not sure he wanted to hear the rest of the story. But Luxa did. And it was about her uncle.

"Under Hamnet, the humans and their fliers launched a surprise attack. The rats, most of whom were playing in the garden with their pups, were thrown into chaos. But they quickly regrouped, herded the pups into the surrounding caves, and turned to do battle. They fought so viciously that the tide began the turn in their favor. But Hamnet had a backup plan provided by his mother. If the rats should prove too strong, he was to open the sluice gates and flood the field. Then the rats would have to swim, and the humans on fliers would have a great advantage. So Hamnet opened the gates."

In the pause that followed, Gregor remembered Hamnet's words to Vikus: "I do no harm. I do no more harm." He knew he was about to find out what that harm had been.

"The river was high, the dike was centuries old. As the water burst through the sluice gates, the surrounding mortar and stone crumbled and the whole dike gave way — not merely flooding the plain, but reclaiming it under twenty feet of water. Hundreds of rats were drowned in the deluge, and many humans and fliers were caught as well. But the carnage didn't end there. Having filled the plain, the water rushed into the cave entrances, drowning the pups that had been hidden there for safety. You could hear their shrieks for miles around," said Ripred.

"Miles around," Lapblood softly echoed. "Miles around."

"What did Hamnet do?" Luxa asked.

"He began a desperate effort to rescue the drowning, human, rat, bat, whatever, but it was useless. His own flier, his bond, was dragged into the water by two rats trying to save themselves, and she never resurfaced. Hamnet was pulled out by Mareth, who had to knock him senseless in order to keep him from diving back into what was by this time a lake of corpses," said Ripred. "When Hamnet regained consciousness in Regalia, he was, for all practical purposes, mad. For days, he recognized no one and spoke in strange, garbled sentences. Then his reason returned and he stopped speaking entirely. A few nights later he fled Regalia. The last person who saw him must have been Nerissa, who was just as unstable as a child as she is now, I might add. But she never mentioned it. A year after his disappearance he was pronounced dead and all efforts to locate him ceased," said Ripred. "And that is the story of your Uncle Hamnet."

"What happened to the garden?" asked Aurora.

"It lies underwater. And those golden apple trees won't grow anywhere else in the Underland," said Ripred. "So they were lost as well."

For a while, all Gregor could hear was the occasional crackle of the lantern and Boots's soft snoring as she slept on his chest. Then a strained voice came from the path on the left. "Telling tales out of school again, Ripred?" Gregor didn't know how long Hamnet had been sitting there on Frill, holding his sleeping son. Long enough, though.

"You know my theory on that, Hamnet. The more tales told, the less chance of repeating them," said Ripred. "Maybe it will help your niece out one day."

Luxa and Hamnet exchanged a look. "Maybe," said Hamnet. "Depending on whose ears she inherited."

"Any luck out there?" asked Ripred.

"I think so," said Hamnet. He held up a handful of plants. The roots still dangled from the stems. Above his clenched fist was a cluster of star-shaped leaves.

CHAPTER 22

"Starshade," said Ripred. "You found it."

"You found it?" Gregor started to jump up, forgetting Boots was asleep on his lap. He set her on the ground and hurried to Hamnet. "You found the cure?"

"It fits your description," said Hamnet. He settled Hazard on Frill's back and slid down the lizard's tail. They all gathered around him.

"What do you think, boy? Does it look like the picture in the book?" Ripred asked Gregor.

"Exactly!" said Gregor excitedly. They had found the cure! Finally, something was going right! He plucked a leaf from the plant and took a deep sniff. The clean, refreshing scent made his nose tingle. "Mmm, smells like lemons. This must be it. It smells . . . like it could heal you. Where is it? Can we go get it now? And then get back to Regalia and —"

"Slow down, Gregor. I know we are all eager to obtain the cure. But first things first. We must sleep. Frill will keep watch. And then we will begin," said Hamnet.

Gregor lay down next to Boots. He was tired, but keyed up, too. He held the starshade leaf in his palm and let the light dance over it. In his hand was life for his mom, for Ares, for all of the Underland. He pressed the leaf against his nose, and comforted by its lemony essence, closed his eyes.

The next thing he knew, Hamnet was shaking him awake. They ate some leftover fish and a few plums. But when they started to get in their previous formation, Hamnet stopped them. "I did not tell any of you save Ripred this last night because I did not want to disturb your slumber, but this final leg of the journey will be treacherous. The field is nearby, but to reach it we must traverse a very dangerous path. As a group, we will need to move with all possible speed."

"I've designed a formation that should give us the highest rate of survival," said Ripred. "Hamnet will show you. Do exactly as he says."

Hamnet left Frill at the front of the line with the two bats and Hazard on her back. He instructed Temp to crawl beneath Frill's back legs. Flanking the lizard to the right was Ripred, with Boots and Gregor riding on his back. Luxa was to travel on Lapblood on the left. Hamnet was to run at the back.

"I can travel fast enough on my own two legs," said Luxa. She clearly didn't want to ride Lapblood.

"No, Luxa, you cannot," said Hamnet. "And trust me when I say you will be grateful for Lapblood's speed."

Luxa reluctantly settled herself on Lapblood and reached up to stroke Aurora's fur. Gregor placed Boots up by Ripred's shoulder blades and sat behind her. He had to keep his knees slightly bent so his feet wouldn't scrape the ground.

"We ride on here?" Boots asked him, puzzled.

"Just for a little way, Boots. Then you can go back on Temp," said Gregor.

Boots crawled up on Ripred's neck and poked him on the top of the head with one finger. "*R* is for rat," she said.

"Yes, and *B* is for bite," said Ripred in a singsong voice. "Be careful the rat doesn't bite your fingers!" He snapped his teeth together for emphasis.

"Oh!" Boots quickly scooted back against Gregor and held her hands close to her chest.

"Was that really necessary?" said Gregor.

"Absolutely. You want her going up and trying to pet rats? Not in this day and age," said Ripred.

Ripred, as usual, had a point. In general, Gregor did not want Boots petting rats. Most of them would kill her in a second. But then . . . if the humans and rats taught their babies from birth to fear each other . . . how was anything ever going to get better? He had a feeling this was a much bigger question to answer than he had time for at the moment, so he just wrapped his arms around Boots and said nothing.

Everyone was in place. "We will only travel a short while when I will give the command to run. At that point, do not stop until you have reached the field of starshade," Hamnet said. "Let us go."

This path was narrower although similar-looking to the one that had brought them this far. But as they turned a corner, Gregor saw a long corridor that was so lovely it looked unreal. The vines were covered with a million tiny silvery-white blossoms that seemed to sparkle in the lantern light. There was a soft, tinkling sound of bells. It was like entering the pathway to some magical fairy-land. And the smell . . . oh, the smell of the flowers made him dizzy with happiness.

"Run!" he heard Hamnet shout.

Ripred sprang forward with such power that Gregor almost lost his seat and had to fling himself forward across Boots and grab hold of the rat's ears to hang on. Boots gave a squeal of protest, since she was pretty much flattened into Ripred's neck, but Gregor didn't dare let go.

The scent of the flowers was making it hard to hold on, though. He could feel his mind beginning to get cloudy and for no apparent reason, he started grinning.

"Hang on, Overlander!" Ripred snarled.

It was the funniest thing Gregor had ever heard, and now he was laughing. He saw the bewitching vines begin to shoot out at them, and he wanted to reach out his hands to meet them. Just then, Frill caught his attention by rearing up on her hind legs and breaking into a sprint. The sight of the big lizard bicycling along on those big legs made him laugh so hard that tears began to stream down his face.

Then Gregor could see a green field. . . . That must be the starshade. . . . What a dumb name for a plant since there were no stars down here or shade, either, since there was no sun. Which was a star. Since the star was a sun . . . No, the sun was starshade. . . . No . . . "Maybe they should call it 'Never-seen-a-star-shade!' " Gregor yelled. The idea was so hilarious that he lost his grip on Ripred's back and fell off onto the path. The plants . . . the pretty plants . . . wove around his arms and fingers. . . . He had never seen anything so amazing in his life!

Something yanked him from behind and he was being pulled back and forth because his new friends, the silvery-flowered vines, did not want him to leave so soon. They bit deeply into his arms before they finally snapped. "Bye!" Gregor called as he was dragged away. "Nice knowing you!"

Then he was lying in a cool, green, lemony world, still chuckling about the "Never-seen-a-star-shade" joke when he realized there was nothing funny about it. Alarm shot through him and he sat up quickly. The group was strung out along a large rectangular field covered in starshade. Boots was curled up in the leaves next to him giggling about her thumbs. Nike was hiccuping, which had Luxa and Hazard in stitches. Aurora, who apparently could fly again, was making lazy loops in the air. Most of his other fellow travelers seemed disoriented, too. Ripred and Hamnet were both taking deep breaths of the starshade, so Gregor did the same. His head began to clear almost immediately.

"What happened back there?" he asked.

"Those flowers put out a scent that gives a feeling of great happiness and well-being," said Hamnet. "And then, my guess is, they drag you into the Vineyard and dismember you."

"Whoa! You might have given us a heads-up on that one!" said Gregor.

"We were afraid you would try to fight them," said Hamnet. "That would have guaranteed your destruction."

"We could have fought them," said Luxa, but then Nike hiccuped again and she fell over, laughing.

"Oh, please," said Ripred rolling his eyes. "As it was, Hamnet and I had to drag half of you out of there, or don't you remember that part, Your Highness?"

Gregor could see the confusion on Luxa's face and guessed that part of the ride was as much a blur for her as it was for him.

"It affects the smallest the fastest," said Hamnet. "Luckily, Frill and I had Hazard with us last night. He began to babble almost as soon as we encountered the silver flowers. It warned us what we were up against." He wrapped his arm around Hazard and gave him a squeeze.

"Are we going to pick the leaves now?" asked Hazard. "Can I help?"

"Yes, we can all help," said Hamnet. "The sooner we can harvest these plants the better."

But before they started, Hamnet insisted

that everyone eat a handful of the starshade leaves.

"Why do we need it?" asked Gregor. "None of it has the plague."

"But we are all no doubt being exposed to it. 'In the cradle lies the cure,' " said Hamnet. "That means the plague breeds here in the Vineyard. I do not know exactly where or how. All of us have scrapes and wounds. Your feet, Gregor. These cuts from the vines." Hamnet turned Gregor's arm around and revealed a crisscrossing pattern of marks where the vines had ensnared his arms. "If the plague germ floats in the air or grows on the plants or sleeps dormant in this earth where we stand, be sure it will make its way into your blood as well."

"Boots!" said Gregor. "Come on, we have to eat this stuff!" He stuffed a wad of leaves in his mouth and chewed. They weren't bad, actually. Sort of like lemon and mint and tea all in one. Boots resisted eating the leaves, since she was not big on greens, until Hamnet made it into a game of who could eat a leaf the fastest. Hazard and Temp played with her and had the sense to let her win almost every time, so she soon had a fair number of leaves inside her.

The starshade was easy to pull from the

thin layer of soil in which it grew, but no one could think of the best way to package it for the trip home. The plants were only about eighteen inches tall, so they were not long enough for tying around bundles of the stuff. Then Gregor remembered the duct tape and took it from his pack. "Here, this will work!" He pulled out a strip of the tape to show them. By cutting the wide tape into thin strips, they could secure a really big haul.

"This is most excellent," said Hamnet. "Thank you."

"Don't thank me, thank Mareth," said Gregor, and then caught himself. Now that they all knew about the Garden of the Hesperides and Mareth saving Hamnet, somehow he felt awkward mentioning the name. "Sorry," he mumbled.

"Why?" asked Hamnet. "Mareth is one of the few people I do not mind being in debt to."

"Yeah," said Gregor. "He's a good guy."

"Come, let us begin the harvest," said Hamnet.

Initially, everyone gathered the starshade from the field, but it soon became apparent that the humans would be most useful taping bundles of the leaves together. None of the other creatures had the hands to do it.

Boots and Hazard really weren't much help, either, so they went back to picking plants. That is, Hazard did, while Boots sang "The Alphabet Song", then chanted " 'Turn and turn and turn again' " while she did her spinning dance until she fell over with dizziness. Occasionally, she presented them with a few leaves, too. Aurora and Nike, who, with their injuries, were also fairly limited in what they could do, made sure she stayed safely in the field. When she began to get too interested in the jungle again, Gregor dug around in his backpack and pulled out her ball and the top Dulcet had packed for her. He also gave her the hand mirror Nerissa had given him — Boots was very fond of making faces at herself.

Gregor ended up working mainly with Luxa, cutting strips of tape and wrapping up bundles of starshade.

Hamnet gathered the bundles and began to build them into a haystack of sorts. When he was out of earshot, Gregor turned to Luxa. "So, that was some story Ripred told us about Hamnet."

"Yes, it explains a great deal about why he left," said Luxa. "He was mad. But it does not explain why he did not come back to Regalia when his senses returned."

"Because they would have made him fight

again, Luxa," said Gregor. "And he couldn't stand killing anymore."

"There is no great joy in killing for any of us," said Luxa. "We do it to survive."

"So, what are you saying? You think he's a coward?" said Gregor.

"Not a coward in that he is afraid to die. But I think it is easier for him to live here in the jungle, than return and face his true life," said Luxa.

Gregor thought about it. First of all, living in the jungle was no picnic. And Hamnet had left everyone he loved behind. He couldn't have known he would meet an Overlander woman and have Hazard. He probably didn't think he would even live. He had given up everything, his home, his loved ones, his life, because he felt so strongly that what he did for Regalia was wrong.

"I don't know, Luxa. I think he made a pretty brave choice. And I think in his mind it was the only one he could have made," said Gregor.

"Perhaps. I do not know." Luxa gave her head a shake. "But would you have abandoned your family, Gregor?"

"That's different. My family doesn't even allow hitting," said Gregor. "Your family's always in a war."

"So is yours, now," said Luxa and ripped off a piece of duct tape with her teeth.

Hamnet had assembled all the available bundles in the haystack, so he came to help them tape up some more. Luxa and Hamnet avoided speaking much to each other. It was too bad, really, since Gregor actually liked them both and they were related and all. He wasn't exactly sure how to get them to talk, but he gave it a try.

"Man, you two sure look alike," he said. "You even smile the same."

Luxa and Hamnet glanced at each other warily but said nothing.

"So, Luxa must look just like her mom did, huh? Ripred said she was the spitting image of your twin," Gregor continued.

It was more of a question, so Hamnet had to answer. "It is remarkable how much she resembles Judith. Even as a baby —" He broke off.

"Oh, yeah, you must have still been around when Luxa was a baby," said Gregor.

"Yes, we were good friends then, Luxa and I. I took her on her first flier ride outside the city," said Hamnet.

"To the beach with the crystals," said Luxa softly.

Hamnet looked at her in surprise. "You

remember that? You could not have been more than two years."

"Just bits and pieces. I still have a chunk of crystal. It is blue," said Luxa.

"And shaped like a fish," said Hamnet. "I remember." Suddenly, his eyes filled with tears. "Of everything I left behind in Regalia, Luxa, you were my greatest regret. You and your mother."

"You could have come and seen us," said Luxa and her voice sounded very young.

"No. I could never have left twice. You know how Solovet works. She would have had me leading an army again in no time," said Hamnet.

"She could not have forced you," said Luxa.

"Bet she could have," muttered Gregor. Solovet would have found a way to make her son fight again. Guilt. Shame. Duty. Something.

"I could not do that again," said Hamnet. "Not after . . . I still dream of it every night. . . . The voices crying out for me to save them. . . . And what did it solve? That battle at the garden? Nothing. It solved nothing at all. When it was over, the humans and gnawers hated one another more than ever. The Underland only became a more dangerous place."

There was a long pause in the conversation before Gregor spoke up again.

"So, don't you ever fight now? I mean, what if something attacks you or Hazard?" he asked.

"I do fight on occasion, but only as a last resort," said Hamnet. "It is a method of survival I have learned from Frill. It turns out there are many alternatives to violence if you make an effort to develop them."

"Like what?" asked Gregor.

"Well, say that Frill is in danger. Her first reaction is to make herself unseen. Camouflage," said Hamnet.

Gregor remembered the first time he'd seen Frill. He wouldn't have noticed her if she hadn't opened her mouth to catch Boots's ball. "Oh, right. So, what if that doesn't work?"

"Then she attempts to scare off whoever is threatening her. She hisses and opens her ruff, which makes her look much larger and more frightening," said Hamnet.

"Didn't work on Boots." Gregor laughed.

"No, Boots tried to frighten her right back." Hamnet grinned. "If Boots had been a true threat, Frill would have begun to lash her tail on the ground."

"And if something still tries to attack?" asked Gregor.

"She runs. Very fast, too, once she gets up on those hind legs. She runs to a place where the vines will support her weight and climbs high above her attacker," said Hamnet.

"But if there are no vines, and she is cornered, and something is trying to kill her?" said Luxa.

"Then she fights. She has very wicked teeth if she chooses to use them. But it is always her last choice, as opposed to the Regalians, who seem to conclude it is their only option almost immediately," said Hamnet. "Living out here, I have found that many creatures would prefer not to fight. But if your first instinct is to reach for your sword, you will never discover that."

Gregor did not know if Hamnet had convinced Luxa he'd done the right thing, but at least she seemed to be considering it.

The field of starshade was about half harvested. They had a huge pile of the plants now. With every bundle he taped, Gregor could feel his heart grow lighter. They had the cure. All they had to do now was get it back to Regalia and into the victims. His mom would get better, and they could all go home. And if she still wanted to move to Virginia then, Gregor would be the first one packed.

For a few minutes he let his mind wander to his dad's family's farm in Virginia. It was pretty nice there, even if it was kind of far away from, well, other people and buildings and stuff. He loved New York City, he would miss his friends, but if it meant his family didn't have to spend every minute afraid, it would be more than worth it.

He was just thinking about how maybe he might learn to ride a horse when he saw Aurora's head snap up. Nike's went up, too. And suddenly, Ripred and Lapblood had their noses in the air. They were all facing the far end of the field.

"What? What is it?" said Gregor. Usually, the bats reacted to rats, but the rats were reacting as if something dangerous were around, too. "Is it some kind of plant?" He still felt shaky from the silvery flowers.

"No!" snarled Ripred. "How did they even get in here?"

"They ate their way in, I imagine," said Nike. Her wings were beating open and shut in apprehension.

"Who?" said Gregor, grabbing Boots up in his arms. "Who ate their way in?"

But before Nike could answer, Gregor saw the red wave beginning to seep into the field. They were so close together that they appeared to be one entity, a thick bloody liquid oozing toward him. He shot the beam of his best flashlight in that direction and could see the wave was made up of individuals.

Ants. Hundreds of red ants were descending on the field, destroying everything in their path.

CHAPTER 23

Ripred took command of the situation immediately.

"You!" he called to Aurora. "Get those pups and fly out of here. Take them to the nibblers and then back to Regalia if we don't show up in twenty-four hours!"

Hamnet swung Hazard and Boots up onto Aurora's back. "You look after Boots for us, all right, Hazard?" he said, giving his son a hug.

Gregor began to object. "No, I don't want Boots to go!"

"Aurora and I are bonds. We do not separate!" said Luxa.

"Your sister, Overlander, is about to be torn apart by cutters," said Ripred. "And I need you on Nike, Your Highness. Your bond is in no condition for battle."

"Battle?" said Gregor numbly. "The ants are here for a battle?"

"Well, they aren't here for a picnic! They're here to destroy the starshade and all the warmbloods along with it! Now move!" Ripred snapped his teeth at Aurora's shoulder and she shot into the air.

"Boots! Hang on!" cried Gregor. He caught a glimpse of her puzzled face peeking over Aurora's neck before Ripred pushed him hard.

"Wake up, Warrior! You've got your sword. What about light?" said the rat.

Gregor glanced at the flashlight he usually kept at his waist. That would be worthless to him in a battle. He remembered a trick he had used on the last quest. "Luxa! Here, quick!" he said. He pulled out two flashlights and duct-taped one to each of their forearms.

"Five-point arc!" shouted Ripred. "I'll take the tip. I want the Overlander and Lapblood on my right, Hamnet and Frill to my left." The rat turned to Hamnet, who seemed suddenly to have frozen to the ground. "You are fighting, right?"

"I — I —" Hamnet stuttered.

"The cure is at stake. Think of it as a way of redeeming past actions," said Ripred. "Think of it as a way of saving your son. Think of it any way you like, but arm yourself or get out!"

Hamnet looked over at the sea of ants coming down the field. Already, a quarter of the starshade plants had been shredded, chewed, trampled to bits. "Yes. Yes, I will fight," said Hamnet. He ran to Frill, ripped open the pack under her neck, and pulled out a sword.

"Fight cutters, too, I will, fight cutters, too," said Temp.

"Oh, Temp," said Gregor. "You should have gone with Aurora." Gregor knew the cockroaches weren't known for their ability to battle. They were good at fleeing. That was how they survived.

"Fight cutters, too, I will, fight cutters, too," insisted Temp.

"All right, Crawler, position yourself in that stack of starshade. If they make it in, do your best to disable them," said Ripred. Temp scurried to the pile of starshade and concealed himself. "In the air, Your Highness, give us as much cover as you can," said Ripred. Luxa's face was grim as she mounted Nike's back and took off, her sword already drawn. "The rest of you, take your positions."

Ripred bounded toward the ants and crouched down about ten yards from the oncoming army. Hamnet took his place about five yards behind Ripred off to the left, and Frill backed him up by the same distance. Gregor looked around in confusion.

"Do as Hamnet does!" said Lapblood. "I'll be behind you."

So Gregor ran up as far as Hamnet was, but on Ripred's right side. Lapblood fell into place behind him.

"Hold your positions as long as you can before you fall back. When we reach the stack, circle around. Don't save each other, save the plants! Remember, it's the starshade we need. Defend it at all cost!" said Ripred.

Gregor stared at the ants. Each was about five feet long and about two feet tall. Apart from their size, they seemed to be anatomically like the ants in the Overland. Each had six legs, two antennae, and a pair of razor-sharp mandibles that opened and closed horizontally, shearing the starshade to bits. They were aligned in a clear formation, shoulder to shoulder, like a well-trained army. Hundreds of soldier ants. Headed right for them.

"Warrior!" Ripred shouted. "Look at me!" Gregor tore his eyes off the ants and turned to Ripred. "If you can rage, do it now! This is life and death, boy! Life and death, understand?"

Life and death? Not just for the handful here in the field, but for all the warmbloods, for Lapblood's pups, for Howard and Andromeda, for Ares, for his mom. The ants were only a few paces from Ripred when Gregor realized he had not even drawn his sword. It came out now, in a smooth even movement. The buzzing swept through his body and his vision splintered as the rager sensation roared through him.

"Take off their legs, decapitate them, drain them, do whatever you have to do to stop them!" bellowed Ripred. And with that, he sprang straight into the column of ants.

In the period that followed, Gregor lost all sense of where he was, of his companions, of himself. There was heat, sweat, the taste of his own blood in his mouth. His sword knew where to go — to the joints of the legs, napes of the neck, the thin waists. But there were so many . . . so many! Where each ant fell, another appeared to take its place. Slowly, reluctantly, his feet shifted, as their sheer numbers forced him back. Eventually, he could feel the starshade bundles scraping the backs of his calves as he took one final stand at the stack . . . and then they swarmed over him, knocking him into the bundles of plants.

"No!" he heard himself scream. "No!" Gregor fought his way back to his feet and plowed after the army as he tried to stop the demolition of the plants, but it was no use. The stack was gone in less than a minute, and the rest of the field was completely vulnerable. As he staggered behind the disappearing army, a pair of teeth caught his shirt from behind and dragged him quickly back from the jungle. He struggled to free himself, to follow the enemy in among the vines, but whoever held him was too powerful to resist.

"Let them go! It's over, boy! It's over. We've lost," said Ripred, as he yanked him onto his rear end.

The force of the impact helped bring Gregor back to reality. He was sobbing in fury at the ants, in revulsion at the battle, and in despair because the field . . . oh, the field was a wasteland! Ruined bits of plants lay ground into the earth, which was sodden with an evil-smelling lilac goo. He scooped up a handful of the stuff and watched the last shreds of the starshade dissolve into greenish liquid and vanish.

"It's gone," Gregor wept. "The starshade is gone. The cure is gone."

"All gone," said Ripred quietly. "It's all gone now."

Luxa and Nike landed beside them. Through his tears, Gregor could see the blood streaming from the cuts on Luxa's pale legs. He realized he was covered in stinging wounds himself, where the mandibles had found their way through his defenses.

"If it's any consolation, the jungle has finished our work for us," said Ripred.

Gregor looked up at the jungle where the remainder of the ant army had disappeared. It had plowed into the area that Hamnet had raced their party through. Into the pretty white blossoms that made you deliriously happy. The ants must have been susceptible, too, because the jungle was filled with vines ripping obliging insects to bits. It didn't take long. In minutes, the ants were dismembered and dropped to the jungle floor where the roots shifted and covered them. And the silence returned.

Gregor wiped his eyes and struggled onto his feet. Ripred and Lapblood were hunched behind him. Luxa still sat on Nike's back. Surrounded by dead ants, Frill's beautiful blue-green body lay sprawled across the field, the skin scored with hundreds of cuts. Gregor looked for motion in her chest, but it was still as a stone.

Temp was hovering over something at the edge of the jungle. Gregor realized the form on the ground was Hamnet.

"Uncle!" Luxa cried, and then she was sprinting across the field to him.

When they reached him, they could see Hamnet was not long for this world. A gaping hole just under his ribcage was pumping out blood so it formed a pool around him.

Luxa knelt beside him and grasped his hand. "Judith," he whispered. "Judith . . ."

"Yes, it is Judith. I am right here," said Luxa.

"Hazard . . . Promise me . . . he will not be . . . let him be . . . anything but a warrior," said Hamnet.

"I promise," said Luxa. "Hamnet? Hamnet?" But his violet eyes were vacant now. He had slipped away.

"Anything but a warrior. Like me," thought Gregor dully. "Oh, let him be anything but me."

Luxa slowly reached up and shut Hamnet's eyes. Then she trailed her fingers along his cheek, removing a spot of blood.

"Now cracks a noble heart," said Ripred. He brushed Hamnet's head with his nose. "Take a lock. For his parents," he told Luxa. She cut a wave of Hamnet's hair and tucked it carefully into her belt.

They all sat near Hamnet's body in the wasted field, mindless of the blood and viscous lilac substance that the ants had spread. Their friends were gone. The starshade was gone. And with it went all of their hope.

CHAPTER 24

Gregor stared at the ground for a while, before he realized he was looking at something he recognized. Obscured by the muck was the mirror he had given to Boots to play with. She must have dropped it. He pried it up and slowly wiped it clean on his shirt. "At least Boots and Hazard didn't have to watch the battle," he thought. Hazard hadn't seen his dad and Frill die. And Boots hadn't seen Gregor hacking away at the ants.

"Why did they do it?" Gregor said finally. "Why did the ants want to destroy the cure?"

"They view us as an enemy," said Ripred. "All of us warmbloods but the rats in particular. Hasn't helped much that the humans pushed us up against their borders."

Gregor vaguely remembered Ripred talking about this, when was it? Before he had gone after the Bane. At dinner in Regalia, a long, long time ago. Ripred had accused Solovet of starving the rats, of driving them up against the ants' borders.

"It was an excellent plan, you have to give them credit for that," said Ripred. "All they had to do was come, obliterate this field, and their problem with the warmbloods would soon be only a memory."

"How did they know where it was?" asked Gregor.

"Oh, that wouldn't be hard to find out. Probably the whole Underland knew we'd gone after the cure. And you can't take a mixed pack, as Hamnet called us, into the Vineyard without causing a lot of gossip. All they needed to know was when and where we'd found the cure. Any number of insects would have been happy to supply that information, right, Temp?"

"Any number," agreed Temp. "Hated here, the warmbloods are, hated here."

"Why?" asked Gregor.

"We have the best lands. The most plentiful feeding grounds. What we do not have and covet, they say we take. We are thought to be lacking in respect for other creatures," said Nike with a sigh.

"Well, you are. I mean, you all treat the cockroaches like trash," said Gregor. "Like when everybody laughed at Temp at that meeting. Do you make fun of the ants, too?"

"The ants are a completely different situation. They have little sense of self. Everything they do is for the collective benefit of the colony. So you see there would have been no trouble sending an army into the jungle. If they lost a hundred, a thousand, ten thousand soldiers, it would be nothing if it meant our destruction," said Ripred. "And every one has such blind loyalty to the queen . . . No, we don't make fun of the cutters much. They can be too dangerous, as we have all just witnessed."

Gregor's eyes wandered across the field. It was littered with dead ants. But they had done their job. Not a stalk of the starshade was left standing.

"What shall we do now?" said Nike.

"What is there to do but go home, and choose a good place to die?" said Lapblood. "The starshade is gone."

"It does not make sense," said Luxa. "We did all the prophecy asked. Brought the warrior and the princess. Joined with the gnawers to seek the cure. Why have we not succeeded?"

"I do not know. But I do not believe we have ever understood the prophecy. Possibly we fail because we still do not see the when," said Nike.

"What?" said Lapblood.

" 'You see the what but not the when,' " Nike quoted from the prophecy.

"I've seen the when. It was when the cutters destroyed this field, and we didn't see it coming," said Lapblood.

"Maybe, but if you are wrong . . ." Nike trailed off.

"What are you thinking, Nike?" said Luxa.

"Perhaps, the cure still exists somewhere. Perhaps there is more starshade right here in the Vineyard," said Nike.

"Doesn't seem likely somehow. Doctor Neveeve said there was only a single field. I think we're sitting in it," said Ripred. "If this is the cradle, then this was the cure."

"Then there is no hope at all," said Luxa.

A long silence followed. Gregor could hear the tinkling of the white flowers and thought how easy it would be to walk into them and never come out. So much easier than going back to Regalia to watch his mom die. So much easier than watching Ares, if by some miracle he still lived, give up when he found out Gregor had failed. He didn't know if he and Boots would ever make it home. Probably they'd been infected with the plague. Would that handful of leaves they'd eaten be enough to keep them safe?

"Not the cradle, unless this be, not the cradle," said Temp.

Since everyone had drifted into their own dark thoughts, Temp's comment made little sense. Besides, no one ever much listened to the crawlers.

"What, Temp?" asked Gregor, more out of politeness than anything else.

"Not the cradle, unless this be, not the cradle," repeated Temp.

It took Gregor a bit to swap Temp's words around and make sense of them. Unless this be . . . not the cradle. The last one who had spoken before Temp had been Nike, who had said there was no hope. Unless this be not the cradle. Yes, Temp was right. . . .

IN THE CRADLE FIND THE CURE FOR THAT WHICH MAKES THE BLOOD IMPURE.

The cure could still be somewhere if the Vineyard of Eyes were not the cradle!

"But this is the cradle," said Lapblood.

"Is it?" said Ripred. His eyes began to come back to life. "Who says it is? Some dusty book written by humans years ago? Why, we don't even really know if this is the same plague, or just one with similar symptoms. And if Temp is right, it would explain one thing."

"What?" asked Luxa.

"The point of having a crawler on this

whole hellish trip! Honestly, how has he added to anything of significance? No offense, Temp, you've been a real champ about babysitting, but what have you contributed? Nothing! Maybe this is it! Your big moment! Maybe this is why Sandwich put you in the prophecy," said Ripred. "To see this wasn't the cradle!"

The big rat began to pace back and forth, the wheels turning in his head. "Let's roll it around the ground a bit and see where we get. All right, say this isn't the cradle, and the starshade wasn't the cure. We saw the what, which is still the plague, but not the when. So, what is the when? Think, everyone! Just say anything that comes into your head!" said Ripred. "You saw the plague but not when — !"

"Not when it would take my pups," said Lapblood as if she could not help herself.

"Not when the cutters would use it against us," said Nike.

"You saw the plague but not when — !" Ripred turned sharply to Luxa.

"Not when Ares got it," Luxa burst out. "I mean, if he caught it from those mites, none of us saw that. And not only when but why? Why don't Gregor and Aurora and I have it?"

"That's what Mareth and I were saying.

Especially me. I rode on his back for days with open cuts on my arm and he was bleeding and . . . and . . . how can I not have the plague if he got it when the mites bit him?" said Gregor.

"Let's say he didn't," said Ripred. "Let's say your other mates, Howard and Andromeda, they caught it when they brought him in sick from his cave. So, where did Ares get the plague?"

"Well, the answer could be anywhere!" snapped Lapblood in frustration.

"No," said Nike. "It could only be somewhere Ares had been."

"Somewhere he had been *and* somewhere that the plague could exist," said Ripred. "Luxa, you know his habits best. Where would he have gone?"

"To find Aurora and me, probably," said Luxa. "Back to the Labyrinth. And his cave . . . the flier's lands . . . Regalia."

"No, he did not go into your city or the flier's lands," said Nike. "After his trial, no one saw him in either place."

"Yeah, he was afraid he'd be executed. He wouldn't even go to the hospital to have his wounds treated. He went . . . He went . . ." Gregor found his eyes locked on the pool of Hamnet's blood that had spread almost to his toes. He could see the light reflecting back from the red surface. It was strangely familiar. "Where did I see that before?" he wondered. And in an instant, everything began tumbling into place. Somewhere that Ares had been . . . and somewhere that the plague could exist . . . "Oh, geez. Oh, geez," he said.

"What, Overlander? What?" said Ripred.

But Gregor couldn't speak his thoughts yet. The red pool of blood in Neveeve's office . . . The fleas gorged on blood . . . The empty plague container . . . brand-new . . . because the old one had broken. Not that day, or the day before. Neveeve had said it had broken months ago. She had had the plague months ago, before Ares had even gotten sick!

"Ares went . . . he went to the lab . . . for his bites . . . to get medicine . . ." he stammered.

"Yes, so what?" said Ripred.

"Neveeve, she had the plague there," Gregor said.

"She had the plague germs there, yes, to study them, to try and find a cure," said Nike. "After the plague started."

"No, I think . . . I think she had it way before," said Gregor. "She said a plague container broke months ago. Ares must have been there in the lab when it happened!

That's when he caught it! And that's why I don't have it! Or you, Luxa! Or Aurora!"

And Neveeve — jumpy, twitchy, nervous Neveeve. She wasn't just stressed because there was a plague, she was stressed because she had started it!

"That makes no sense. What use would the plague be to the humans?" said Luxa dismissively.

"A great deal, Your Highness, if they had the cure as well. They could wipe out every gnawer, every warmblood who displeased them, safe in the knowledge that none of them could die!" said Ripred. "Oh, that's a fine weapon indeed to be brewing up in your labs."

" 'The remedy and wrong entwine, / And so they form a single vine,' " said Nike with an agitated voice. "That could be Doctor Neveeve. She could be the vine. Both the remedy and wrong in one."

"This seems like wild conjecture to me," said Luxa.

"Really? It seems very plausible to me. But I suppose if we can't convince you, we can't convince the other humans, either. Think harder, boy! What else do you have?" said Ripred.

What else did he have? There must be something. Gregor was clutching the mirror so tightly it hurt his hands. The mirror! He thought of the hours he'd spent before the bathroom mirror, holding up the prophecy, trying to make sense of it. "The mirror!" he said holding it up urgently for them to see. "You know how you need a mirror to read the prophecy? You have to look in a mirror . . . and when you do, you see . . . What do you see?" He flipped it around and pointed it at each of them.

"Yourself, you see, yourself," said Temp.

"It was the humans. They had the plague all along!" spat out Lapblood.

"No, even in the worst times we humans would not create something so destructive to so many. Something that could turn against us," said Luxa defiantly.

"Turn . . . yes, 'Turn and turn and turn again,' " said Ripred, his ears sticking up. "'That's it! Don't you see? It's like Boots's annoying little dance." Ripred glared into the field. "We started out heading toward the jungle looking for the cure. But if you turn . . ." He turned 180 degrees. "And turn . . ." He swung back around to the jungle. "And turn again . . ." He spun halfway around again. "You're not facing the jungle, Your Highness. You're facing Regalia."

CHAPTER 25

"I do not — I cannot believe this is true!" said Luxa.

"Hope it is, for all our sakes. And if the Overlander is right and you have the cure in your lab back in Regalia, I want your first action to be to send it to us," said Ripred.

"There is no cure in Regalia," said Luxa stubbornly.

"But if there is — ?" said Ripred.

"If there is . . . on my word, the gnawers will be served first," said Luxa.

"All right then. Fly back to Regalia and straighten this mess out. Lapblood and I will head home to deliver our latest theory. I expect to hear from you very soon," said Ripred. He turned to Lapblood. "I think our best bet will be to follow the ants' trail back. It should lead close enough to the tunnels, and the plants won't have had time to recover yet —" Ripred noticed no one was moving. "What are you waiting for? Get on your flier and go!"

"What about Hamnet and Frill?" asked Gregor, not wanting to leave them lying there. But the soil was too thin to bury them. And Nike could never carry them all.

"They belong to the jungle now. Likely the starshade will grow back here. So they'll be in a good place, right?" asked Ripred.

"I guess," said Gregor. But he did not really feel any better about it.

"On your bat now," said Ripred, nudging him toward Nike. Gregor and Luxa climbed on Nike's back. "Don't forget the crawler. He may have saved us all," said Ripred, scooting Temp up behind them.

"If he did, it wouldn't hurt if you spread that information around," said Gregor. Then maybe the warmbloods wouldn't be such snobs about the bugs.

"If he did, I will become the biggest bore in the Underland, as I will talk of nothing else," said Ripred. "Fly you high, boy."

"Run like the river, Ripred," said Gregor. And Nike lifted into the air up over the vines and headed out of the Vineyard.

It was a surprisingly short trip back to the pool in the nibblers' land, where Aurora had taken Hazard and Boots. They had barely touched down when the words were coming out of Hazard's mouth. "Where's my father? Where's Frill? Will they be here soon?"

Luxa gave Gregor a sad glance. It occurred to Gregor that no one knew better than Luxa what Hazard was about to face. She slid off Nike's back and took Hazard's hands in hers. "They are not coming back, Hazard. We had to battle to try and save the starshade. Hamnet and Frill died fighting the cutters. I am sorry."

Hazard just looked at her for a moment, uncomprehending. "But . . . they couldn't have," he said. "They wouldn't leave me here alone."

"They did not want to, I promise you that," said Luxa. "Only they could not help it. Sometimes, you cannot help the things that happen."

"Oh," said Hazard. His large green eyes filled with tears. "Like when my mother left me. She didn't want to go, either. But she had to." He tilted his head down, and the tears slid down his cheeks and onto the stones.

Boots came over and tugged on Gregor's shirt. "Gre-go, he's crying." She was always thinking he could fix things he couldn't.

Gregor picked Boots up in his arms and gave her a squeeze. "I know," was all he could say.

Luxa knelt before Hazard and wiped his tears with her fingers. "The same thing happened with my parents. They both died, too," said Luxa. "My mother and your father were brother and sister. Did you know that?"

Hazard shook his head. "I don't have a sister."

"I do not have a brother, either. But I was thinking, that if you would come back to Regalia with me, it would be like I did," said Luxa. "Will you come?"

"To Regalia?" said Hazard. He seemed so lost. "I live here in the jungle."

"But who will you live with now, Hazard? Who will take care of you?" said Luxa.

"I want my father! And Frill!" said Hazard, beginning to sob. "They take care of me!"

"I know. I know. But they are gone," said Luxa. She wrapped her arms around the little boy, and he clung to her. "Oh, Hazard, Hazard. Please say you will come with me. It is not so very bad in Regalia."

"My grandfather . . . lives in Regalia. He said . . . I could visit . . . any time I wanted to," Hazard choked out.

"Oh, yes! Vikus will be very glad to see you," said Luxa, stroking his dark curls. "Everyone will."

"And you'll be my sister?" said Hazard. He looked over at where Gregor was holding Boots. "Like she's his sister?"

"If you will have me," said Luxa.

"All right," said Hazard. His tears didn't stop, but he wiped his nose on his sleeve. "Can I ride on your flier?"

"Any time you wish. And when we get back, maybe you will meet a flier of your own to bond with," said Luxa. "Would you like that?" Hazard nodded. "Let us go home, then."

They took only a few minutes to drink from the pool and wash their wounds. There was nothing with which to bandage the cuts from the mandibles. Everything had been destroyed. But at least the lilac goo the ants had doused the field with did not seem harmful to them. It didn't burn like the acid from the yellow pods, and it rinsed off easily in water. No, it seemed it was only destructive to plants.

A trio of mice appeared and dropped a few dozen plums at Luxa's feet as they were about to go. "Thank you," she said. "I will never forget your kindness to myself and Aurora. Know while I have breath, you will always have a friend in the Underland." She removed the band of gold from her head and laid it on the stone before them. "If ever you have need of my help, present my crown to one of our scouts, and I will do whatever is within my power to come to your aid."

Then Luxa laid her hand on each of their heads, and they squeaked out good-byes to her in high-pitched English.

Neither Nike nor Aurora was in very good shape, but both insisted they could make the journey home. Luxa took Hazard with her on Aurora, and Gregor, Boots, and Temp climbed upon Nike's back.

Gregor couldn't wait to get back. What if the cure was there, in Neveeve's lab, but it was still a secret? Then his mom, Ares, his friends . . . if they were still alive, every second was precious.

The bats lifted high over the vines and sped toward Regalia. Gregor thought of the agonizingly slow progress they had made on foot and shook his head. He guessed it hadn't been realistic to fly in. The rats would have been too heavy to haul very far, let alone Frill, but still. How much time could they have saved? He could have been to Regalia and back ten times.

"What did you do up here, Nike, while you were waiting for us to catch up with you?" asked Gregor.

"I went in circles. Both in the air and in my head, is I was trying to break the prophecy," said Nike.

"It's broken now, though, don't you think? That we're right about the humans

311

starting it?" asked Gregor.

"As Ripred says, I must hope we are. But Gregor, when the rest of the warmbloods learn the plague was the humans' fault, it will be very ill indeed," said Nike.

"What will they say?" said Gregor.

"Most humans and their allies will be ashamed. Their enemies will say it only confirms what they suspected all along. That humans lie and will do anything to get what they want," said Nike. "The awful thing, is . . . no one will truly be surprised."

Although he hadn't been born in the Underland, Gregor felt a natural kinship to the humans down here. He was still mad at them for putting him and Ares on trial when they hadn't killed the Bane, but he had chalked that up to being a misunderstanding. When Nerissa had explained the truth, the humans — at least the majority of them — had listened. Gregor's view of the rats was very different. He had always thought of them as essentially the bad guys, with a few exceptions like Twitchtip and maybe Ripred. The idea that the humans could be as bad as the rats, or even worse, threw him for a loop. But was he truly surprised? He remembered the council's attempt to deny the rats the flea powder. No. He couldn't say he was.

Boots and Temp chatted back and forth in Cockroach while Gregor mulled the whole thing over, trying to make sense of it. After a while, he realized they were coming in for a landing. Shining his light down on the ground, he saw the piles of skeletons stretched out around the Arch of Tantalus.

"We're stopping here?" he asked Nike.

"Do not worry. It will only be for a brief time. But Aurora and I must rest," said Nike.

"Oh, sure, of course," said Gregor. He was impatient to get back, but they needed to give the bats a break, especially since they were both hurt.

They had no water, but plenty of plums. The seven of them gathered in a tight circle and ate. Four kids, two bats, and a cockroach. Gregor thought they must look like an easy meal, and kept a close eye on the jungle.

Luxa was so lost in thought, she did not even seem aware of their surroundings. She held an uneaten plum in her hand while she stared fixedly at the skeleton of some large rodent.

"Luxa? You going to eat that thing?" asked Gregor.

She snapped back to reality. "Why? Do you want it?"

"No, you should eat it. But we can't stay here very long," said Gregor.

Luxa nodded and took a bite of the plum, but her face was troubled. "I have been thinking of what Ripred said. About the value of such a destructive weapon. He was right. Having the plague at our command would give the humans total control over all the warmbloods."

"So you think I'm right? You think Neveeve started the plague?" said Gregor.

"It still seems impossible to believe. But there is one way we will know for sure," said Luxa.

"What's that?" said Gregor.

"If during your absence she has come up with a cure, then you will be right. For the cradle and the cure will be one, and no other cure will exist now that the starshade is gone. There will be no argument left," said Luxa.

Aurora said the bats were ready to fly, so they all mounted up. Nike suggested that Gregor sleep on the way back. He lay down with Boots, who soon drifted off, but he could not sleep. In the quiet dark tunnels, the battle was beginning to come back to him. He could remember more of it than the time he'd fought the squids, now almost a complete blank. This time, he could call up very specific images of his sword as it severed the life of ant after ant. Who were the ants, anyway? Not just animals, not just a natural force. Ripred had talked about them as intelligent creatures that had formed a clever battle plan. Did they all have names? Did they have parents and children and friends? Who exactly had he killed?

He could not sort out his feelings. At the time, he had only thought of protecting the starshade. His own life had been at risk as well — look at what had happened to Hamnet and Frill. But on the battlefield, Gregor had not been fighting for his own life as much as he'd been fighting to save what he'd believed to be the cure. Sometimes you had to fight. . . . Even Hamnet had agreed to that . . . and he must have thought today was one of those times. Gregor had done what he had to do. . . . But still . . . he felt horrible when he envisioned the twisted bodies of the ants in the field.

And even though Gregor had raged, they had not succeeded in saving the starshade. Hamnet had fought, too, when backed against the wall, but Gregor knew he hadn't wanted to. That he didn't really think it was a solution to anything. Maybe if they had all taken that approach, they could have still deciphered the prophecy, and there wouldn't be all those corpses waiting to be covered by vines. But what would the peaceful alternative have been? It had been too late to think of one when the ants were marching in on them. A solution would have needed to have been thought up a while ago. And so many parties — the humans, the rats, the ants — everyone would have had to agree that it was for the best.

All of this was complicated by the fact that if Gregor was correct about Dr. Neveeve, the loss of everyone's life today was utterly pointless. Because that thing they'd all gone to battle over — the starshade — had never been the cure at all.

The more he thought, the more his mind reeled in confusion. We were right to fight. It was wrong to fight. We had to fight. It was pointless to fight. He simply did not know where he stood, and it made him feel crazy. No wonder Hamnet had run off to the jungle.

After several hours of tormenting himself with the events of the day, flickers of light began to appear in the distance. Regalia was just ahead. A squad of four Underlanders on bats materialized to block their way. Then they saw Luxa.

"Queen Luxa!" burst out one guard in

disbelief. "You live!"

"Yes, I live, Claudius," said Luxa. "And I must have immediate access to the council regarding the cure to the plague."

"Yes, by all means," stammered Claudius. "But there are several checkpoints meant to screen those who would bring the plague into the city."

"We must bypass them in the interest of time. Believe me, even if I carried the plague, that would pale in importance to the news I bring," said Luxa.

"Yes, but we have very strict orders . . ." said the guard.

"Which I overrule now," said Luxa. "Clear my passage to the city. It is a direct order for which I take full responsibility."

Claudius looked at the other guards in hesitation, then called out, "Clear the queen's passage to the city!" He flew with them, waving aside any resistance they met. "The queen! The queen returns!" he cried out, and the Underlanders fell aside.

As they flew across the city of Regalia, Gregor could see people on the ground pointing up at them and shouting. He guessed they recognized Aurora by her beautiful golden coat, and were hoping that Luxa might be on her.

As the exhausted bats skidded on their

bellies across the High Hall, two female guards ran up to help.

"Get Aurora and Nike to the hospital at once," said Luxa. "Both are injured. Is the council in session?"

"Yes, Your Highness. They have only just convened," said one of the women. Then she quickly placed her hand over her mouth as if suppressing some great emotion. "Oh, Luxa, you are back."

"It is good to see you, too, Miranda," said Luxa with a half smile. "We must make haste, Gregor." She took Hazard by the hand and headed off.

Gregor scooped up his drowsy little sister and he and Temp followed Luxa through the hallways to the council room. The full council was there, including Solovet and Vikus, and Nerissa presided at the head of the big, stone table. Doctor Neveeve was in the process of addressing them. Before her sat a large, square rack that held hundreds of glass vials filled with an orange liquid.

When the five of them walked in, Neveeve stopped speaking mid-sentence and a gasp went up around the table. People were rising, starting to move toward them, but Luxa raised her hand.

"Please, I have a matter of great urgency that takes precedent over my own happenings. Sit and let me speak," she called. Confused, everyone returned to their seats. Still holding Hazard's hand, Luxa crossed to the table directly across from Dr. Neveeve.

"We have been to the Vineyard of Eyes and found the starshade. The entire field was destroyed by an army of cutters. The cure is lost," said Luxa. "What say you to this, Doctor Neveeve?"

"It is tragic news, indeed. But we have been working night and day in the labs to try and create a cure of our own. These vials you see before me are the fruit of our labors," said Neveeve, gesturing to the glass vials.

Luxa looked down at the vials for a moment, then took a deep breath before her next question. "And have they been tried on the plague victims yet?"

"The patients in the hospital are responding favorably. Both the Overlander's mother and his bond have shown improvement," said Neveeve.

Gregor felt his knees go weak with relief. "Oh!" The sound came out of him on its own. They were alive! Somehow they had hung on!

Neveeve gave him a smile. "Yes, we have much hope that this remedy may be effective."

There were murmurs of approval and appreciation around the table. The cure was working. Neveeve was a hero.

Luxa's voice cut through the others like a knife. "I expect it shall be highly effective. I expect it will cure the plague."

"I hope we may deserve your confidence," said Neveeve, but she gave Luxa a nervous look.

"Oh, I think we both may be confident. Certainly you look well enough," said Luxa. "And if the cure works for you, why should it not work for the rest of us?"

Neveeve flushed bright pink. "I do not know what you mean."

"I mean that you started the plague in your lab. That was the cradle. So it makes sense that the cure came from it as well," said Luxa.

There were exclamations and objections from around the table, but Luxa forged ahead.

"Do you deny, Doctor Neveeve, that Ares was infected in your lab while you were breeding the plague germ?" said Luxa.

Now the color drained from Neveeve's face, leaving her pale as a ghost. "I . . . I . . . did not . . ."

"Was he or was he not infected in your lab?" insisted Luxa.

"There was an accident. . . . It was no one's fault. . . ." said Neveeve. "He was there for something else entirely. . . ."

"And you led others to believe that the cure was in the Vineyard of Eyes, all the time knowing that you had it in your hands?" continued Luxa.

"I could not . . . reveal that. . . . The research was secret and . . ." said Neveeve.

"So, to conceal that secret you let it spread and kill and sent an unsuspecting party on a deadly fool's errand. Is that it?" said Luxa.

Now Neveeve was wildly looking around the room. "I was told to study the plague! My assignment was to find an antidote so that we could use it as a weapon. . . . I was only doing what I had been told to do!" Neveeve cried out.

Most of the council members looked stunned. But Gregor couldn't help notice a few faces that reflected Neveeve's fear. "Some of them knew," Gregor thought. "Some of them knew exactly what was going on."

Vikus rose shakily from the table and nodded to a pair of guards. "Take Doctor Neveeve into custody. And alert the tribunal that their services will be needed."

Guards took Neveeve by the arms. She

did not even put up any resistance. "I was only following orders," she said softly as they led her away.

"Contact the lab to find out how many doses of the cure they have. And take these down to the hospital immediately," said Vikus, indicating the vials of orange liquid.

"No," said Luxa, her face as hard as flint. "Our first act will be to send aid to the gnawers. I gave Ripred my word. And it will be done."

No one in the room dared to object.

CHAPTER 26

After this announcement, a wave of fatigue seemed to wash over Luxa. She looked down at Hazard, who had never let go of her hand. "You must be hungry," she said. He gave a nod. "Have food sent," she said to the guards on her way out of the council room.

They did not go far. There was a small chamber just across the hall with a couple of couches. Luxa sank into the corner of the nearest one, drawing Hazard down beside her. She rested her elbow on the arm of the couch and leaned her head into her hand. Gregor collapsed on the couch across from her with Boots on his lap. Temp sat at their feet.

"You did great in there, Luxa," said Gregor.

She made a noncommittal sound in her throat. He could see she was upset.

Vikus and Nerissa appeared in the doorway. Vikus came to Luxa and gently laid his hand upon her cheek.

"How will we survive this, Vikus? The retaliations from our enemies . . . and our shame," said Luxa.

"We will survive it together," said Vikus. "If we are attacked, we will defend ourselves. But we will first try and temper the anger with apologies and aid. Give back land, supply food and medicine. As for our shame, we can only hope to learn from it." He lifted her chin. "It is so very good to see you again."

"And you," said Luxa. Her eyes went to her cousin. "How did you enjoy the throne, Nerissa?"

"You can well imagine," said Nerissa with a quivery laugh. She took the small golden crown off her head and settled it on Luxa's. "I think this fits you better."

Luxa sighed and gave the crown a little shove back on her head. "It seems I only lose one of these to find another. Thank you for standing in for me."

"It is a truly dreadful job. I do not know how you bear it," said Nerissa. She reached out and touched Hazard's hair. "And you must be Hazard."

"Luxa says I can live here and be her brother," said Hazard uncertainly. His eyes traveled around the room, taking in the unfamiliar surroundings. Gregor realized he had probably never even been in a building before.

"You are most welcome," said Vikus. He

looked at Luxa and said softly, "Hamnet . . . ?"
Luxa just gave her head a small shake.

"He died. He won't come back now," said Hazard. "Right, Luxa?"

"No, he will not. So we shall have to hold him very carefully in our hearts," she said, wrapping an arm around him.

Vikus gazed at Gregor, his wounds, the sword at his waist. "So, Gregor the Overlander, how fare you?"

"I'm still here," said Gregor. He wasn't the least bit interested in talking about himself right now. "So they're alive? They're getting better?"

For the first time, Vikus smiled. "Come and see."

The food was just arriving. Nerissa stayed with Hazard, Boots, and Temp so they could eat while Gregor and Luxa went with Vikus down to the hospital.

"They have been receiving Neveeve's cure for several days, so they are in recovery. Of course, they worsened after you left, Gregor," said Vikus as they walked down the hospital corridor that led to the plague wing.

Just before they turned the corner to the hall of glass walls, Gregor caught Luxa's arm. "They're going to look really bad. Just so you know."

"I have seen many disturbing things, Gregor," said Luxa.

"Okay, but the first time I saw Ares . . . I threw up," he said. "Your aunt told me people faint and stuff. It's a shock."

A flicker of doubt crossed Luxa's face. "Well, what can I do? I must see them."

"I don't know. Here, hang on to my hand, and if you feel sick or something, just squeeze it," said Gregor.

Luxa looked down at their hands and intertwined her fingers with his. "Let us go then."

They rounded the corner and immediately caught sight of Ares through the glass wall. He looked dreadful. Most of his fur had fallen out and he was still covered with big purple bumps. But Gregor grinned because his bat was actually up out of bed. "Hey, look. Ares is on his — ow!" Luxa had squeezed his hand so hard he was sure she'd broken at least three of his fingers. He turned to tell her to ease up and saw her pale white skin had an undeniably green tinge. "It's okay, Luxa. Really, he's a lot better than when I left."

She couldn't speak. She just stood there, clutching his hand, her eyes taking in the ruin that was her friend.

"Truly, Luxa, he is mending," said Vikus.

"And the sight of you two will be like a tonic." He rapped on the glass, and Ares turned his poor wreck of a head in their direction. His wings fluttered and he took a few hops toward them, but then he had to stop and rest to catch his breath.

"Smile at him, Luxa," said Gregor through his teeth, attempting to follow his own advice. "Aurora's — down — there!" Gregor mouthed the words slowly and pointed down the hallway to indicate she was in the hospital, too.

Ares's head bobbed up and down a few times to show he understood.

"Come, we are tiring him," said Vikus. He gave Ares a wave and moved down the hall. In the next room, Howard and Andromeda lay asleep in their beds. They both were covered in the purple bumps as well. One of Howard's burst as they were watching and Gregor lost the feeling in the tips of his fingers as Luxa, impossibly, tightened her grip. "We almost lost Howard the day before Dr. Neveeve began to administer the cure. But he is gaining in strength each day," said Vikus. "Let us see your mother, Gregor, and then you two need medical care yourselves."

His mom was in bed, but she was not asleep. The fingers of one hand were compulsively stroking a purple bump on her cheek. She stopped when she saw Gregor. They just stared at each other, as if no one else existed. After a long time he saw her lips form the word, "Boots?" He nodded and pretended to spoon food into his mouth to show that his sister was eating. His mom closed her eyes, but he could see tears slipping from under her lashes.

"She looks really sick," said Gregor.

"So she is, but now she will heal," said Vikus. "Come, you two, and let us heal you as well."

"How many others are here?" asked Luxa, glancing down the corridor.

"More than a hundred," said Vikus. "We have lost about thirty so far. The Fount was hit harder. Eighty have died there."

Luxa did not let go of Gregor's hand until they were directed into separate bathrooms to wash. Before her fingers left his, she whispered, "Thank you, Gregor. For warning me."

Gregor bathed, reopening the cuts the ants had given him. Or maybe they had never closed over at all — some of them were pretty deep. He lay on a hospital bed while a whole team of doctors went to work on him. Besides his battle wounds, he had the vine scratches on his arms and raw, acid-eaten toes. Apparently, he needed stitches — a lot of them. One doctor gave him a light-green liquid to swallow and that was the last thing he remembered for a long time.

When he came to, he was swathed in white bandages from head to toe. For about ten seconds, he thought it was kind of cool to look like a mummy. Then he wanted to rip them all off. As he started to tug at one on his wrist, a voice stopped him.

"No, Overlander, you will open the wounds again," said Mareth. The soldier was sitting in a chair by the bed, his crutch by his side.

"Hey, Mareth, how you doing?" asked Gregor.

"I cannot complain. How are you feeling?" said Mareth.

Gregor shifted around. "Kind of sore. How long have I been asleep?"

"Some sixteen hours. They roused you once to administer the plague cure, but you never really awoke," said Mareth.

"The plague cure? Why did I need that?" asked Gregor.

"Everyone is being given a dose as a preventative measure," said Mareth. "There were thousands and thousands stored in the caves off Neveeve's lab. Just sitting there, while so many suffered." Mareth shook his head in disbelief.

"Man. So was I right? About the broken container?" asked Gregor.

"Yes. Neveeve confirmed it. When Ares was in her lab to receive treatment for his bites, he accidentally upset the container with his wing. It broke, the infected fleas escaped, and both Ares and Neveeve were bitten. She said she could not tell Ares what had happened but that she intended to find some way to give him the cure the next day when she treated his wounds. Only he never appeared. He had gone to look for Luxa and Aurora in the Labyrinth. That is when he unknowingly spread the plague to the gnawers," said Mareth.

"Where is Neveeve?" asked Gregor.

"Gone. She has been executed. The tribunal passed judgment while you were sleeping and she was found guilty of high treason. It all happened very quickly," said Mareth.

"You mean . . . she's dead?" Gregor had thought they would lock her up in the dungeon, not kill her. What good did that do?

"Yes. It was the most serious of crimes," said Mareth.

"Did Luxa go to the trial?" asked Gregor. He knew the queen could stop executions.

"No, she was asleep as well. But she would have been excluded from the proceedings, anyway. You see, Neveeve was under orders to produce the plague as a weapon. She revealed Ares's accidental infection to no one, so that blame was hers alone. But others knew the plague was there." It was hard for Mareth to even get out the next sentence. "Solovet . . . for one. And as she is related so closely to Luxa by blood, the queen could not be involved in the trial."

"Solovet gave the order to make the plague?" asked Gregor.

"Apparently, she heads a highly secretive weapons committee that approved the research," said Mareth.

Gregor felt sick when he thought about Solovet being behind the plague. Not only because his family and friends had been victims. It was too evil a weapon to inflict on anyone.

"Are they going to execute Solovet?" said Gregor.

"I doubt it will come to that. But she and the rest of the committee are being confined and questioned," replied Mareth.

Another thought struck Gregor. "Vikus didn't know, did he?"

"No, but he has always been so vehemently opposed to this sort of weapon that . . . no one is taking this harder than he," said Mareth.

"I'll bet," said Gregor. The news that his wife had been instrumental in such a catastrophe for the warmbloods must be crushing the old man.

A doctor came by, checked on Gregor, and ordered food for him. Mareth stayed and ate, too. It was bland, but the simple soup and bread tasted good.

The food energized Gregor and he suddenly felt too restless to stay in bed. "Is Luxa still here in the hospital?" She was probably having a bad time with the news about Solovet, too.

"They wished her to stay, but she insisted on leaving to be with Hazard," said Mareth.

"He's a nice kid," said Gregor.

"So was his father," said Mareth sadly.

Not being a queen, Gregor wasn't sure he could get the doctors to let him leave the hospital, so he just slipped out when they weren't watching. He had to admit it might not be the best idea. His whole body hurt inside and out. But his muscles loosened up a little as he moved, even if his stitches tugged more.

It must be the middle of the night. No one was in the nursery, but he knew Dulcet would have made sure that Boots was in good hands. He wandered around until he found a guard and asked for directions to Luxa's room. The guard looked a little unsure, but led him through the palace to the royal wing. It was, as Gregor expected, very ornate and had several sets of sentries posted around. After waiting for a few minutes, he was allowed to enter.

He'd never seen where Luxa lived. She greeted him in a big living room with a fireplace, and he could see that several rooms led off of it. It was like she had a big fancy apartment to herself. He thought of his bedroom, which was actually a storage space, at home. "Wow, is this whole place yours?" he asked.

"Since my parents were killed," she said. She adjusted one of her many bandages as her eyes swept the room. Gregor suddenly felt incredibly grateful for his apartment, which was over-packed with people he loved. "But now, Hazard will live with me here." Her face brightened at the thought.

"How's he doing?" asked Gregor.

She waved at Gregor to follow her to a doorway. It was a bedroom, softly lit by candles. Hazard and Boots were snuggled together like puppies on the giant bed, sound asleep.

"It is very hard for him. He is so unused to living indoors. And then, of course, Frill and Hamnet were his whole world. . . ." said Luxa.

"Yeah, I know," said Gregor. "He's got you, though."

"Do you know what he said just before he went to sleep? He said, 'My father ran away from here to the jungle. He ran away from all the fighting. But it followed him, anyway,' " said Luxa.

"Like my grandma said to me about the prophecy. I could try and run away from it but it would find me," said Gregor.

"Vikus says that wars find everyone," said Luxa. She picked up something from a dressing table and held it out for Gregor to see. It was a crystal. Pale blue. Shaped like a fish.

"From your first flight with Hamnet?" he asked.

"Yes. It really does look remarkably like a fish, does it not?" she said.

It did. But Gregor couldn't think of anything else to say about it. Nothing good, anyway. The little chunk of rock was a reminder of so much tragedy.

They went back and sat in the living room. Gregor wondered if his next question might be a little too personal, but he asked it, anyway. "Is Vikus okay?"

"No," said Luxa. "He is devastated by what Solovet has done. Still, he organizes the aid missions, conducts diplomatic matters. The rats are beside themselves with fury, of course. Vikus does what must be done, and I do the same. You must be getting on with your life, too, Gregor. You must be getting home."

"Yeah. I guess we'll go back in a few days. You know, as soon as my mom's well enough to go home," said Gregor.

"To go home?" said Luxa in a surprised tone. "But Gregor, that will not be for many months."

CHAPTER 27

He could hear Luxa calling after him as he sprinted down the hall but he couldn't stop to explain now. Many months? They were planning to keep his mom down here for many months! Well, that just couldn't happen!

As he bounded down the stairs, he could feel stitches popping open, but he ignored it. He scrambled around the hospital until he found a guy who looked like he was in charge, and it turned out he was because the doctor gave one terse order and suddenly Gregor was literally being carried back to his bed. No one was particularly paying attention to what he was saying about his mom; they were far too concerned about the damage he'd done to his wounds. Blood was starting to stain the white bandages. "Listen," he said, "my legs are fine but I need to talk to someone about my mom staying —" He was cut off by an Underlander pressing a dose of medicine against his lips. Taken off guard, he swallowed. The drowsiness began almost immediately. "No . . . no . . . you don't understand. . . ." he insisted as the world slipped away.

When he awoke, who knew how much later, it took him a moment to recollect what had happened. He bolted up when he remembered, but a hand appeared on his chest. A very weary-looking Vikus pressed him back down into the sheets. "Stay, Gregor, or they will have to restrain you."

"What's that mean?" asked Gregor.

"Tie you to the bed," said Vikus. "You need to let the wounds heal over. It is for your own good."

"Luxa's out of bed. She's upstairs, I saw her," objected Gregor.

"Luxa is not running wildly through the palace — and she did not fight on the ground. Her wounds are fewer and more shallow," said Vikus. "Please, Gregor, it will not be so long if you will only cooperate."

Gregor stopped resisting less because of what Vikus said than how he looked. Which was terrible. He had big bags under his eyes, which were bloodshot, and his whole face seemed to sag. Gregor didn't want to give him any more trouble. "It's just my mom," he said, settling back in bed. "Luxa said you're going to keep her here for months. And you can't."

"We must. She is too ill to travel, even the

short distance to your home. And once she was there, who could care for her? This is an Underland plague. If she is not completely healed of it here, she may carry it home with her. What if it began to spread in the Overland? Your doctors would have no idea what it was, let alone how to cure it."

"But I thought she was getting better," said Gregor.

"So she is, but the plague has not yet been eliminated from her blood. She must become fully well. And you must help me to convince her of that, Gregor, because you know how badly she wants to return home," said Vikus.

"The thing is . . . we need her, Vikus," said Gregor, suddenly feeling closer to Boots's age than his own.

"I know this. And you will have her back. Only not quite yet," said Vikus. "Will you help me?"

Gregor nodded. What was the alternative? They couldn't take his mom back and risk starting a plague epidemic at home.

"Thank you. This is one less worry on my mind," said Vikus. Man, he looked bad!

"What's going on with Solovet?" asked Gregor tentatively.

"She is confined to our home while the investigation takes place. As you might guess, things are not easy between us," said Vikus.

"Why did she do it?" said Gregor.

"To have the plague in our control . . . it would have given us total domination over the warmbloods," said Vikus, searching for words to explain. "From a military standpoint, it is a highly desirable weapon. Lethal. Unstoppable to those without the cure. Such a deadly weapon . . . such a seductive one . . ." He rubbed his eyes, and Gregor was afraid he was going to start crying, but he didn't. "We are very different people, Solovet and I."

"Yeah. It's kind of weird to me that you're married," said Gregor, and then wondered if that was a really obnoxious thing to say.

But Vikus only smiled. "Yes. It has always been something of a puzzle to both of us as well."

Gregor had to spend the next two days confined to his bed. He had plenty of visitors, but it still drove him crazy. He kept thinking of the jungle and everything that had happened there. He thought a lot about the prophecy, too, and one thing still confused him. When Nerissa came by to sit with him, he asked her about it.

"Hey, Nerissa, you know what I can't figure out about 'The Prophecy of Blood'?" he said. "How come we had to go on that whole search for the cure at all? Neveeve had the cure to the plague right here. She'd even started to treat people before we got back."

"The prophecy does not say the plague will destroy the warmbloods, Gregor. It says, 'If the flames of war are fanned, / All warmbloods lose the Underland,' " said Nerissa.

"So . . . so, what?" said Gregor.

"Say the quest for the cure never happened. Then we would have never known the truth about Neveeve. She would have produced the cure, yes, but do you think it would have been given to the gnawers?" asked Nerissa.

"Probably not. You guys weren't even giving them the yellow flea powder," said Gregor.

"Exactly so. The minute the gnawers found out about the flea powder, they were determined to get it. Now imagine if it became known that the humans had the actual cure for the plague and were not giving it to the gnawers. What do you think they would have done?" asked Nerissa.

"Attacked you. I mean, what would they have to lose if they were going to die of the plague, anyway?" said Gregor.

"Yes. There would have been a war. And *that* is why Sandwich was saying the warmbloods would not survive," said Nerissa. "War has been averted . . . for now."

The longer Gregor stayed in bed, the more restless he became. He had to see his mom! When he was finally given permission to get up and visit her, the doctors said he had to walk slowly and quietly. He agreed.

His mom was propped up in bed with a tray of food before her. Not much of it seemed to be getting in her. Gregor came up to her bedside.

"Hi, Mom," he said.

"Hey, baby," she said hoarsely. The purple bump on her face looked a little smaller, but she seemed almost too weak to hold her spoon. "How you doing?"

"Oh, I'm good," said Gregor. That was not really true but he didn't want to add to her worries. He tried to think of some funny anecdote to tell her from the trip to the jungle, but absolutely nothing came to mind. "You seen Boots?"

"Not awake. I didn't want her to get scared seeing me like this. A girl brought her and held her up at the window, though, while she was asleep," said his mom. "The girl didn't look so hot herself."

"That must have been Luxa," said Gregor, and for some reason he felt himself blush.

"I liked her. I could tell she's got real attitude," said his mom.

"I thought you'd say that," said Gregor. He scooped up a spoonful of broth and held it up to her mouth. "Come on, Mom. You're not going to get better just looking at it."

She allowed him to feed her a little broth before she spoke again. "Have they told you I can't go back now?"

"I've been thinking, maybe Boots and I can just stay down here with you until you're better," said Gregor.

Distress contorted his mother's face. "Oh, no, you can't! I want you out of here. You take my baby and go home now!"

He had to promise he would go, over and over again. His mom made sure he knew she thought he had broken that promise once before, when he had left for the jungle instead of New York City. There was no cure to seek now, though. He knew he had to do what she asked.

A few hours later, he and Boots were saying goodbye in the High Hall. Luxa, Hazard, Nerissa, Mareth, and Temp had come to see them off. He had made the rounds in the hospital already, telling everyone he'd see them soon. He would, too. Vikus said they could come and visit his mom as often as they wanted.

As difficult as his own life must be, Vikus took the time to personally fly Gregor and Boots home on his big gray hat, Euripedes. He had arranged for their father to meet them at the laundry room instead of the Central Park entrance. The currents were in full force, and Euripedes barely flapped his wings as they rode the misty white vapors up, up, up to the world above.

And there was his dad, arms extended for Boots, then pulling him into the laundry room. And there was Lizzie, her little face pinched with the strain of the last few weeks, but smiling, too, at the sight of them.

"Fly you high!" he heard Vikus call as Euripedes dropped back into the mist.

"Yeah, fly you high, too, Vikus," he called beck. The old man needed all the good wishes he could get at the moment.

Boots was delighted to be back home and ran to get her poison arrow frog toys so that she could tell Lizzie about the real ones she'd seen. While she prattled on about "I see red, I see blue, I see yellow fogs!" and hopped around the living room, Gregor tried to catch up some with his dad. It was all still pretty hard to talk about. The plague, the jungle, the battle, the deaths, and the huge hollow in the apartment that his mom usually filled.

It was after midnight on Friday night. He had been down less than two weeks. All that had happened in less than two weeks.

There was no argument when his dad told them it was bedtime. Gregor gratefully crawled between his covers and fell asleep at once. In his dreams he kept looking for someone but it wasn't until he woke the next morning that he realized he'd been trying to find his mom.

While he was still lying in bed, Lizzie peeked around the corner of his doorway. "Hey, Liz, come on in." He pulled back the blanket, and she happily curled up next to him. She held out an envelope to him. "What's this?" Inside was a handmade card that read, "Happy Birthday, Gregor!" in bright marker. His birthday. It had been sometime last week. He must have turned twelve in the jungle.

"Wow, that's beautiful, thanks, Lizzie," he said.

"Dad said we could get you some presents when you got home and make a cake, too," said Lizzie. "But, Gregor, I don't know what's going to happen now about money."

Their mom made the money, but she was too sick to even come home.

"Dad says he's going back to work, but his fevers have started coming back in the after-

344

noons, so I don't think he can," said Lizzie.

"He's sick again?" asked Gregor.

"I read the paper they sent that time from the Underland. It said people can have re-lap-ses. The dictionary says that means it comes back again," said Lizzie.

His dad had seemed okay last night, but afternoons had always been when he was the sickest. Gregor began to feel worry gnawing inside him, but tried not to let it show. "Well, Vikus said he had them pack some more money from the museum. That should get us by for a while." He hoped. "Don't worry, Liz, it will work out okay. It's Saturday morning, right? I better get over to Mrs. Cormaci's." They would need that forty bucks.

"You had another flu," said Lizzie.

"What?" said Gregor.

"You had another flu. That's what I told everybody who asked about you," said Lizzie. "Mrs. Cormaci said you better get a flu shot next year. Oh, and Larry and Angelina brought over your homework." She pointed at a stack of books on his windowsill, the sight of which made Gregor feel kind of sick for real.

"Man, two weeks of homework," said Gregor.

"We had two snow days, so it's really only

eight school days," said Lizzie encouragingly.

"Okay, then things are looking up," said Gregor and poked her in the stomach. It was nice to see her laugh.

The cold snap was over, and when he opened the window a crack there was a soft, springy smell to the air. Gregor pulled on a pair of baggy pants over his bandaged legs and found a long-sleeved sweatshirt. It wasn't until he'd put on his socks that he realized he had no shoes except the Underlander sandals he'd left Regalia in. His boots had been destroyed by acid in the jungle. His last pair of sneakers had disintegrated before Christmas. Not knowing what else to do, he put on the sandals over his socks and tugged his waistband down to his hips so his pant cuffs would help hide his strange footwear.

He tiptoed in to give his grandma a kiss while she slept and tucked a blanket up around Boots. Around her on the pillow were the plastic poison arrow frogs. "I better come up with some way to get rid of those," he thought. His dad was still asleep on the pullout couch. In the daylight, Gregor could see what Lizzie had said was true. The strange tone to his skin, the tremor in his hands . . . He was sick again.

At ten o'clock, Gregor was knocking on Mrs. Cormaci's door. She eyed him closely, said he looked washed out, and gave him a big plate of scrambled eggs. Before she handed off the list of errands for the day, she made him come sit in the living room so she could give him his birthday present.

"You didn't have to get me anything," he said, turning the gift over in his hands.

"I figure I owe you these, much as I make you run around," she said with a wave of her hand.

He opened the box to find a pair of sneakers. Not any sneakers, but great sneakers, cool sneakers, the kind he never really even imagined owning because he knew they cost too much. "Oh, they're fantastic," he said.

"Why don't you try them on, because if they don't fit I've got the receipt, and we can go back and exchange them," she said.

But Gregor didn't move. Because to try them on would mean to take off his weird sandals, which he had carefully tucked under the coffee table, and then he'd have to explain those. And he couldn't. He couldn't because his mind was too preoccupied with his mom being miles under the ground with the plague and his dad relapsing and Lizzie's worried face and the impossibility of managing all that. What were they going to do? If his mom was gone for months, if his dad got bad again and couldn't even take care of them let alone go back to work and even if he could go back to work, then who would take care of his grandma and Boots and where was the money for all this going to come from, anyway? And whoever he was in the Underland, in the real world Gregor was just an eleven — no, a twelve-year-old kid who had no idea what to do.

"Gregor? You going to try on the shoes?" said Mrs. Cormaci. "If you don't like them, it's okay to say so. We can exchange them for another pair."

"No, they're perfect," he said. "It's just that . . ."

"What's the matter, honey?" she said.

He was going to need help. His whole family was going to need help if they were going to keep going. But Gregor was not good at lying, and he was so very, very tired.

"Gregor? What is it?" said Mrs. Cormaci. She sat in a chair across from him. "Something's wrong, I can tell."

Gregor fingered the laces of the shoes, took a deep breath, and made a decision. "Mrs. Cormaci?" he said. "Mrs. Cormaci . . . can you keep a secret?"

About the Author

Suzanne Collins's debut novel, *Gregor the Overlander*, the first book in the Underland Chronicles, received wide praise both in the United States and abroad, as did its sequel, *Gregor and the Prophecy of Bane*. Also a writer for children's television, Suzanne lives with her family in Connecticut.